Royal Treatment

Also by Parker Swift

The Royal Scandal Series

Royal Affair
Royal Disaster

Royal Treatment

A Royal Scandal Novel
Book 3

PARKER SWIFT

FOREVER
YOURS

New York   Boston

Copyright © 2017 by Parker Swift
Cover design by Elizabeth Turner. Cover copyright © 2017 by Hachette Book Group, Inc.

Forever Yours
Hachette Book Group
1290 Avenue of the Americas, New York, NY 10104
forever-romance.com
twitter.com/foreverromance

First published as an ebook and as a print on demand: June 2017

Forever Yours is an imprint of Grand Central Publishing. The Forever Yours name and logo are trademarks of Hachette Book Group, Inc.

The publisher is not responsible for websites (or their content) that are not owned by the publisher.

The Hachette Speakers Bureau provides a wide range of authors for speaking events. To find out more, go to www.hachettespeakersbureau.com or call (866) 376-6591.

ISBNs: 978-1-4555-9809-0 (ebook), 978-1-4555-9810-6 (print-on-demand edition)

To ER, because always.

Acknowledgments

A resounding thank-you to Lexi Smail and everyone at Forever Yours for bringing Dylan and Lydia's final chapters to life.

The writing of this book occurred in exactly two locations: Metro-North and my friend Sukey's couch. To the riders of Metro-North, you're welcome for using a privacy screen while I wrote. And to Sukey, I clearly cannot thank you enough for all of those perfect late summer nights in the backyard chatting about life and story ideas, the sushi shared before diving into our respective writing projects, strategizing about the best ways to kill cockroaches, making me laugh so hard my sides hurt the next morning, and providing literal shelter for me and my laptop. This entire series wouldn't have happened without you—I know it, you know it, and now the readers do too.

Kimberly Brower, as all of your authors know, you are the best agent in the whole world. Thank you for knowing just what to say and when to say it. Thank you for seeing this story through with me. I can't wait to see what's next.

And, Ethan, bring me this page of this book, and I will tell you how insanely grateful I am for all you did so I could write. There is no limit. You deserve to hear it every day.

Chapter 1

Lydia

Five months.

Five blissful months.

Five months of walking around with a stupid smile on my face. Five months of bursting into laughter in the middle of the workday like a fool. Five months of rolling over in my sleep and humming in pleasure when I realized I was in *our* bed in *our* house, and it *hadn't* been a dream.

How on earth had it been *five months* since we'd gotten engaged?

And a better question was: How had we managed to keep it a secret for that whole time?

When Dylan had asked me to marry him, I assumed that after a few weeks of hiding away and indulging in our newly-engaged world, I'd be just as ready as Dylan to announce it to everyone. It was while telling my best friend Daphne about our new status, discussing it all out loud, that I realized I wanted more of that private time, that I didn't know exactly *when* I'd be ready to go public with our engagement.

Daphne and her family had come to spend Christmas with me in London. It was Dylan's first Christmas as Duke of Abingdon, and, as head of the family, he had to be at Humboldt to preside over the holiday for the extended family. He'd just lost his father, just been thrust into the role of duke, and all eyes would be on him. We knew that nothing would start the gossip mill turning like him bringing me home for Christmas. Plus, it was *my* first Christmas without my father too, and I wasn't sure how much I'd feel like celebrating. So, as much as we hated it, we resigned ourselves to spending the holiday apart. And Dylan did what he always seemed to do when trying to cheer me up or give me a surprise—he flew Daphne over. And this time, her parents as well.

It was Christmas Eve when I finally got the chance to tell my best friend that I was engaged. Daphne's mother had just finished telling a story when she paused and complimented me on the thin diamond band on my pointer finger. It was the ring Dylan and I had bought as a placeholder, a subtle symbol of our engagement just for us.

"Thank you," I said. "It's new." I paused again, looking at each of them, debating for only a second before I continued. "Can you all keep a secret?"

Daphne's features immediately settled into an expression of extreme skepticism. "Lydia?"

"Dylan asked me to marry him." I smiled in a way that surprised even me, feeling the corners of my mouth stretching across my cheeks. "And I said yes." God, it felt so good to say it out loud.

"*What?!*" Daphne shrieked in a register not audible to humans and literally flew out of her seat. "But. But. But. Oh my god!" She was now jumping up and down and flapping her hands like some kind of bird, making me laugh, which surely wasn't her intention, not to mention it made it difficult to actually hug her, which I wanted desperately to do. Her mother and father were now standing together by the fire, letting us have this moment. There was more hugging and jumping, and then my hand was back in hers, and she was closely examining my ring. "I have to admit, knowing Dylan, I would have expected a ring that went a little farther in screaming, 'Lydia Bell is going to be mine forever,' but this is definitely gorgeous. And why isn't it on your ring finger? And why have I not seen this splashed across every newspaper?"

I was still laughing at her eagerness. "Did you forget the part where I asked if you could keep a secret? This isn't an official engagement ring. It's kind of a secret engagement ring. Something just for us—I wanted something to symbolize it, but we're not quite ready to make it public."

"Another secret?" She asked it lovingly, but I could hear the thread of concern in her voice.

"This time the secret was *my* idea." I turned to her parents to include them in the conversation, but they each gave me a quick hug in turn before heading to the kitchen. "He asked me to marry him just after you left at Thanksgiving. You were there—you know how much had been going on. You saw how relentless the press was when we went public with our relationship the first time. Then our breakup was gossiped about and spread across the papers and Internet. Throw in a cyberstalker"—I shuddered at the thought of Tristan Bailey, an employee of Dylan's father, who'd sent me threatening emails all fall—"and, well, I just felt so exposed, trapped by all of that. So once we were back together, I wanted a few weeks of peace and quiet, just for us. And Dylan agreed. I just wasn't ready to share the news with the world. *Our* world, okay, but not *the* world."

"How are you even managing to keep it a secret? I feel like the paparazzi are like lethal weapons over here," she asked in a tone that suggested we'd managed to solve some kind of unsolvable puzzle in our ability to keep the press at bay.

"If there's one thing Dylan's an expert at, it's keeping his private life private. He keeps saying that if we want it to be a secret, we just have to avoid giving the media anything to chew on—no pictures of us on the red carpet, no candids of us canoodling around town, no nibbles about our private life. Eventually they get bored and move on to whoever is giving them the money shots, whoever is providing the juiciest gossip. And an engagement *definitely* would be juicy gossip, as you may imagine."

"I'm sure," she agreed.

"Right, so we're lying low. No big kisses in front of throngs of reporters this time, no splashy red-carpet parties. His office confirmed we were back together, but otherwise we're just keeping our life private."

"And it's working?" Daphne tucked her knees underneath her and held her wine close—we'd settled back onto the couches in front of the fire, the lights from the Christmas tree we'd decorated making the room glow.

"It seems to be. It hasn't been that long. The first couple of weeks there were definitely stories—the *Daily Mail* printed the story about me moving in with him. But it feels like it's dying down."

"So when *will* you announce it then?"

"I don't know," I said, realizing that I really wasn't sure. Daphne was still holding my hand in her own when I could see the concern about the secret turn into something a little deeper, her smile straightening out a little, her eyes going a little foggy the way they did when she was thinking about how to say something. "What?" I asked her.

"I…Lydia, I like Dylan a lot. And I think you guys are incredible together. That man would, like, eat a crocodile if you asked him to." I smiled a little, loving Daphne's bizarre humor. "It's just that, well, what's the rush? Your father died less than a year ago. Dylan's died a *month* ago. He just became the youngest duke in England. I'm worried that maybe it's not the time for you to be making life-altering decisions. It's not that I think you shouldn't marry Dylan. I mean, shit, girl, he's a duke and madly in love with you—marry that dude. But you just got everything started here with your job and life outside your relationship. Maybe marry him in four *years*, not four months?"

Daphne wasn't being critical. She was being *protective*. I knew she felt like I was supposed to be sowing my wild oats or something.

"I *know*," I said reassuringly. "I said yes to him for a reason, Daph. I *do* want to marry him, and not four years from now. But not today either, and announcing our engagement will be as good as getting married in the eyes of the world." I thought about what it had been like to wake up with Dylan each morning knowing we were engaged, that he was the man I was building my life with.

"And, the fact that marrying Dylan will change my life is exactly *why* I don't want to announce it yet," I continued. "I came to London to finally figure out what *I* want to do, to take risks, to start my life, and in most ways I still feel like I just got started. And I can only really keep doing that, keep figuring all that out, if we keep the engagement a secret. Once we announce it, the floodgates will open. Once people know Dylan has a fiancée, there will be a million questions about me, my life, our life. I'll be in the spotlight, well, forever." As I said the words out loud, I realized how true they were. I *wasn't* ready to be in the spotlight again, wasn't ready to have my life change so dramatically. "There's just more I want to accomplish before I'm doing it under the watchful eye of the British aristocracy." As I said this, I realized it was going to be more than a few weeks before we announced our engagement, realized I wasn't anywhere near ready to open those floodgates. "So, I guess, I don't know when I'll be ready."

"And Dylan is okay with this? The waiting?" she asked, eyebrow raised.

I laughed and rolled my eyes lovingly. "The man waited a decade to have his first real relationship; he can certainly wait a bit longer to have a wife." I knew Dylan would be frustrated that he was going to have to wait any longer. "Plus, he's not *really* waiting. We do *live* together. And I *did* say yes. The only trade-off is that I'm not attending any of the parties and palace events with him—but we have a lifetime of those ahead of us."

"You sound pretty smart about this, I gotta say. And I mean, that man *does* love the crap out of you." She couldn't hide the smile creeping over her face. She looked like she was thinking for another moment, then she reached for the bottle of wine sitting on the floor by our feet and refilled our glasses. "To the court jester and my best friend! To their long engagement and the crazy aristocratic marriage that will follow!"

I rolled my eyes at her nickname for Dylan, and she raised her glass again, clearly on a roll now. "To my favorite lady—" Suddenly her gaze widened and a mischievous grin started to curl her mouth. "Oh. My. God. You're going to be a lady! You're going to be a *duchess*! Holy shit!"

And the jumping started all over again, and now I was laughing harder than ever.

"Oh, I'm never going to let you live this down," she squealed. I could see her wheels turning and could only imagine the steady stream of royalty jokes that would be continuously flowing from her for the foreseeable future. "I'm really happy for you. No one deserves this happiness more than you do. And I think Dylan deserves a little happiness thrown his way too. He's damn lucky to have you."

*　*　*

When I'd told Dylan that I was going to need more time, he was disappointed. I could feel it. But he was also supportive—he'd seen what that spotlight had done to his friend Grace: His childhood friend had taken her own life when the press mistakenly reported that she was Dylan's girlfriend. The resulting media whirlwind wreaked havoc on her life. In fact, he'd spent his entire adulthood believing that the duties and constraints that came with his life meant that he'd *never* get married. So, as reluctant as he was to wait, he agreed to as much time as I wanted.

And the miracle was just how right Dylan had been about the media. After a few weeks of stories about our reunion accompanied with boring pictures of us entering the house or getting into the car, the news died down. We gave as few photo ops as possible, and for the most part we'd spent our weekends at Humboldt Park, the grand mansion that had been passed down through generations of Dukes of Abingdon and that had become Dylan's the moment his father died.

This was how, five months later, I found myself on a Sunday

morning sitting at the large mahogany table in the library at Humboldt, with our engagement *still* a secret.

I momentarily glanced up and out one of the enormous windows, onto the huge rolling park behind the house. The sun was shining in, warming the room, and I couldn't believe that this massive place was Dylan's, that it would be *ours*. It was startling how a place like Humboldt—with its eighty-odd rooms, butler, gardeners, and ancient tapestries—could start to feel like *home*.

It was also startling how much work it took to run it properly.

Our weekends up here had been punctuated by tasks to do with bringing the estate up to Dylan's standards. We would have long talks with the gardeners, farmers, and dozens of staff and tenants who made the place live and breathe and function. While alive, his father had apparently neglected the actual business of running the estate, and his death was so sudden that Dylan hadn't had any time at all to adjust to being the 17th Duke of Abingdon. He'd been thrown in, and his primary concern was making sure that everyone associated with Humboldt was well taken care of and that it was running properly. At that moment we were going over all of the leasing agreements for the estate, trying to figure out which to renew and which to terminate.

"Thank you, damsel, for taking on this mess with me," Dylan said, sighing and running his hand through his dark brown hair, letting his hands flick at the ends, which had just the slightest bit of curl to them. He'd started keeping it a fraction longer, and I loved it. Watching him run his fingers through it both turned me on and told me when something was on his mind. And running my own fingers through it was something I thought about doing on an hourly basis. There were still moments when I found myself breathless looking at Dylan—his lean muscular frame, the way his tailored shirts hugged his biceps or cuffed around his forearms, the way his carved jaw rested on my head when he held me against him. Then there were those lapis-colored eyes framed by those outrageous eyelashes. He was, without a doubt, stunning.

"Shall we stop? I'm famished," I said, closing a folder in front of me and trying to focus on the fact that we were in a *library* and not our bedroom.

Dylan leaned back in his chair for a moment, looking at me, drinking me in the way he did sometimes. He came around to my side of the table and stood behind my chair. I felt his hands land on my shoulders, and he leaned over so his lips were right next to my ear. "Thank you, baby, for doing this with me," he said, not letting me ignore him. I could feel the blood rising to the surface of my skin as it always did when he was near, my breathing getting shallower.

"Of course," I said, sighing, and I leaned my head back until it came into contact with his shoulder. He kissed my exposed throat, and his lips rested there for a moment, warm and constant, and I began to feel desire pool low in my belly.

"Let's get you some lunch, then I'll thank you properly," he whispered, making the goose bumps rise to the surface of my skin. He took my hand and urged me towards the kitchen. I groaned in frustration, suddenly not feeling as hungry for food, and Dylan just laughed as he pulled me down the grand hallways of the mansion.

As we entered the bright kitchen, we found Mrs. Barnes, or Christine as I called her, putting together a salad at the counter, and she greeted us with a warm smile.

"Ahh, there you are. I was beginning to wonder. Was about to come and fetch you two for a proper lunch," she said, and gestured to the table, indicating we should sit. I loved hearing her lilting northern English voice. Christine was Dylan's former nanny, Humboldt's current housekeeper, and an incredible cook. In many ways she was like a mother to Dylan. And unlike Dylan's actual mother, Charlotte, she welcomed me with open arms.

I was pretty sure Christine suspected Dylan and I were engaged, even if she'd never pry for confirmation. Meanwhile, I wasn't even sure Charlotte was aware we were living together. Had she been around Humboldt at all, she surely would have figured it out or asked us directly. And we both knew that I, a quirky commoner who'd grown up in the States, wasn't exactly her first choice for the next Duchess of Abingdon. But Charlotte preferred to grieve the loss of her husband from abroad, from the comfort of cruise ships and European resorts, so she, like most of the public, was in the dark, thankfully. We both knew that telling *her* we were engaged wouldn't be a pleasant conversation.

"You two have been in there for hours," Christine said, interrupting my unpleasant thoughts about Charlotte and glancing at Dylan, who was already at the table with an apple and a beer.

"Yes, well, Father left things in quite the state." Dylan grimaced, taking another swig. Christine came over, swiped the bottle from his hand, and poured the contents into a glass, giving him a scolding *you-should-know-better* look.

Dylan came close to rolling his eyes like a teenager before taking a second apple. "Now, don't fill up. I'm making a cottage pie, and it's nearly out of the oven." Dylan looked chagrined, and I couldn't help but laugh out loud, which earned me a stern look as he put the apple back in the bowl.

"Christine," I said, gasping, never ceasing to be surprised

when Dylan responded to her reprimands. "What's your secret? If I told him to put down an apple, he'd..." But I didn't finish my thought, because Dylan was so used to being in charge that if I did tell him what to eat, he'd probably try to take me over his knee or something, which would probably just end in us having sex in the kitchen. I could feel the blush creep into my cheeks.

Dylan laughed, and I looked over to see him smile knowingly. "Bastard," I whispered.

Christine's voice bellowed over mine. "Yes, well, my dear, it helps if you were once the one changing his nappies. Also, you should know this one listens to no one more than he does you." She was gesturing between us, her hands already covered in flour as she delved into making some kind of dessert that looked like it was going to involve chocolate and pecans.

We ate our lunch sitting in that kitchen, homey in spite of its twenty-foot ceilings and enormous country table in the middle, and I thought about how here, inside Humboldt's walls, working at that table in the library, behind closed doors, I was already Dylan's duchess. And if Dylan had his way, I knew we'd be opening those doors.

I thought about what I'd told Daphne, that I wanted more time, and I thought about how in spite of Dylan's nagging, he'd been so patient. He put down his fork with a thud and drank the dregs of his beer. Christine had left the kitchen, and it was just us.

"Remember when you flew Daphne over for Christmas?" I asked, just as he was pulling me from my seat at the table onto his lap so I was straddling him.

He wiped a crumb from the corner of my mouth and kissed where it had been. "You mean when I flew over that daft girl who somehow convinced you to take a bloody eternity to agree to announce our engagement?" He flashed a smile to convey that he didn't truly mind, that he'd wait forever.

"So impatient, knighty," I scolded and kissed him back. I rose so I was standing on my knees and reached for his lapels, pulling him closer. "You know, I'm *going* to marry you." I kissed him on the lips. "Eventually." Then I felt his palm wrapping around the base of my head, and another under my ass, pulling me up and against him.

"Impossible girl. Time to get you upstairs, don't you think?" he asked, pulling his lips away from mine.

"Dylan," I protested as he stood, and I wrapped my legs around him. He moved his mouth to my ear, biting it briefly and signaling to my body it was time to come to attention, as if it weren't already there.

"Shhh, damsel." His voice was a husky whisper. "No more sounds, understand? Mrs. Barnes doesn't need to hear your sweet little moans when I taste you."

"Sweet little moans? You'd think I was a mouse," I prodded in my own soft whisper.

"Fine. Your depraved riotous moans." He gripped my ass tighter, and gave it a firm smack, making me shriek and laugh into his shoulder, all while the blood was thumping through my veins. "Now, if you're done correcting me, you saucy thing, I'd like to get to the business of showing you exactly how much I want you to wear my ring."

I still loved it when he released his dominant bossy side, when he acted as though he were desperate to march me down the aisle. Because I was pretty sure that as much as he wanted to marry me, our *bed* was the destination that was most often on his mind.

Chapter 2

Dylan

Five months.

Five sodding months.

Five months of watching her light up in the mornings when I woke her with my touch. Five months of twisting that bloody ring on her finger and wanting to replace it with something proper. Five months of pulling her into dark corners and keeping the press guessing. Five months of delighting in the way she went soft on me when she forgot she was supposed to be marching through her independence—in those moments she'd relax into me, melt under me, and make me fucking crazy for her.

The number ran through my mind as I drew circles across her warm naked back. I'd just given her the afternoon shag she needed—I needed—and now she slept, her petite frame draped over me like a gorgeous blanket, her caramel-colored hair tickling my arm, her wide brown eyes hidden behind her sleepy lashes. We lay there in our room at Humboldt, the one we'd recently refitted, and I fucking cursed those five months.

When she'd told me that she wanted time to "adjust to the

idea"—I think those were her words—to think about how she was going to handle a life that would be "full of compromises," I understood. Fuck, I wanted that for her too. There'd been a reason I'd wanted us a secret in the first place—I'd *seen* what being in a public relationship with me could be like. "Normal" it was not and "full of compromises" it definitely was. There'd be paparazzi, there'd be spreads in architectural magazines about our homes, there'd be parties, ceremonies, monthlong international diplomatic trips, and there'd be a generation of girls wanting wedding dresses that looked just like hers. She wasn't quite ready to tell the world, and as much as it fucking killed me to wait, I'd give her the time.

A year ago I wouldn't have entertained the idea of ever being in this position—desperate to publically claim a girl as my future wife. But bloody hell, Lydia, that chaste, delightful, brown-eyed, smart-as-a-whip, fierce-yet-gentle-as-a-goddamn-bunny damsel of mine had turned my world upside down. Without my quite realizing it, she'd taken the reins and was now the one guarding our relationship from the world. Had she been a business associate and not my fiancée, I would have considered myself one hundred percent rightly played, except there wasn't a Machiavellian bone in her little body. The girl just wanted a few months of normalcy and independence before hitching herself to my chaotic star.

At least I'd taken advantage of the situation. I put the time to good use. For the past five months I'd been reorganizing my life now that I was duke. Overnight I found myself juggling two companies. I was acting president of Hale Shipping, the family company my father had led into bankruptcy and that was in desperate need of stable leadership. I'd spent hours every week acquainting myself with the company, slowly developing a plan to reestablish it, and figuring out how in the hell I was going to run a bloody *shipping company* in addition to my own architecture firm. There was also the task of getting Humboldt Park back in order—it had become evident that my father had left our estate in no better shape than he left Hale Shipping.

And as if that wasn't enough, there were my father's misguided efforts to save the shipping company from his own mismanagement. In some act of desperation, he'd taken a loan from a Russian crime family, the Bresnovs, under the condition that both Hale Shipping and Humboldt Park would be collateral. And I wouldn't be able to undo any of this mess until the criminals were apprehended. *This* lovely disaster was how I found myself working with MI6—in an effort to save my family's legacy, I'd agreed to help them in exchange for the amnesty for Hale Shipping. Somehow I'd ended up in the plot of a bloody James Bond movie. A bleeding mess was what it was.

All of this meant I had certainly been occupied over the previous five months, even without a wedding to think about. But I also wasn't sure how much waiting I had left in me. I just looked at her and turned into some kind of caveman, wanting to mark her like a bloody animal, wanting to march her down the aisle, over my shoulder if necessary.

I'd had the ring ready since December, and I couldn't wait to get it on her finger. Not the delicate little band she liked to call her engagement ring—that was all well and fine while we kept it a secret, but I was ready to put *the* ring on her finger, to open up the floodgates, and make a three-carat canary-colored announcement that she was mine.

I'd known exactly which ring I wanted her to have—it just had to be resized and cleaned before I could slip it on her finger. And she had to agree to wear it, of course—something I'd mistakenly thought would be a minor detail. I recalled feeling downright eager when the squat kind-faced old jeweler, in his neat suit, the same man who'd been serving my family for approximately fifty of his seventy-odd years, handed me the velvet pouch, heavy with the jewelry inside it.

"The resizing was not a problem, sir," he said, eyeing me through his bifocals.

I nodded as I removed the ring and stared at it, the memories flooding back to me. My grandmother had worn it her whole life, and I'd seen it daily as a child. I didn't think I'd ever seen her *without* it. A brilliant square canary diamond guarded by four small exquisitely clear white diamonds, all nestled in the antique platinum setting. It was unique and delicate—not a hint of severity—regal and elegant. Quintessential Lydia.

"Thank you," I said, letting the weight of the ring sink into my palm as I looked back to the jeweler. "Charge it to my account?"

"Of course, my lord," he replied. He was one of the few people, a member of the old guard, who said my title in a way that didn't make me jerk slightly with ambivalence. It was a term of habit and respect for him, not sycophantic or servile. "And might I say, sir, that whoever the lovely lady is, I sincerely hope she enjoys it. I cleaned and repaired that ring many times for the duchess, your grandmother, god rest her soul. And I remember the very first time your grandfather brought the stone in to have it set. I was just a lad then myself."

I nodded. I'd heard the story, or stories rather, about the ring so many times as a child, and my grandfather's leathery voice was alarmingly vivid in my mind. He'd ask my sister, Emily, and me, sitting by his feet in the library at Humboldt, fire roaring behind us, "Now you children know where I got that special yellow stone in Grandmamma's ring, don't you?" and we'd look wide-eyed at him, ready for whatever tale he was about to spin for us. "From a gentleman tiger across the high seas." Another time he'd said it was from a pirate he'd had a scuffle with whilst sailing off Samoa. He'd tell us a different adventure story every time. Eventually, I couldn't be sure when, I'd learned the truth: The stone had been a gift from the king of Monaco, and he'd had it set as a gift for his engagement to my grandmother.

I found myself smiling at the memories, at the idea of sharing them with Lydia, and it was as though the ring announced itself in my palm—she was going to bring new life to it. To me. She already had.

"Thank you," I'd said. "And, I hate to mention it, of course, but I know I can count on your discretion."

"Of course, sir."

That was months ago, and I'd never intended to let my damsel get away with waiting so long before we went public with our engagement, but the truth was I'd probably give her anything she wanted. Not to mention, being secretly engaged had turned out to be one of the sexiest goddamn things I'd ever experienced.

I turned onto my side and brought my girl with me, gently stroking her arm, urging her into wakefulness.

"Damsel," I said, kissing her warm cheek, loving the fucking adorable way she grumbled when she was waking. "We need to get back to London, baby. Time to wake up."

* * *

A day later, an otherwise normal Monday night in April, I was reminded just how unbelievably hot it could be to be secretly engaged to Lydia. I was also wondering how the fuck I was going to make it through the dinner party we'd just walked into when all I could think about was the gorgeous woman beside me. My damsel. My *fiancée*.

There were ten of us seated snugly at the dining table in the newly purchased flat in some new modern monstrosity in Hampstead. The other couples, mostly married or engaged, all swank and pompous, were blissfully unaware that there was a vixen in damsel's clothing in their midst.

Given that we were trying to keep our relationship low profile, we didn't do this often, venture into the social sphere together. But dinner parties in apartments seemed relatively safe as far as paparazzi went, plus this social obligation would just be too fucking boring to attempt without her. The flat belonged to Roger, a chap from Cambridge, and he'd just moved into the place with his French model girlfriend. I kept forgetting her name. Madeleine? Mathilde? Manon? I couldn't keep it straight, which was almost certainly due to the fact that I could see Lydia's garter out of the corner of my eye. She'd allowed her innocent-looking floral skirt to slide high up her thigh. And I knew she wasn't wearing knickers, which meant she was *only* wearing those stockings with the garter belt. *Bloody hell.* Now I was hard at the dinner table.

I'd bought her the garter belt when I happened by a lingerie shop whilst walking from the office, thinking of nothing but her like some kind of sodding teenage wanker. I was beginning to think I'd bought my own instrument of torture.

"Hale." Roger's three-drinks-in voice interrupted my thoughts. "Saw in the *Financial Times* today that HS might merge with Maersk—is it true?" Ever since my father had died, business interests were lined up to see where I'd take the company, how I'd run it, looking to see if it might be for sale. "Is an acquisition on the table?"

"Ahh, Rog, you know never to believe what you see in print," I started, putting on my best public show, knowing that whatever I said would be spread across town by noon the next day. "I honestly can't tell you where that rumor started—I wouldn't be surprised if it was a member of the board, hoping to drive up interest, nab an offer I wouldn't be able to refuse." This was *actually* what I thought—the board would be thrilled if I were to sell.

"Does such an offer exist?"

I raised my eyebrow at him. "You know that Hale Shipping has been in my family for three generations. It will stay in the family."

"You'll run it then?" a woman from down the table chimed in. "*And* the architecture firm?" Christ, this was like talking to my mother.

"Working on the details, but I have no doubt it will resolve itself soon." Lydia took my hand under the table and squeezed it. I loved her for knowing when to do that. She knew, more than anyone, that I had no idea how I was going to solve that little conflict at the moment; she also had an unwavering belief that I'd figure it out.

"Stay in the family, eh?" another one of the guys asked, sitting across from us, eyes wide, hoping for gossip. "Does that mean we hear wedding bells for you two?" He gestured towards Lydia with his wineglass, the arse, then his eyes were on me. "What do you say, Abingdon? Going to make an honest woman out of this one?" It was a shocker we got through the starters before any of this had come up. They were digging. As a rule we hadn't confirmed anything about our relationship for months, and it was driving them all bleeding mad.

"Oh no," said Lydia immediately, her warm body so close to mine at the table that I could feel the heat radiating off of her. "I can't imagine Dylan ever settling down, can you?"

She said it as though she couldn't give a frog's arse, and she looked at me with that sly little smile making me pause mid-swallow of wine. That delicious little wench. If fifty minutes earlier in the car, we hadn't been joking about whether or not Lydia should really wear white at our wedding, I might have actually believed her. "I mean, this is *the* Dylan Hale we're talking about."

"Oh, well, it's hardly just me," I said, leaning back in my chair, taking a sip of wine and playing along, doing my best to maintain a stoic believability. "Lydia is brilliant, of course, but she's a workaholic, aren't you, darling?" I gripped her knee under the table, but the cheeky little thing took my hand and moved it between her legs, mid-thigh. Then she lifted her napkin daintily to her lips, as if to suggest *that* was what her hand been doing, moving about in her lap.

"I learned from the best. I just don't think we're the marrying kind, are we?" she said, looking briefly down at her engagement band—the thin diamond ring she wore on her pointer finger. She twisted it against my hand, reminding me of just how much the marrying kind we were. The table bought our little show, seemed to find it dull if anything, and I was infinitely relieved to hear the conversation turning to Manon's, or whatever her name was, modeling career. I took the opportunity to make the entire evening worth our while.

I slid my finger farther up her thigh, and my damsel had the nerve to spread her fucking legs beneath the tablecloth. She was going to be the death of me. I could practically taste her from where I sat. How did this woman make commitment sexier than all bloody get-out? Then she calmly took a sip of wine—a bloody sip of her *wine*—as I slipped my finger into her. As though she were completely unaffected.

I'd created a monster. No one would believe this innocent-looking girl with her big brown eyes and generous smile was waltzing around London without her knickers and letting her fiancé feel her perfect pussy at dinner parties.

I could feel her pulse within her, and my own was beating like a goddamn marching band in my head. Getting through this dinner was going to be torture.

For another hour, we took turns provoking each other. I "dropped" my napkin and grazed her bare thigh with my teeth after picking it up from the floor—she didn't even flinch or miss a beat in her conversation about fashion commerce with the American finance arse. A moment later she looped her foot around my ankle and pulled, forcing my leg towards her just as her hand landed in my lap. My balls were so fucking tight, my jaw tense, and my fingers itching to explore every inch of her. There was something about being secretly bound to this woman, being the only one to know that she was *mine*, that was better than goddamn Viagra. Doctors should bottle *that* shit.

We finally left, politely declining the offer for another round of post-dinner drinks and dodging more inane questions. There was no goddamn way I was waiting until I got her home before getting inside her. I'd been hard for an eternity, and I needed to get my girl under me, against me, whatever.

I had Lydia's hand firmly gripped in my own as I pulled her closely behind me, down the stairs of the house, and onto the sidewalk. She was laughing, giggling at her success in having worked me up, and fuck me if I wasn't laughing too. I felt sorry for my pathetic younger self—I'd spent a decade not understanding how *fun* it could be to love someone. But then again none of the someones had been Lydia.

She tried to move towards the car, logical little thing, but I pulled her past it and against my side. She obviously had no idea just how serious I was about getting my hands on her, and I didn't want to be inside that confined space with our driver, Lloyd, just a few feet away. I was feeling too goddamn randy for that.

I could hear her heels hitting the cobblestones beside me, could feel her palm warm in my own. I eagerly dragged her around the side of the building, down some darkened cobblestone mews, and lifted her little body up against the brick wall behind her. It was a cold night for April, fucking freezing actually. But I didn't give a shite, and thankfully neither did she.

For a moment, I just held her there, against the wall, my palm on her face, her eyes fixed on mine. I swept her long hair from her cheek and tucked it behind her ear, really just another excuse to touch her. She was smiling, and I knew I was too, but she was also as primed as I was. Then she was kissing my neck and unbuttoning her coat, and I was hiking that evil skirt above her hips. Because apparently neither one of us could wait another second.

Christ, I fucking loved this woman.

She was muttering her delightful sighs and eager little pleas that did nothing to calm my greed. She wrapped her long legs around my waist, her arms around my neck with a desperation that matched my own. I could feel her breaths get shallow the way they always did when she was turned on, little gasps that had me ready to come on a dime. Had there been enough light, I'd see her cheeks flush and the pink spread across her chest.

Taunting me had ripened her.

I reached into her coat, held her where her back met her perfect ass, and I slid my free hand between her legs, stroking her with my fingers.

"You like provoking me, don't you, damsel?" I whispered, knowing I sounded needy as fuck. To be fair, I was. I wanted nothing more than to remind her who she belonged to. To sink into her. To remind her just how engaged we were.

"I don't know what you're talking about," she panted, playing dumb in the sexiest possible way. Steam came with my breath and met with the steam coming from hers.

Our faces not a hair apart, I kissed her. I kissed her to remind her, to show her. Our first kiss flashed before my eyes—the deepness, the desperation of that moment on a moonlit path in Canada flooding my mind. Fuck, how had we gotten from there to here? And how had I not seen how utterly perfect for me she'd be?

"One of these days, damsel, I'm going to put my ring on that finger of yours, make it official, show the whole goddamn world…," I whispered as I unzipped my trousers and lifted her onto my cock. She panted deeper, gasping for breath, and I knew she was already close. I only regretted that I couldn't see her clearly. When she came her face was fucking majestic. "And there'll be no denying just how much the 'marrying kind' we are." I barely recognized my own hushed demanding voice.

We fucked as quietly as we could against that brick wall—our harsh exhales and desperate inhales the only audible hints as to what was occurring tucked away in that mews—and it was thrilling as hell. Fucking was never just fucking anymore. It would never be "just fucking" again. It was simply the most feverish version of what we did to each other. Lydia was strong, willing, and she trusted me to know when we could take risks like that one, me bringing her to the edge of getting caught.

I loved it, respected it.

"But in the meantime, this is pretty fun," she whispered as she kissed my neck, coming down from her high.

"I love you," I said, because, fuck me, I really, really did.

"I love you too."

Chapter 3

Lydia

I couldn't stop thinking about it. My back against that brick wall. My legs wrapped around Dylan's waist. The cold night air skating across my bare sex moments before he plunged into me. I felt that rush of electricity across my skin at the memory. The previous night was hotter than engaged sex had any right to be.

"Lydia? Helloooooo? Lydia?" Emily's voice snapped me back to attention.

I'd taken the morning off, and Dylan's sister and I had met up for coffee and a quick mani-pedi at her insistence. She'd said my nails looked like I'd been in a fight with a cheetah and a gorilla. I didn't even know what that meant, but I knew it wasn't good. Also, I knew the real motivation was so she could hound me about wedding planning. My nails were now painted something called Fire in Fiji and we were, predictably, standing outside Vera Wang on Brook Street. Emily had known about our engagement since January, and she was certifiably obsessed.

"Are you *ever* going to look at wedding gowns?" she sighed, glancing longingly from the gown in the window back to me

with an irritated look of defeat. I could practically feel her thinking up outlandish yet tasteful centerpieces and creating a "concept" for the whole affair. She was like a dog with a bone, only
we'd demanded she keep the bone a secret.

Emily was one of those women who would have you believe
she was a brainless socialite with her big sunglasses, shiny dyed-
to-perfection locks, and of-the-moment handbags, but the truth
was she was sharp as a tack. If I let her, she'd probably have
our wedding planned according to the highest standards within
days, and all with an efficiency that would boggle my mind. She
was amazing. She was also the only person in London we'd actually told we were engaged. Or she was supposed to be. The day
we told her, we also ended up telling Dylan's best friend, Will.

I'd told Dylan that even though the engagement would be
a secret, we had to tell Emily. She would somehow be able to
smell it on us whether we told her or not—she was like a blood-
hound that way—and wouldn't he rather it come from us than
she figure it out? Plus I knew we might need an ally if we expected to keep it an actual secret for any period of time. So we'd
taken a Saturday and visited her at Cambridge, where she was
getting her degree in art history. Sometimes I forgot Emily was
only twenty-two and still in college. She always seemed much
older than that.

We'd driven up mid-morning—Dylan had wanted to show
me around, do the whole memory-lane thing from his "uni
days." He'd recounted stories steadily from the moment we left
London straight through till we arrived at the town center. Stories about him and Will and their band of mischievous aristocratic friends. When the two of them got together and began
reminiscing, it was as though a film reel of all their memories
was playing live before their eyes. So maybe I shouldn't have

been surprised when we'd stopped for a drink before our dinner with Emily and the man himself, *Will*, walked through the door. Apparently he'd been up for the weekend too, giving a talk about entrepreneurship to a group of young students—he'd become something of a local celebrity since the restaurant he ran and co-owned with Dylan had been given its first Michelin star.

So what we'd planned to be a quiet dinner in which we told Dylan's only sibling became something more boisterous, more joyous, closer to a mini engagement party than a close-knit family conversation.

"It's just as well you're both here," Dylan had started, and Will and Emily exchanged confused looks. "Lydia and I want to talk to you about something." Dylan gripped my hand under the table.

"Dylan—" Emily had started, reaching for her wine, but Dylan raised his hand to stop her from speaking. I knew this look—he'd gotten a similar look of determination on his face when he'd proposed, like he had started and he couldn't brook interruption or the whole thing might fall apart. He squeezed my hand under the table once again, but instead of holding it and stroking my thumb there, hidden under the table as he normally would, he raised our entwined fingers and placed them on the table between our glasses.

"First, you must swear to me. Swear on all that is holy. Swear on your goddamn shoe collection. No, no." Dylan interrupted himself and got a look of total mischief on his face, the kind of delighted cunning you only see between siblings. "Swear on Miss Midgy—" Emily gasped and looked horrified all of a sudden.

"Miss Midgy?" I asked, looking between them.

"Swear on Miss Midgy that you won't tell a soul what I'm

about to tell you." Emily was turning bright red, and Will started to giggle. And that giggle turned into full thigh-slapping laughter.

"Miss Midgy?" Will asked, barely getting the words out, following my lead in chuckling that was quickly turning into full-on hysteria.

Emily patted her reddening cheeks and spoke through gritted teeth. "Well, Lydia and Will, I do hope you've enjoyed being acquainted with my darling brother, because I am now about to throttle him, and it's doubtful he'll make it out alive." Emily sighed, her fury brimming over the edges.

"Miss Midgy is Emily's stuffed kangaroo," Dylan explained formally, as though giving a recitation about a rare mammal species and trying to contain his gloating but failing miserably. "Apparently, the delightful Miss Midge actually came to life while we were at school and was a top-notch barrister in the animal world. *And*, if I'm not mistaken, I spotted her on Emily's couch the last time I was at her flat. Isn't that right, Em? Still sleeping with her as well?"

Emily's face was in her hands, and her words were muffled as she said, "That is between me and Midge." Then after a moment, when I swear steam was coming from her ears, she silently flung her balled-up napkin across the table at Dylan. "Fine, you petulant tosser. I won't breathe a word. *Some* of us can keep important secrets."

Dylan chuckled, but quickly resumed the task at hand. "And you," he said, looking at Will, "you—"

"Oh, for Christ's sake. No. Whatever bollocks you're going to blackmail me with, just don't. I swear on my career as a chef, on the entire bloody restaurant, I won't breathe a word." He was giving Dylan a look of death. Dylan must have some amazing dirt on Will—I was going to have to get it out of him later.

Dylan's shoulders relaxed just a hint, and he looked at me. He smiled—not so much that anyone would notice but me, but I saw it, how the pride and excitement caught in the corners of his mouth as his eyes met mine. "Lydia and I are engaged to be married."

I was looking back at Dylan so contentedly, taking him in, that it took a minute for me to process the shrieking happening on the other side of the table. I looked up to see Emily clapping her hands. Then she reached across the table for my left hand, pulling me halfway across the table as she searched for a ring.

"Ah, so you're up the duff then, are you?" Will clasped his hands, rubbed them together and leaned back in his chair, looking entirely too pleased. And Emily gasped, looking intensely from Dylan to me and back to Dylan as though we were a tennis match.

"Up the duff?" I asked, looking at Dylan.

"Calm *down*," he said sternly to Emily, freeing my hand from his sister's grasp. "First, *William*, no. Lydia is not pregnant. And, Emily, do you think if we want this to be a secret, she'd be wearing a ring?"

Oh lordy. It was clear that was going to be what everyone thought when they found out we were engaged after dating for only a few months. One more reason to wait as long as possible to spill the beans. Not that being pregnant would be a bad reason to get engaged, but I had a feeling that would be a tad more scandalous in Dylan's world than it was in mine. As if we wouldn't have enough media attention to deal with once the announcement was made.

"Oh, you're no fun. Fine. Which ring *are* you giving her?"

Emily asked, calming a bit and sulking a little at the realization that we weren't embarking on an extravaganza quite yet, but she was now leaning over the table, her chin in her palm, with rapt attention.

"Yeah, Dylan, which ring *are* you going to give me?" I said, smirking, and grasping his hand just a little tighter.

He chuckled and squeezed my hand gently in return. "Cheeky girl," he whispered in my ear as he moved in to kiss my cheek.

"You don't think I'm going to tell her, do you?" he said, still smiling, directing his question to Emily. "You're a girl—you should know how these things work. Isn't it meant to be a surprise?"

Emily raised her eyebrow at her brother, and Will laughed at Emily's defiance and ran his hands through his hair—clearly enjoying the sibling dynamic as much as I was. "Have you *ever* done anything as it's meant to be done, Dylan?" his sister asked him skeptically. "For all I know, you intend to abandon the ring altogether and give her a Thoroughbred or a house in the Maldives."

"Oh, now there's an idea," I said, enjoying feeding into this frenzy. "I mean no to a Thoroughbred, yes to the Maldives."

Dylan looked slightly frustrated with our shenanigans, but Emily resumed before he could get a word in. "I mean I've always been able to count on you to *not* do it as it's meant to be done. Don't disappoint me now."

I laughed out loud and Dylan gave me a look that said *not you too*.

"Oh, trust me, when the time is right, there will *be* a ring, you pain in the arse."

"All right, all right, my turn," said Will, who was rising from his chair. He rounded the table and slapped Dylan on the back.

"Finally, mate, you're *finally* making something of yourself. You've been *such* a disappointment in the love department," he said jokingly.

"Oh, really?" said Dylan, looking up to his best friend. "Well, maybe it's time you start reining in whatever it is *you* have going on—"

But Will cut him off. "Now, now, bridegroom, don't go casting stones. There's more important business to attend to," he said, halting Dylan and moving in my direction. At this point, assuming there were no serious skeletons in Dylan's closet, I realized I no longer cared about his colorful sexual past. I just knew, under my skin, with total certainty, that I was different to him than any other girl had ever been. This realization was floating through me when I found myself being lifted into the most joyous encompassing hug in Will's arms. He was literally shaking me. I couldn't help but laugh and hug him back.

As he put me down, he said quietly, so I was pretty sure only I could hear, "Smartest decision that dolt has ever made. Welcome to the family, you wee yank." I smiled big and hugged him back again—it felt like after years of being mostly alone, my family was expanding rapidly, and it was incredible. Will was the steady force of true friendship in Dylan's life. They'd opened a business together, and anyone who knew Dylan knew he wasn't good at sharing control, so that spoke volumes of the trust between them. And Will was the one guy I'd seen who'd ever made Dylan truly *laugh*. When Dylan had been ready to go public with our relationship the first time around, to announce to the world he had a girlfriend for the first time in nearly a decade, Will was the first person he'd introduced me to. And now, the guy was holding me tightly in a firm hug, one that said more than words could about how happy he was for us.

"Thank you," I whispered back.

When Emily was done sulking that she had to keep things quiet, she fully embraced this new reality. I showed her my non-engagement engagement ring and told them the PG parts of Dylan's proposal. And Dylan and Emily exchanged some sibling look that I'd probably never understand, but looked to me like the end of a conversation they'd been having, like Emily wholeheartedly approved of our decision to get married.

So, while telling Emily had been planned, telling Will was a surprise. But now, after those drinks and the boisterous dinner that followed, I was glad they both knew. If for no other reason than it meant that in those rare moments when we *didn't* want it to be a secret, we had friends we could talk about it with. But sometimes, like that moment standing in front of Vera Wang, it could also be downright annoying.

"I'll look at gowns when I'm ready," I finally replied to Emily, hands on my hips.

"Well *I'm* ready," she said, "and have been for years—"

"It's only been five months!"

But Emily waved her hand in dismissal. "If you dare even *think* about trying on gowns without me, I will disown you as a sister-in-law," she said, on the verge of shouting indignantly at me.

I grabbed her hand and dragged her past the store as I looked around for paparazzi. "Emily!" I whisper-shouted. "You can't say that in public!"

She huffed, "Oh, please. No one heard me. Although, I am half hoping someone does. Then we could get the show on the road, as you lot say."

I raised my eyebrow at her. "You are shameless, you know that?"

"I do," she said, smiling, and I threw my hands up in the air as we walked towards the coffee shop on the corner.

"Besides," I said, smirking, "having it be a secret is so much fun, I'm not sure I'll ever want to plan the wedding." I knew I was blushing, but I didn't care.

"Ew. Stop being vile. I don't want to hear about it."

"I didn't say anything!" I protested.

"You did. You think I don't know that look, Miss Lydia Bell? You *shall* not ever allude to my brother's...my brother's...well, I can't even say it."

"Fine," I huffed out between chuckles, "but then no more wedding talk."

"You," she started firmly—you could really imagine Emily commanding a room someday, she was so no nonsense sometimes—"are evil. And I'm questioning this entire enterprise," she said. "Now. Let's get some coffee, shall we? And for lord's sake, let's change the subject. How's the store going?" she asked as we walked into the cafe.

She was referring to the store I helped open for Hannah Rogan, an up-and-coming fashion designer. It was her first brick-and-mortar store, a flagship in Mayfair, and it was my idea. In what felt like a crazy how-am-I-so-lucky-to-get-my-dream-job kind of moment, we'd gotten the investors on board and gone to work. We'd rushed the launch—something that was only possible with the help of Dylan's contacts in the design world—in order to open before Christmas, which meant we were past the "new store" phase, settling into being part of the couture London shopping scene, and I was finally getting over the feeling of not believing it was really happening.

"Well," I said. "I mean, I *think* it's going well. We're moving merchandise, and the press has been decent—"

"Decent?" Emily asked skeptically, eyebrow fully raised. "I'd say a full-page full-on crush piece in the *Sunday Times* is a bit more than 'decent.'" Emily had been incredibly supportive, bringing in her posh posse of school friends and talking up the store. And as one of London's "It Girls," her opinion mattered. "Also the fact that she is sending you to New York to open a pop-up store is a solid indicator that *Hannah* thinks you're doing well. When is that happening again?"

"First week of May—wow, next week actually." Hannah and I had been planning the pop-up store for months. I'd be gone for a month, preparing the store, launching it, and breaking it down. The goal was to showcase her spring line as well as some resort wear for summer. It'd been my idea—part of my big "say yes to everything, go after things I want, enjoy pre-duchess life" plan. "I can't believe it's coming up so soon—we've already shipped the merchandise. Your brother would obviously prefer I not go, or I'm certain he'd come with me if he weren't so busy. He's convinced I'll get mugged or lost or who knows what, As though I didn't manage to live my life perfectly safely before he came around."

"What? My brother is being overprotective? Impossible!" We both laughed—if anyone knew Dylan's protective side as well as I did, it would be his little sister. "I will say you've made him far more reasonable. At least he has the good sense to say, 'I know you won't listen to me,' before he tells me not to take the Tube at night or tries to interfere in my dating life. Thank you for that."

"Yeah, poor guy. He knows I'll give him the death glare if he goes too far. I'm half tempted to walk around bad neighborhoods at three in the morning just to drive him crazy." Emily looked at me mischievously as though she wished I really would—she had the terrorizing look of one sibling out to torture another, which always made me laugh. "Anyway, I'm hoping that announcing the New York pop-up might even drum up business here."

"You know what would ensure a steady stream of customers for the foreseeable future, don't you?" she asked, and I prepared to take mental notes. "For the director of sales to be involved in a stylish and fabulous wedding-of-the-century to her famous boyfriend," she finished, smiling in victory.

I couldn't help smile through my sigh. "You never give up, do you?"

"Never," she replied, and we leaned on the counter in the window of the cafe, chatting. And she was right. I knew much of the press attention we'd gotten so far, any puff pieces about the launch, had something to do with the fact that I was linked with *the* Dylan Hale, the preternaturally gifted architect, the rock-my-world-attractive 17th Duke of Abingdon, and irresistible former bad boy.

Chapter 4

Dylan

Lydia had spent the morning before work with my sister, but I'd spent it dealing with the last of the legal proceedings against Tristan Bailey.

The case was pretty open and shut—I mean the arse had *confessed* in front of three witnesses. He had cyberstalked and harassed Lydia for a month, taking and recording private, personal photos and videos, threatening her, scaring her, all in an attempt to dismantle our relationship, fuck with me, and ultimately expose me. Had his stunt succeeded, the company that had been in my family for three generations, Hale Shipping, likely would have gone to him. And because of the unfortunate deal my father had made with the Bresnovs, the Russian criminals who had bailed the company out, Tristan could have walked away with my estate, Humboldt Park, as well. The whole disaster had been thwarted, thank god, but even after Tristan was behind bars, there was still plenty to sift through, plenty of damage to undo.

I'd spent lunch with Jack Bickford, the MI6 agent I'd been working with on the Bresnov case, who was also a mate from my

Cambridge. In reality, if it weren't for Jack's involvement, I probably wouldn't have even listened to the mad plan the agency had up its sleeve. After that lunch, I'd found my way to Will, at the restaurant. I'd needed, wanted, to run the entire situation by my best friend, make sure I wasn't completely mad to be even considering what I was considering.

"Am I completely mad for even considering this?" I asked him, taking a sip of an amarone he was thinking of adding to the wine list. We were sitting at one of the rear tables, away from the bustle of the chefs at work in his kitchen.

"Take me through it again." Will leaned back, patient.

"Well, the goal is get to this guy, King. Russian, ruthless, and so far, the highest-ranking identifiable member of Eastern European organized crime. He's been untouchable for over a decade and essentially, from what anyone can discern, the boss. Six different human-trafficking rings are associated with this fucker—"

"Christ." Will rubbed his forehead, as disgusted with the concept as I was.

"Right, so according to Jack, the problem isn't evidence, it's actually getting their hands on the fucker—they've been trying for a decade with no luck. There's a chance their man, an undercover agent who's been on the ground in Moscow for over a year, will get close enough to isolate him. If that works, I'm off the hook." While Will had been becoming a restaurateur, and I'd been building my firm, our friend Jack had managed to work his way into the upper echelons of Britain's foreign secret intelligence service.

"Got it. We're hoping for Moscow Man to succeed." Will took a sip of the wine and made a disapproving face.

"Yes, well, I have a feeling if that were a real option, Jack wouldn't be talking to me, and yet here we are. Their backup plan, so to speak, is to get at King through the Bresnovs, who have climbed the ranks in recent years and apparently have rather reliable access to him. And to get to the Bresnovs, they use me. From what I understand, I am the only uncompromised asset with direct contact with these people, thanks to good old Dad."

"So how would this all work?" Will looked partially alarmed and partially skeptical that any of this was real, which mirrored how I felt exactly.

"Essentially, when they get word that King will be in London, I'd approach the Bresnovs and offer a deal good enough that they'd want to include King in the negotiations. I'd say I'd need to meet King directly—apparently Moscow Man is confident all this can be done. I meet with King, then Jack and some other agents follow me, intervene before anything foul happens, and all is well."

Will was looking at me as though I were definitely a touch mad for considering this. "And then you're in the clear. With King apprehended, MI6 would have no use for the Bresnovs anymore—they would swiftly be taken into custody. You'll be able to remove Humboldt from Hale Shipping's assets without any risk of the Bresnovs trying to retaliate, and you finally get the company back in order and get out of the goddamn shipping business. Easy peasy." He wiped his hands back and forth, mocking the idea that wrapping up this insanely complicated situation would be at all easy.

I rolled my eyes at him. "That is the idea, yes. They have plenty of evidence against the Bresnovs—needing them as bait I'm afraid is the only reason they haven't been taken in. And if I were to make any moves on putting Humboldt back in my name, it would alert the Bresnovs that I am no longer willing

to play ball with them, alert them to my involvement, and presumably put this whole plan at risk. So, according to Jack, the
agency is hoping that I continue to sit tight and play nice with
these Russian arses until this is done." I finished the glass of wine
and went to work on some pork-belly-related appetizer Will had
made. God, he was a good chef.

"Crikey. Does Lydia know about this?" Will leaned forward,
resting his hands on the table. I nodded. "Is *she* all right with it?"

I sighed, exhaling deeply. I knew the plan made Lydia nervous. Every emerging detail added to the feeling of risk. "She
is." I sighed again—I hated thinking about the fact that Lydia
would be affected by this. "She knows I need to do this. But I
also know she'd prefer I *not* be involved. She doesn't want me
to know she's nervous about it, but I can tell she is, of course. I
mean, Christ, every time I think of the massive amount of utter
crap I have going on in my life, it's utterly clear that it's a full-on
miracle she's agreed to marry me at all."

"Well, that's true. She's measurably superior to your sad arse."
Will took another swig of his wine. "Look, mate, I'm not sure
you have much of a choice. You could refuse, of course, but it
honestly seems like the fastest route to having this all sorted.
And it's Jack, right? I'll concede that it sounds exceedingly idiotic, even for you, but I can't imagine that Jack would ask you to
do this if there were a real risk."

I nodded. "And according to him and his team, after this
there won't be much *left* of this branch of organized crime once
King is out, and those that are left will be rather relieved he's
gone. The agency will provide some cover, deny my involvement,
obviously. So after the actual event, the risk of retaliation is minimal." Even just saying it out loud I felt satisfied, albeit no less
apprehensive. I could do what they needed me to do. And I

would. But there wasn't a moment I thought about it that I didn't resent the fuck out of my father for leaving me in this position. "Thanks, mate." I ran my hand through my hair—this whole plan would have been fine before Lydia was in the picture, before it felt like I had anything to lose.

We spent another hour talking about the restaurant and a new sous chef he was hiring. We chatted about a redesign he was thinking about for his house in Camden, and whether I thought he could accomplish an addition. And eventually we made our way to the kitchen, where in spite of my protests, Will insisted on trying to teach me how to make something involving braised rabbit and polenta.

* * *

On my way home I sent Lydia a quick text to see if she was close. After my day I wanted to lose myself in her, completely.

> TUESDAY, 6:15 pm
> Home soon, damsel? I've got something in mind that I'd like to do to that pussy of yours.

> TUESDAY, 6:16 pm
> How am I supposed to keep working when you say things like that?!

> TUESDAY, 6:16 pm
> Now you're getting the idea.

This. This is what I needed—just texting with Lydia already had my shoulders unwinding.

> TUESDAY, 6:16 pm
> Sadly (for me), I'll be home late tonight I think.

TUESDAY, 6:17 pm
Be good then, baby, and later I'll show you what I had planned.

> TUESDAY, 6:17 pm
> Always talking such a big game, Hale.

I didn't have a chance to reply, when my phone rang.

My goddamn mother.

The woman had been perpetually absent, grieving in absentia, floating between Cannes, Paris, and occasionally Italy with friends, generally avoiding her new reality: a dowager duchess. We'd speak for a few minutes a week about Humboldt, but otherwise in classic fashion we were staunchly avoiding the issues running beneath our conversations as of late. We were grieving in parallel, dealing with life without my father in our own ways. Lydia encouraged me to be patient with her, reminded me she'd just lost her husband, but *fucking hell*, the woman was so self-absorbed it was shocking she remembered she had a son at all.

"Hello, Mum," I said, trying to disguise the disappointment I had at the interruption.

"Are you alone?" Her subtext was clear—*Is Lydia there?* My mother knew Lydia lived with me. Knew without having asked, never having confirmed, and never once inquiring about our relationship. However, I was certain she still had no idea I'd asked Lydia to marry me. Finding out that Lydia would be the next Duchess of Abingdon was going to ignite a fight I wasn't looking forward to. The fight would of course be worth it—I didn't give a shite what my mother thought. But Lydia wanted us a secret, as much as it killed me, and I didn't trust my mother not to use that secret against us, against me, as soon as she knew.

"Yes, Mum, Lydia's at work. What can I do for you? How's Cannes?"

"Crowded. I called to talk to you about Humboldt." No she didn't. "But now that I have you, I also wanted to ask you about Prince Arthur's party on Thursday—" Ah, there it was. The queen's husband's annual charity event was two days away, and obviously my mother saw it not as a philanthropic affair but as a way to further her bloody agenda. It was a command performance—I was duke, and I'd be there. My mother knew that.

"What about it, Mother?"

"You're not going alone, are you? It's getting a bit ridiculous, snubbing people the way you have been."

"Mother, I'm not taking anyone to the party, and *not* inviting women to things for meaningless dates could hardly be described as snubbing them."

"Dylan, you can't afford to continue on this way."

"What are you saying, Mother?" It was truly astounding how quickly conversations with this woman devolved into something unpleasant. Either that or I'd just honed my ability to cut through her crap.

"Dylan, don't be coy. You know as well as I do that it would be wise to think about the future, that this party might be an appropriate occasion to bring a companion with you, an *appropriate* companion. I know we all have our way of grieving, Dylan, but it's time you take things more seriously. It's time you tie up loose ends, wrap up this thing you're doing and—" *Fucking Christ.*

"Let me stop you, Mother, before this gets any more unpleasant. And let me remind you that Lydia and I—"

"Dylan—"

"Fucking hell—" I was practically shouting. We were speaking over each other—our mutual frustration the only clear signal. She was going on about me inviting someone or another, but I'd stopped listening.

"Mother!" I said the word loudly and clearly enough to stop her in her tracks. "We'll speak when you get back about the changes at Humboldt. Safe travels."

Hanging up on my mother was not something that came easily—I'd worked for years to learn to do it without flinching. But at this point, the skill was well honed, and I did it without a second thought.

She had never been so blatant about Lydia before. The day had just gone from shite to a fucking rageful disaster.

* * *

It was nearly nine when I heard the telltale sounds of Lloyd pulling the Jaguar into the garage and the car doors closing announcing Lydia's arrival home. She'd have anyone believe she was carefree about her work, but I saw the way she snuck in extra hours, got up early, sent emails from her phone while she dressed for work. She was a tigress, determined, and it was fucking sexy.

Of course she'd said she'd take the Tube home, but I'd sent Lloyd. It had nothing to do with keeping her safe, or not entirely. I *had* actually gotten better about tamping down my overprotective tendencies. No, I simply wanted her back in my bloody arms as soon as was humanly possible.

And there she was in the doorway to my study not a moment later. Her long legs in one of her deliciously trim little pencil skirts, the kind that hugged her ass in a way that bloody well undid me. Blue high heels that most girls wouldn't dare think of. Some kind of floaty blouse with animals on it—the woman was a savvy wildcat dressed as a sweet innocent.

And she looked tired—her hair falling across her shoulder, resting on the top of her breast, looked like at some point in the day it had been in a bun. She'd pulled the pins out, and now I needed to do the same with the rest of her body, still wound tightly from her day.

"Get over here," I said, patting my lap. She snickered one of her cheeky laughs and rolled her eyes, but she still kicked off her shoes and came to me—I fucking loved that she came to me. Nothing in the world felt better than being able to touch this woman when I wanted to, the privilege of getting to end my days with my skin on hers.

She crawled onto me, her petite frame fitting perfectly over mine, and nestled her face into the crook of my neck. Fuck, just the feel of her warmth calmed me down. The floral smell of her, the subtle feel of her eyelashes fluttering against my neck. She was a like a goddamn Xanax, the way she relaxed me. Her body shifted with my exhales.

"Hi," she said softly, and she turned to unbutton my shirt, starting at the collar and loosening my tie.

"Damsel," I whispered firmly, ready to take her, ready to command her. I took her earlobe between my teeth. I wanted to forget about my mother completely. I was mortified by my her snobbery, hated that she was so predictably horrible. I leaned in to start kissing Lydia's soft neck, but then I noticed she'd stopped her unbuttoning.

"What is it, baby?" I asked her, raising my eyebrow.

She just looked at me, searching. She knew I was upset, could probably tell instantly. "Everything okay?" she asked, searching, and I sighed in defeat. I knew this look. It meant she knew *my* look, and wasn't going to let me just roll this away. "How was your meeting with Jack?"

I rubbed my temples. I knew by the look on her face that it made her edgy, nervous.

"It was fine, baby. He's still going to try to make it work without me," I said reassuringly. "They're giving that option another month or so before going with the plan that involves me. So, there's a chance all this will be for nothing." She closed her eyes for a moment, and I took her hand and brought it to my mouth, kissing it. "It will be *fine*, baby."

I tilted my head from side to side, trying to remove a tightness in my neck, and Lydia caught me. That nervous expression gone, her curiosity back.

"What else is wrong?" she asked. Christ, she missed nothing. I'd be fucked if my clients could read me this well.

"Nothing, damsel. Everything's fine." I ran my nose along her collarbone, but she didn't move. She was waiting. I'd promised her once I wouldn't keep her in the dark, and my stubborn girl was going to hold me to it. "I talked to my mother tonight—she was just being her lovely self, I'm afraid. Typical rubbish." I felt her shift in my arms as I took a deep breath. "It's not worth talking about."

Would she let me get away with that? *Please let her let me get away with that.*

She raised her eyebrows at me, indicating that there was no way in hell she was letting me get away with that.

"Baby, it was just the usual." I didn't want to hurt her, and everything my mother said would hurt her. "She wants what my father wanted." Marriage to a daughter of a member of the peerage, a devoted traditional ducal life, and fucking heirs.

Lydia kept looking at me. Patient. Then she prompted, because she already knew, "For you to get married. Just not to me."

I paused, not being able to actually voice the confirmation she could see on my face.

"It's so odd." She had a look of puzzlement on her face, like she was trying to work something out.

"Which part?" I sighed again and wrapped my arms more tightly around her.

"Well, most of the time I don't think about it, but it's odd that I'm going to fill her shoes. I mean, is your mom what a duchess is supposed to be like? Is that what all the duchesses are like? Because I can assure you, in case you need assuring, that even if you forget my American accent and propensity to swear, I will probably never fit in."

Of course she thought of this—I was such an idiotic prat. How could she *not* look at my mother and wonder if those were the expectations? "You could never be like my mother, baby, because with few exceptions, she and her lot are stiff and lifeless, and you, damsel, are rather stunning and vibrant." I reached for her neck with my lips again but she pulled back.

She half rolled her eyes at me, giving me her *oh-please* look. As though I'd let that slide.

"Damsel," I warned, my tone shifting to get her attention, the tone that pulled her out of herself. I took her chin, brought her eyes to mine. Her face went receptive and her body sank just a bit deeper—I wondered if she knew how her whole body responded when I took control. If she could feel how she melted into me. "I look at that life, the one my father chose to live with my mother, and I don't want it. I never have. The only reason I can do this at all and not drown myself in whisky is that I am determined to be the Duke of Abingdon that the title deserves. And you, damsel, are a key ingredient to that. If I wanted one of those women, I'd have married bloody Amelia Reynolds a decade ago and spent my weekdays playing polo."

"You'd never."

"Precisely." I shifted her so she was straddling me, her skirt riding up her legs and pooling between us. Her toned thighs gripped my own, and I held my hands clasped at her lower back, pulling her just a little closer. "You, damsel, are radiant. You're already twice the duchess she ever was."

She wrapped her arm around me and held her lips against my neck.

"You deserve so much more than my horrible family," I said. I loved the feeling of her against me, loved the way I felt when she was there.

"I deserve *you*." Her voice had descended to a whisper.

"Yes, well, it's too late anyhow," I said, wrapping my fingers around the base of her head, holding her where I could see her. "I won't be letting you out of our engagement, even if you did despise my wretched life. The deal is rather binding, I'm afraid." She laughed, and her laughing undid me every time, and my dick remembered what it had been wanting the entire goddamn day. I slipped my hand into her blouse, cupped her perfect tit, and kissed her exposed neck, hard.

"You, damsel, are already my duchess," I said, lifting her and moving us to the leather love seat in my office. Fucking hell she was so warm, so *soft*. I couldn't help myself—my thumbs moved to the creases of her legs of their own accord. And in perfect time those darling goose pimples rose to the surface of her skin. I slid my hand further and found her bare, freshly waxed, with no knickers between us. *Good girl.*

I heard my own breath hitch. Her smile was playful, relaxed.

"Your mother will panic when she finds out I'm going to be her successor, won't she?"

I kissed the corner of her mouth. "Perhaps," I whispered. "But I don't care." Her lips felt like velvet against my neck. "You know, baby, if you'd agree to wear my ring, she'd fall into line—there's nothing she'd be able to do. No more ridiculous propositions about any woman other than you." I practically grunted the words, weaving in and out of coherent thought. I was losing my mind, wanting to be inside her.

"Not yet," she breathed and shut her eyes, arching into my touch. "Soon." Goddammit, she was going to be the end of me. There was a part of me that wanted to own her, tell her, rule her, insist she let me take her in the most public possible way and then build a fortress with her, against the world, the press, my mother, who-the-fuck-ever. But I'd be patient because I adored her, and because I bloody well needed to be. *Christ*, her slender arms wrapped around my neck, the pull of her, felt amazing.

"Maybe she'll finally stop bugging you about heirs when she finds out," she whispered back, and I shifted my lips down her neck.

"No heirs, damsel." I mumbled my automatic response to the thought of children, then quickly returned to the task at hand. I kissed her mouth like I had nothing else to do, running my tongue along that sweet crease in her lips, prying them open, slipping inside. She demanded patience from me, and I would demand it of her, the little minx. Her warm tongue slid into my mouth, desperate, hungry. She tasted like oranges, vanilla, double cream. She put her fingers in my hair and pulled, trying to get me to move faster, harder, but I just kissed, holding her and everything else at bay.

Chapter 5

Lydia

Oh god.

That felt so good.

When Dylan decided to slow us down, force me to just kiss, to receive him, to taste him, let him taste me, it reminded me what an alarmingly amazing kisser he was.

When I tried to reach between us and move my hands to the bulge in his pants, he gripped my wrists firmly in his hands and held them against my lower back, pinning me in place. The position allowed him to pull away and dive into my mouth at his leisure, keep me from indulging completely in him, forcing me to submit to him, and it made me *want*.

He was wiping away the stress that had clouded the room when I'd entered, and he was replacing it, kiss by kiss, with us.

My breathing was hard and desperate against his mouth, as though my body couldn't be bothered to understand this whole need-for-oxygen business while there were more important things happening, like how my legs were becoming twitchy and needy, wanting to close, wanting to be spread, to be gripped, to be held still while Dylan did what I so badly wanted him to do.

But all he let us do was kiss.

"Damsel." Dylan's words were like crystal—hard and clear and unwavering. In a swift move he was standing above me, and I was fully on my back, the leather seat cool against my bare shoulders, my legs bent to accommodate the short seat, my knees closed in an attempt to calm the embers collecting at the apex of my thighs. Dylan shook his head in disapproval. "Now, now. Show me."

My eyes never left his as I pulled my skirt further and spread my legs, exposing myself to him, for him. "Pervert."

He laughed but still managed to keep the thread of dominance in his eyes. Dylan used one of his large hands to press my knee into the seat back and his other to move my other foot to the floor, spreading me further. "Beautiful."

It probably should have bothered me when he called me beautiful and was obviously just staring between my legs, but it didn't. I knew he thought all of me was beautiful, and that adoration made me feel coveted, hot. It coaxed those embers into flames, and made me want to thrust that part of myself right up to meet him.

"Darling, I'm going to fuck you right here. Because we can, because I want you, and you want me, and because, unlike that other wretched lot, we've got blood running through our veins."

I smiled and bit my lip as I watched him lower the zipper on his trousers. "So it's a protest fuck then?" My heart was racing and that familiar need was spreading through my limbs. I had made a joke, but I knew what he meant. It wasn't a protest anything. It was a reminder. He was shedding whatever conversation he'd had with his mother, leaving it behind like you would an ill-fitting garment.

He just shook his head and then leaned down and bit my ear, inciting a throaty groan. I could hear the jangle of his belt unfastening, his zipper dropping, all while his mouth stayed fixed on mine.

"And when I'm buried in you, you'll squeeze around me, because it bloody *ruins* me when you do that."

I threw my head back as he entered me, and welcomed every tangy sensation, every tiny place where his thrust met my need. Holy hell this was good.

I moaned, louder than I should have, and Dylan clamped his hand over my mouth. "I want you quiet, darling." And he replaced his hand with his mouth, fiercely kissing me in time with his thrusts against my core.

After that conversation, after thinking about just how off-kilter I was in his world, how at odds I was with the role I was supposed to fill, I *needed* this, to be reminded of *us*.

He lifted my hips effortlessly, and suddenly he was hitting me directly in the neediest of places. The spasms around his hard cock were clingy, out of my control, and spiraled me into the orgasm that had me ignoring any demands to be quiet and screaming his name into the room. Calling him *knighty*, and *Dylan*, and *wicked*, crying *I love you*. Tiny fireworks ricocheted over my skin, bouncing from surface to surface and prompting me to pull Dylan against me to calm the riot of sensation.

He stilled as his lips met mine and he came too, that last thrust sending him just a little deeper, wider, harder.

"Fuck, baby. You know you're bloody brilliant at that, don't you?"

I could barely catch my breath as I sank back into reality. "What? Letting you have sex with me anywhere you please?"

Dylan's lips curled into a smile that I could feel in my hair, and he kissed my cheek, holding back a laugh and whispering. "Making me lose my mind anytime I'm around you."

"It's a special skill." I rose onto my elbows as he rose to put himself back together.

"Indeed. Now shall we go take a shower, and then you can get some revenge in our bed?"

"Revenge for what?" I looked at him curiously—his attitude had shifted from regretful to mischievous in the past ten minutes.

"Doesn't matter. Make something up. I love the way you shag me when you're trying to get back at me for something."

I laughed, shaking my head, as I straightened my skirt. "Well, you are a crazy bossy fiend who drives me crazy, so it all works out."

With that, Dylan landed a smack on my bare thigh and chased me to our room, where, within minutes, I was exacting my revenge.

* * *

An hour later I was staring at the ceiling. I couldn't fall asleep. He lay there with his strong arm over my stomach, his fingers wrapped around my waist, pulling me into him, and I loved it, feeling his warmth against me. Feeling the reverberations of my orgasms making my skin tingle. Being home with him.

But my mind was on our conversation in the study. Or one particular part of our conversation. *No heirs, damsel.* I wasn't even sure if he knew he'd said it out loud. He'd said similar things before, and I knew it was a habitual response built over years of believing his own steadfast rules—he'd never get married, never have children. His own upbringing had made him feel that loving others was truly off the table—for nearly a decade he'd avoided love, the mess of it, the vulnerability. But then he let me in. He'd broken that rule. So I knew this rule, about becoming a father, might one day be broken too.

But we had talked about children only once.

It was Marriage 101. I knew that. You don't agree to spend the rest of your life with someone without asking the big questions. What are your hopes and dreams? How do you envision handling finances? Do you expect me to stop working just because you're a duke? (Okay, maybe that one was just me.) And, of course, do you want kids? And if so, how many?

I had a pretty good sense of the answers to most of those. I knew we'd live in England forever—there was too much family history and life here for Dylan, and I loved it here too. I wasn't worried about the financial aspect, partly because being married to Dylan meant not really having to worry, but mostly because I'd always been independent, and Dylan was way too proud of my accomplishments to ever ask me to stop working if I didn't want to. I knew, with confidence, that in that area we were on the same page.

And we were on the same page about kids too, only that page consisted of basically agreeing to table the conversation. The day we'd talked about it, we'd been sitting in the lounge on the first floor of the Belgravia house, a fire in the fireplace, reading side by side.

"So, we should probably talk about children," I'd said, and his eyes went a bit wide. "You know, before we get married."

"Right," he said, closing his book. "Well, I have to be honest—"

"I'm not ready," I said, cutting him off. "And I might not be for a while. My whole life is about to change, and I'm only twenty-five. I just don't think—"

"I agree," he said, cutting me off this time, and he pulled me closer to him on the couch. "Damsel," he started, sighing and rubbing his forehead the way he did when he was stressed. "I didn't have the best example of parenthood. I've never wanted children who will feel the pressures I felt growing up. But, since meeting you, I don't know…perhaps?" I looked at him, hoping for more. "That's probably the best I can give you right now." The more I understood about Dylan's childhood, about the way he was parented, the more I sympathized with his not wanting to repeat that. But when I looked at him and saw how much love he had to give, how he'd lay his life on the line for those he loved, how he wanted to open the world, not just for me, but for every person who walked into any building he designed or every person who set foot onto Humboldt Park, I was sad. Because he'd be an incredible father, as good as my own had been. And I wanted that for him.

"Okay," I'd said. And I went on to tell him how the last year had been a whirlwind, and how I'd spent the years before preoccupied with the very real decisions before my eyes, things about care for my father or balancing work and school. Because that was all true. And now that we were here, starting our life together, I wanted to indulge in each part of it, not rush through it. But it was more than that, more than me wanting time. The real issue, I'd told him, the thing I'd been studiously avoiding, was that even though I knew I wanted children, and I wanted them with him, I was afraid.

I'd never even *had* a mother. What the hell did I know about wanting or not wanting that? I'd seen Daphne with her mom, and could see how great it was, that I wanted *that*. But what if I couldn't do it? What if I wanted to abandon my child the way my mother had abandoned me? What if I didn't want him or her enough?

When I'd said all of this to Dylan, in front of the fire that day, he'd hauled me onto his lap and held me there, just for a moment, kissing my forehead. "There's nothing we can't figure out together, damsel, and thankfully," he'd said, "this isn't something we have to decide today." And I'd nodded into his shoulder, relieved that he wasn't writing it off but noting that he wasn't exactly rushing to reassure me we would make it happen either.

This was the one area of our future that seemed like a question mark. Was I ever going to ask Dylan to make me a mother? Was his answer ever going to be yes? And yet, as I drifted off to sleep, I marveled at how at home I felt lying there next to him, how even when a huge question remained unanswered, I didn't feel that sting of uncertainty. Instead I felt like no matter how we carved out our life, we'd do it together.

Chapter 6

Dylan

The week was flying by—it was Thursday, and Lydia had been working her tight little arse off every night in preparation for her New York trip, a trip I didn't even want to think about. A sodding month without her. Seemed inhumane if you asked me, but no one had.

We were both busier than I wanted us to be. Apart from everything else, it seemed to be the season for parties, parties that I'd attend alone as long as my damsel wanted our relationship to be low profile. Parties my mother continued to see as opportunities to marry me off. Any other girl would jump at the chance to don a gown and waltz down the red carpet at these affairs—fuck, many of the girls I'd slept with in the past had hoped for just that. But as stunning as she looked in a gown, Lydia honestly seemed content to spend those evenings out with her own friends, having some kind of god-awful girls' night with my sister or helping her co-worker Fiona.

That evening's gala was Prince Arthur's annual charity thing, and I cursed its existence as I stood in the closet dressing. Lydia sat cross-legged on the bench, a glass of wine in her hand, wearing nothing but one of my shirts and a pair of leggings. Those leggings should be fucking illegal. No, fuck that. It should be illegal for her to wear anything *but* those leggings. *Christ,* I was definitely going to end up going to this party with a hard-on.

"So what's the party for again?" she asked, taking a sip of her wine and twirling a strand of her hair between her fingers. The dark hair dye from the previous winter had faded, and it was returning to its caramel color. She'd kept that fringe though, which I adored.

"It's Prince Arthur's annual charity thing. My father used to go."

"But now it's your job," she said, standing. She came over to me and took the tie in my hand and brought it back to the shelf. I watched her sway back and forth, side to side on the balls of her feet, as she looked at my ties, and I wanted to devour her. "This one." She draped the thin ocean-blue tie around my neck. "It's different," she added, using the ends of the tie to pull me closer.

I took the ends of the tie from her hands, kissed her, and began the work of a Windsor knot. "I'm tempted to remind you that once the world knows you're the Duchess of Abingdon, you won't be able to escape these things either." I looked in the mirror behind her to straighten the tie.

She just smiled and landed a kiss on my lips, one I couldn't escape even if I wanted to, before she sauntered away. She sang out, "Be good, knighty!" as she sashayed down the hallway, back to the library, where she'd inevitably curl up with her laptop for the evening.

Christ, I was an idiot for leaving that woman at home alone.

* * *

It's not that I truly despised the Prince Arthur's annual spring party in honor of the Racehorse Sanctuary, a place where Thoroughbreds went to retire. I was more than happy to support the animals; although there *was* something a tad hypocritical about the whole business, which you'd know if you went to Ascot and saw just how thoroughly His Royal Highness enjoyed the horses' working years. It wasn't that I'd ever hated these kinds of things—to the contrary, I hadn't thought of them at all. Attending these parties, ones bursting at the seams with every titled lady and gentleman in Great Britain, and some foreign dignitaries to boot, had always just been part of the fabric of my life, lines in my journal, part of the hum.

That year had some kind of casino theme, a James Bond–ish affair, and the great hall at the palace had been set up like a gambling parlor, with all of the proceeds going to the charity, of course. Normally, it would've suited me fine, but tonight felt different. Leaving Lydia, even if only for the evening, felt odd. Being there, in my tux, tumbler in one hand, rubbing two chips together in my other, I felt as though I was playing a part. I'd prefer to have been at home, with my fiancée. No, I wanted her *there*, with *me*.

Had she been there, she would have been charming the bloody pants off Prince Arthur—the man always had a thing for young women, particularly those who didn't play by the rules and had a little life in them. Not that I wanted him ogling my fiancée, but I wouldn't have minded watching her fend him off in that way she always seemed to be able to—with grace and just enough fire in her belly. Like some kind of social ninja, she would extricate herself with a smile, leaving poor blokes standing there somehow thinking they'd won a prize when in fact she'd effectively just told them to sod off. She was bloody brilliant. And she would have worn something perfect, perhaps the dress she'd worn to the Serpentine the previous year, to a party for Jemma and Richard. The back dipped low towards her arse, and made her neck look long in this way that—

"My lord?"

My thoughts were interrupted by the blackjack dealer. I nodded at him, and asked for a card. I already had two eights, but I still couldn't help myself. A four. Didn't get much better than that, but I still felt like something was missing.

"What's the matter, *my lord?*" I turned to see Beatrice Pollard, standing at my side, her arm placed strategically close to mine at the table. "Feeling lonely?" she said in a false, overly coquettish whisper.

Beatrice, or "Beadie" as everyone had called her, was a force. She was, admittedly, stunning. At nearly five foot ten and with her mother's Middle Eastern coloring, she was striking, and had managed to spend most of her twenties modeling. I was also rather certain she had dandelions for brains, and her voice had this treacly quality that made me want to off myself. Of course it hadn't stopped me from sleeping with her a few years back, a mistake of epic proportions since she'd been relentless in her appeals for a solid six months following.

"Not in the slightest, Beadie. Are you well this evening? Enjoying yourself?" The woman had always been an opportunist. Not to mention unoriginal. She was wearing a version of what every woman between the ages of eighteen and thirty-five was wearing—some kind of strapless, solid-colored thing that was purposefully revealing but conservative enough that the old guard would approve. It was like they all got together and decided exactly how far they could push the line.

"Are you still with that girl? I haven't seen you together lately." She frowned with false sympathy, and tried to edge closer to me. The way she said *that girl* gnawed at me, as though Lydia were some fleck of gossip that could be cast aside. But I also found it oddly calming. The more this lot dismissed her, the more they'd leave her alone. Beadie was like a bellwether for the paparazzi. If her dismissal was any indicator, we were doing the job of keeping our relationship low profile rather well, perhaps rather too well if people weren't even sure whether we were together anymore.

I ignored her comment with purpose, refusing to stir any gossip where Lydia was concerned, slid the chips I'd just won into my pocket, and rose to head to the bar. She followed me, abandoning her cards at the table. "How's Nick?" I asked, falling into the politeness routine. Ask about the boyfriend? Check.

"Oh, didn't you hear? We..." I was pretty sure she was telling me a story about how they'd broken up, but I'd stopped listening. My mind was drifting into a calculation about how long I should stay. My mother still hadn't arrived, and I probably needed to be here when she did. And if I was going to make the evening worthwhile, there were a few people I should talk to. I wondered what Lydia was doing at that moment—she'd mentioned she might invite Fiona over so they could work on her online jewelry store. The two of them had put in at least a hundred hours, and the launch of the store had been a success by any standard. Lydia seemed to have a knack for it, not to mention I fell a bit more in love with her every time she did that mad little jumping dance when she had a success with work.

Suddenly my thoughts were interrupted by a screech at my side. I looked down to see Beadie bent over, hopping about and holding her ankle. I'd zoned her out completely, but apparently she'd continued to follow me, and now Amelia Reynolds, of all people, was at her side, doing an admirably horrible job of helping her friend. You'd think that with the decade of finishing school between them they could have kept the shrieks and chaos to a minimum.

What a fucking mess. I set my drink on the tray of a passing waiter, bent down, and lifted Beadie to standing—she gripped my side tightly, plastering herself against me. "Are you all right?" I asked. "What in god's name happened?"

"I tripped. These shoes…" She sucked air in through gritted teeth, indicating she was in pain, and pointed towards a pair of lime-green stilettos that looked more like weapons than shoes. Amelia remained close by, holding Beadie's hand with about as much strength as a kitten. *Totally fucking useless.*

"All right, well, let's get you to a place to sit, shall we?" I wrapped my arm around Beadie's waist and let her put all of her weight onto me as I moved her out of the main room towards a lounge by the toilets. The room had gotten crowded, tuxedos and evening gowns brushing up against one another right along egos and Oscar-worthy social performances. And here I was navigating around drunken chatting groups with a hobbled socialite and her sidekick. *Fucking hell.* These women were a nightmare.

"In here," Beadie said, pointing towards a closed door.

"It's just a big farther to the lounge." I kept moving.

"No, I can't go another step. Please, let's just go in here." I sighed in resignation as Amelia opened the door to the darkened room, and I lifted Beadie over the threshold.

"Now, let's find a place to put you and perhaps, Amelia, you can go fetch one of the staff?" The noises from the party had dimmed behind us, and light shining into the darkened space illuminated a harpsichord and a standing harp but nowhere to sit. Could nothing be easy that night? I pulled a low side table from the wall and gestured for Beadie to sit on it, but she didn't budge; in fact, she leaned in closer.

"What's the rush, Dyl?" Amelia asked, her eyes falling into half-closed seduction. *Oh, fucking Christ.*

I looked down to Beadie, who was still standing, hugged into my side, only now she miraculously seemed to be able to stand perfectly well on her own. They had to be joking. In a flash, Beadie's arms were around my neck, and her face was alarmingly close to mine. Amelia was moving in on my other side, her hands sliding under my jacket lapels, her nails curling to dig into me and her lips perched at my ear.

"What the ever-loving fuck?" I said sternly as I stiffened instinctively and pulled away, not allowing another inch to close between us, expanding the distance as efficiently as possible. The feel of other women touching me, seducing me, and even hinting at that kind of intimacy felt repellant, every cell in my body rejecting the scene they were begging for.

I looked at both of them, their faces lit by the light pouring into the room behind me, neither having any trouble standing on their own at all, and took in their expressions—far too smug to suggest they'd understood the full extent of my rejection. They looked as though my *no* was just a starting point for negotiations.

"To answer your earlier question, Beadie, *Lydia* and I haven't broken up, nor are we likely to. My girlfriend and I live together, and we intend to for some time. And let's be perfectly clear, lest there be a misunderstanding on this point: I will never be unfaithful to her." Amelia had the goddamn nerve to roll her eyes, as though my dating Lydia were some kind nuisance I was inflicting on her, and Beadie just looked confused.

To be fair, I'm not sure either of them ever thought they'd hear a speech railing against infidelity from me, of all people. I often forgot that to the vast majority of people, I was still the commitment-avoidant cad I'd always been. It was funny really, and I couldn't help but smile, because if they had any grasp of who I was was, they'd realize how comically little chance they had at seducing me away from Lydia.

"Now, ladies, for your sake and mine, let's pretend this little interlude didn't happen, shall we? The last thing I'm sure either of you want is that lot"—I gestured back towards the party—"prattling on about how you were rejected for a three-some in the palace music room." The two of them gasped in offense and looked at each other before returning their attention to me. "And I'd appreciate your continued discretion as well. Lydia and I are together, decidedly, but we prefer to keep that private. I'm sure you understand." The two of them had dropped jaws, and I caught a flicker of a scowl at the edges of Amelia's brow. I stepped from the room into the brightly lit hallway and said over my shoulder, "I'll send a waiter with some ice."

Fuck, that had been close. How had I been naïve enough to follow Beadie fucking Pollard into a dark room? Bloody hell. A second longer and her lips would have been on mine. What was an annoyance had been a hair away from being something I'd have a damn hard time explaining to Lydia. The fact was, I was lucky to be walking away from those two women being able to honestly say that nothing had happened. What a god-damn nightmare. I couldn't bloody wait until Lydia and I were married and every twat in this fucking town would understand that they had better luck of getting struck by goddamn lightning—twice—than getting anywhere with me.

I went straight to the bar, ordered a whisky, and emptied the glass like a classless arse before asking for another. As I stood there, softening my stress with liquor, I saw Beadie and Amelia on the far side of the bar, laughing heartily at something some tosser was saying. Amelia caught my eye and gave me a look that confirmed, with zero uncertainty, that I had fully crossed the line from the man she thought she may land one day to being on some list of men she despised. It was probably titled something like *The Real Wankers of London*. Good riddance. After forking over enough dosh and making the polite conversations I was there to make, agreeing to possibly redesign the Majorca estate of the newly married Baron of Essex, and generally having made a presentable appearance, I headed for the exit. I needed to get back to Lydia and get that pretty pussy of hers under my mouth before I lost it entirely.

Chapter 7

Lydia

I was so tired that I could barely keep my eyes open, which was not good.

Hannah had asked me to meet her at her office—I normally went straight to the store, where it wouldn't really matter if my eyes were at half-mast. But I had a ton to get done—it was Friday, and I'd be leaving for New York the next morning. The night before Dylan had come home from that party in a state of near desperation. Presumably the fact that there'd be no sex for a month had just dawned on him—the last time he'd gone a month without sex was probably middle school.

I'd been asleep, sprawled out facedown on our bed, and I'd woken to him hovering above me, his hand sweeping my hair off my back, pushing my T-shirt over my head, laying kisses across my bare back. He had whispered "marry me" and "say yes" as we'd made love. He'd done this before while making love to me, reminded me how much he wanted me to be his. I'd usually say "I love you" and "soon" and make love to him right back. But last night felt just a little more raw, a little more real. And making love had turned into the feverish kind of fucking that included handcuffs he apparently had stowed away in his sock drawer and sounds I should have been embarrassed by in the light of day. It had been nearly two in the morning before I'd fallen asleep again.

"Lydia?" I looked up, fighting a yawn, and saw Fiona glaring at me in a way that suggested she'd probably said my name three times already. "Hannah said she's ready to meet now." She held out a cup of coffee, which I pulled out of her hand with probably a little *too* much enthusiasm.

"Are you in this meeting too?"

She nodded. "Any idea what it's about?"

I shook my head as we stepped into Hannah's crisp white office and sat before her desk. She was beaming, so presumably it was good news.

"Morning, ladies. I'll cut right to it." She looked between us like she was about to tell us we'd all won the lottery. "We're opening up a proper shop on Madison Avenue in New York."

Fiona and I just looked at each other, then back at her. This was amazing. It was everything we'd been working for. Her brand was growing, faster than any of us had anticipated. If we managed to get a New York store up and running within the next eighteen months, it would represent unprecedented growth for a company of our size.

"That's incredible, Hannah. I'm thrilled for you," I said, still in awe, pleased that the Knightsbridge store must be doing well if we were moving forward.

"I'm glad to hear you say that, Lydia. Because my hope is that you'll be the one to do it. I want you to go to New York tomorrow and do the pop-up as planned, but I'd also like you to stay on and oversee the opening of the proper shop." Thoughts started to swarm through my mind. Stay? In New York? "And, Fiona, you can take over for Lydia here. You can work from her office and take over management of the shop in Knightsbridge, if it suits you." Fiona dove right in with the effusive gratitude. I smiled, still struggling to process this.

"Wait, what?" I asked, probably a little more abruptly than was professional. I cleared my throat and tried to refocus while images and thoughts of being back in New York for more than a few weeks flew through my mind. "Um, when would this happen? What's the timeline?"

"Oh, I shan't think you'd need to be there for much more than six months, don't you think? So if you leave at the weekend, you'll be back before Christmas. Or of course if you want a permanent position in New York, I'd be happy to discuss it."

Six months? Why did that number make me feel sick? It was an opportunity. To be trusted to open the shop in New York was a big deal. But something felt off about the whole thing. I couldn't process it here, in Hannah's office. Before I had time to think it through, to respond, to do anything other than the situation required in terms of thanks and enthusiasm, the meeting was over, and technically I was committed to leaving London tomorrow. For New York. For six months.

* * *

After downloading the news with Josh, who was immediately planning Hannah-funded trips to New York, I chose to walk to the store. It wasn't too far, and I needed to *think*. I needed to figure this out.

For the past five months, I'd taken my mission to heart: *Put yourself first. Enjoy the freedom of life out of the spotlight. Get your career off the ground before it competes with running an ancient estate and being on your husband's arm.*

For five months, I'd said yes to all things. Late nights dancing with Fiona and Josh. Girlie nights with Emily. Paris for Fashion Week. Long runs in the park by myself without paparazzi trailing me. Late nights working on the launch of Fiona's online store. Dylan and I had kept our relationship low profile so that I could do all those things, so I wouldn't get sucked into the aristocratic machine, so I could move freely and make choices without fear of how it would look or who would be watching. And it had been great. It *did* feel freeing, like I'd been slipping into a version of adulthood I'd always been waiting for, figuring out who I wanted to be in the world, taking a deep breath while I thought about the reality of being a duchess. But no matter what I did, I was always happy to go home to Dylan, to find him there, to let him find me there. Nothing had changed in that regard—I wanted to be *with him*.

I had figured I'd wake up one day and just know, *now's the time*. And on that day I'd replace *soon* with *yes*. We'd make a big announcement, open the door, I'd officially be Dylan's fiancée and soon after his wife, with everything that came with it. But that aha moment hadn't happened yet, and now there was this. This decision, going away for six months, would change everything. If I said no to Hannah and stayed in London, I knew that, in some plates-shifting kind of way, it meant that I was ready to say yes to Dylan, to all of this, to everything he was asking for. But if I said yes to Hannah, to effectively leaving behind everything I'd built in London for a half a year in New York, my long engagement would be longer than I'd ever really wanted it to be. I knew Dylan would want me to stay in London, with him, to say no to Hannah, to give in to what he'd been waiting for me to give in to. But that meant diving into everything I'd been holding off. Was I ready for that?

With each block I passed through Mayfair, my mind changed, I swayed back and forth. Yes, I'd go to New York for six months. No, I'd stay in London with Dylan. Yes. No. Yes. No. It felt like everything was pitted against one another. London versus New York. My career versus my relationship. My present versus my future.

I was swimming so feverishly in my own mind, my heels clacking on the pavement, my bag swinging against my hip, that I jumped a foot and actually shrieked when I heard a familiar voice say my name. I turned to see Lloyd standing by Dylan's car. In front of our house.

Our house.

I hadn't walked to the store. I'd walked home.

I smiled at Lloyd, who must have sensed I needed privacy, because he walked around to the side of the house where the garage was. I looked in the window, and I could see Dylan in the library on the ground floor. It looked like he was searching for a book, his arm stretched up to one of the higher shelves. He'd been working on a restoration recently and had been researching like a madman. He was wearing jeans and a T-shirt that fitted his muscular frame perfectly. His hair was tousled, uneven from running his fingers through it. He looked at the book in his hands and then stared into the room, thinking. I knew that in a moment he would begin absent-mindedly spinning the pencil in his hand, tapping it against his shoulder, deep in thought. I knew, without looking, that his feet would be bare. I knew there was probably a half-consumed cup of tea on a stool by his drafting table. I knew *him*.

The beauty I saw when I looked through that window made my chest tighten, made me want to take care of him for the rest of our lives. I was looking into a home that had become *mine*, *ours*, and all of the anxiety of the decision fell away. I was looking at my future.

There was no way I could go to New York for six months. And if there was no way I could do that, then I knew in my gut that the plates *had* shifted. I wanted this. I wanted him. I wanted whatever a life with Dylan brought me. There was nothing left for me in the version of the world where my first thought was, *Is Lydia being free, doing everything she should be doing as a twenty-five year-old starting her life in London?* I didn't need that anymore. I didn't want it. I felt freer with Dylan than I ever would without him.

As I watched Dylan disappear from the library, I turned around and began to walk back to the office, practically jogging. I needed to tell Hannah that a month in New York was my limit. Maybe Fiona would want to open the Manhattan store, and if even she didn't, Hannah would still probably need her to take over the London store. The reality was that if Dylan and I were going to be married, I was going to need more flexibility at work.

As I picked up my pace, I let the details and questions and possibilities unfurl in my mind, let the excitement take over. Then I started daydreaming about that night, about what it was going to feel like to watch his eyes fill with satisfaction as he finally got his way, to say yes.

Chapter 8

Dylan

Lydia seemed downright buoyant when I spoke to her on the phone that afternoon. She'd been flirty, giddy, attentive. She hadn't scoffed when I told her I'd upgraded her plane ticket the next day to first class. She hadn't shot me down when I suggested we have a late dinner at San Lorenzo, something we rarely did given that it was a favorite stalking ground for photographers. Nor had she fought me when I suggested she let Lloyd drive her home that night. My only guess was it was due to the fact that she'd be leaving my smitten ass for a month the next day, but I didn't give a shite.

Fuck me, I didn't want her going anywhere for a month without me. If I hadn't been up to my ears with work, I'd have gone with her. And the last thing I wanted to do was have drinks with my mother the night before Lydia left. The weekly phone calls with my mother about Humboldt were fine, but actual in-person conversations? I could count them on one hand since my father had died. We'd been avoiding each other. She knew it, as did I, but I had the distinct feeling we were finally about to have it out. After that phone call earlier in the week, I was madder than hell. And she'd booked a private dining room at Annabel's, which could only mean she had no intention of us being over-heard. My plan was to be in and out and back to Lydia within an hour—like hell I was going to let my mother take my last night with my damsel.

"Darling," my mother said as she joined me at the table, at precisely six thirty. The woman was never late.

"Mum," I said, forcing a smile "How was your holiday?"

She waved her hand in the air, dismissing my question, and for some reason I felt like I could see her sadness more clearly that day. Or she was showing me more of it. "I'm headed to Ibiza tomorrow. I need to get away."

"Why not stay at Humboldt for a while?" On one hand I wanted to throttle her for being the worst snob and a terrible mother, and on the other hand, Lydia's sympathy kept my own alive as well. I could hear Lydia reminding me that we should pick our battles, but restraint was not my forte.

"I can't be there, Dylan." My mother looked at me with a pleading expression, like she wanted rescuing, like she'd grown weary of pushing me away. "I can't be there while all of this hangs in the air." She waved her hands in the air as though all of Annabel's hung in the balance. I had expected her expression to provide some clarity or even unity—weren't we both enduring a substantial transition? But instead I was met with a cold stare of accusation.

"While *what* hangs in the air?" I asked, trying to understand her meaning. She just continued to stare at me with a combina-tion of frustration and disappointment. "Mother, just say what you mean to say."

"You know what I am going to say. You know what needs to

be done. I can't have my mind at ease while the fate of Humboldt Park, this family's future, hangs in the balance."

"Mum, don't start with that bloody nonsense. It's a nonstarter and you know it. You're about to say something you'll regret."

"No, darling. I don't have regrets. You need to devote yourself to Hale Shipping—it's your legacy, Dylan. And—"

"Don't say it—" I tried to cut her off.

"You need to marry. You need to marry *appropriately*. And you need to provide for the future of this family." A baby. She was talking about a baby. With some woman I probably wouldn't be able to stand to be in the same room with. No fucking way.

"First of all, let's get one point straight. Hale Architecture and Design is my legacy, *not* Hale Shipping. I'm well aware the company must stay in the family. I'm wondering if *you* have any sense of what kind of trouble that company is in? Of what I'm having to do to get it back on track? Are you aware, Mother, that Father nearly bankrupted the company? That he made risky deals that lost money, that he fired managing staff who had held the company together for years in favor of sycophants who agreed with his absurdist vision for how to run a company? That the company continues to carry loans it has yet to pay back? That he took a loan from the Bresnovs?"

"That family that your grandfather knew?" she asked, clearly confused.

"Yes, the family that is now firmly entrenched in the Russian Mafia. The family that swindled Father into putting Humboldt Park into the holdings of Hale Shipping and then promptly began to extort the company for its own illegal gains. The family I have been busily trying to extricate us from for the past two years. Mother, are you aware that while Father was busy sitting on his arse before he died, I have been working with MI6 to try to apprehend that *family* so that we can once and for all be done with them and we can return Hale Shipping to its former status, *legally*? And trust me when I tell you that figuring out how, precisely, to sort everything out to everyone's satisfaction is very much at the fore of my life these days." My tone was low, steady, conversational. I didn't care if we were in private; I wasn't going to give my mother the satisfaction of losing my cool. And her expression was stiff, but not blank. "I'll take your silence as confirmation that you were unaware of everything that's been going on. I should hope that we can now agree that I apparently will not be abandoning the company. Now, as for the second matter. I am going to pretend you didn't just suggest I marry and knock up some poor girl I don't love, someone with a goddamn title who may have nothing but waxed cotton between the ears." I was seething, and as I took a swig of my whisky, I found it harder and harder to remain in control. I was speaking between my teeth, my fury rising to the surface. "I'm going to pretend that you didn't just insult my…" I wanted to say *fiancée* so badly in that moment. I wanted my mother to know just how futile her efforts were. And goddammit, I was going to get that ring on her finger soon to put an end this nonsense. "…girlfriend while pretending she doesn't exist, suggesting that I give up the one thing that's actually making me *happy*."

"Oh, don't be ridiculous, Dylan. Stop with the adolescent dramatics. You're far too old for this nonsense. Everything you've just told me about Hale Shipping, while disappointing, just makes my concern all the more important." What was bloody wrong with this woman—had she heard nothing I'd just said?

"So I see you and Father were rather aligned on this point,

were you? Appearances first, no matter the cost," I said, knowing that she often thought my father was overly cruel, that maybe I could point out the absurdity of what she was saying.

"All your father wanted was to help you get some perspective—perspective that will serve you well for the course of your life, Dylan, not just satisfy some passing boyish wants. Please, Dylan, think about someone other than yourself for once."

"Think about someone other than myself? Mother, I've spent my entire life tamping down my own desires, my own goals, my*self* in order to please you and Father. For the first time in my life, I am taking care of myself, and if you haven't noticed, I'm taking quite good care of Humboldt as well. I'm not going to live my life to please *you* anymore."

With Lydia's help, I'd been devoting every spare second to reorganizing the management of Humboldt Park. I'd given overdue raises. I'd scheduled repairs. I may not be eagerly attending leisurely weekend shooting parties with other aristocrats, but no one could deny that I was actively working on behalf of the estate.

"I'm not talking about *me*, Dylan. Or opening Parliament or any of the other duties you've taken on. Of course you're doing what you *should* be doing there. You've been preparing for that you're entire life. That's not what I'm referring to."

"Then what in the bleeding hell *are* you referring to, Mother?"

"Lydia, of course." What was she talking about? "I know you're planning on marrying her—as much as you may think otherwise, my head is not completely buried in the sand. I've seen how you are with her. Has it occurred to you how absolutely selfish *that* would be?"

I was truly stunned, because the fact was I *had* thought her head was buried in the sand.

"Mother, Lydia knows exactly what she's getting into."

"Does she? Do you?" My mother sat there, her hands on the table, somehow knowing without looking that a waiter was coming from behind her, that she should stop talking while he placed our drinks before us. A moment later he was gone. "Dylan, you know that I also went to Cambridge?"

I nodded.

"Did you know I had a first in French? Did you know I was offered a PhD candidacy at Oxford, that I wrote a paper that is still considered a seminal piece on French translations of early modern British literature?"

I hadn't. I hadn't known any of this. And she knew it.

"You see, Dylan, it's all well and good to have these romantic notions of modernity, of continuing onward into life at Humboldt as though nothing has changed, that nothing will. But you haven't a clue what you're asking of this poor girl, do you? Of course it all seemed possible. Of course I thought I'd just take a year off, perhaps two, then I'd go back and continue my work. At first it was just a conference I turned down. Then I put off the position for a year, because it was the queen's silver jubilee, and even though your father wasn't duke yet, it wouldn't be proper for us not to be in attendance. Then I was pregnant. There was Humboldt—it's not a normal house, Dylan. It's an estate that needs a master *and* a mistress. So you see, you may be willing to take things away from her, but is it who you want to be?"

I sat, silently. How had I not known any of this?

"I know you think your father's infidelities were *his* aggressions," she continued. "And they were, of course. But have you asked yourself what *you* will do if your wife, whose independence you adore now, resents you so completely for taking it away from her? What *she* will do if that happens? She doesn't know what is ahead of her, Dylan. She has that excuse. But you do not."

"Mum," I started, but I didn't know what to say.

"It's time to grow up, Dylan."

* * *

When I left the restaurant, I went to the pub a block away from the club. I texted Lydia and apologized about dinner, saying I'd see her at home in a bit, that I had some things to take care of. The darling girl wrote back with a frowny face and a promise to make coming home worth my while. What was I doing to my damsel, asking her to marry me, to give her life to me? Is that what I wanted for her? As the person who knew this life wasn't it *my* responsibility to shield her from a shite life in which she'd resent me, resent us. The puzzle pieces just weren't fitting. I wasn't my father, but I couldn't get my mother's words from my mind. Fuck, it made my head hurt. My heart hurt.

I stopped thinking. I started drinking.

It was well after ten before I got in a cab. I'd sent Lloyd home—I didn't want anyone, even him, to be privy to this.

The cab was rounding the corner onto my street when my mobile rang.

Thomas, my assistant. I reluctantly picked up—he never called at this hour.

"Mr. Hale, have you seen the *Evening Standard*?"

Chapter 9

Lydia

Finally, I heard the door shut downstairs. No, *slam*. It *slammed* shut.

I slipped on Dylan's thick flannel robe and gently padded down the main staircase. As I descended towards the foyer, I heard something else slam in the kitchen, and I turned to look down the hallway. Dylan's arms were braced on the marble island top, and a newspaper was on the surface in front of him. All the lights were off, apart from the one above the stove, lighting his features.

"Fuck!" he practically shouted, and then I noticed the crystal tumbler of brown liquid gripped in his hand. His voice was so loud and stern I jumped back a little, my arm hitting the bannister in the process, and I gripped my elbow to dull the pain.

Dylan caught my movement and looked up at me.

"Damsel," he said, sounding sad, off, like maybe this wasn't his first drink of the night.

"Hey," I said, sidling up next to him. "You're home late."

He exhaled, like he was bracing himself, and slid the *Evening*

Standard towards me. On the front page, in full color, was a set of three photos.

In the center was Dylan emerging from a small jewelry store, and there was snow on the ground. It had only snowed like that once over the winter, back in December. To the right of it, there was a picture of me, standing alone on a street corner. It had been taken a couple of weeks prior. I was looking at my phone and had a distracted look on my face. I had no idea what I must have been thinking in that photo, but I conceded that I looked stressed at best. And to the left was a picture of Dylan standing next to some freakishly tall brunette at a party, wearing that ocean-blue tie I'd picked out. The headline read, *"Dashing Dylan Can't Decide?"*

The caption hinted that the jeweler's apprentice had told sources that, indeed, Dylan had picked up an engagement ring that day.

I found myself exhaling too, and actually laughing a little. These misinformed mishaps on the part of the press used to stress me out, make me question everything. Now they felt inconvenient and offensive more than anything, but not threatening. I pushed the paper away, towards the far end of the island, and pulled the robe tighter. Dylan looked at me with his brow furrowed.

"The little git's been sacked." Dylan's voice was harsh.

"Who?" I asked, confused.

"The jeweler's apprentice. When I went to pick up your ring, the owner of the shop assured me of his discretion. He's been handling our watches and jewelry for decades, and I had a voicemail from him this evening to apologize. And to tell me he'd sacked the little bastard."

I sighed. I honestly didn't care about the jeweler—it just seemed like the kind of thing that was bound to happen.

"So you *do* have a ring?" I was trying to make a joke, to get him smiling, but his lips didn't curve away from their hard line. I sighed, resigned to the mood he was in. "Who is she?" I asked, pointing at the picture of the girl.

"You can't tell me you actually believe this rubbish?" Dylan had the nerve to sound pissed. As though *I* had done something wrong here. It wasn't like I thought *he* had done anything wrong.

"Dylan, no. Of course not. I trust you. I was just curious. If half of London thinks you're just as likely to be engaged to *her*," I said, pointing at the couture-clad femme fatale, "I just kind of want to know who she is." I didn't like how this was moving into fight territory. I moved closer and linked my arm in his, trying to pull him towards me.

"Lady Beatrice Pollard." He threw back another sip of whisky. His arms were locked on the island, and I felt as though no matter what I did, I couldn't get him to relax and look at me, talk to me. "You shouldn't have to put up with this shite." His upper lip was rigid—it was an expression I'd seen before, when he was lost to whatever stress-induced place he was in. There was no way this was just about the newspaper—we dealt with crap like that all the time and it never put him in *that* foul of a mood. He must have had a terrible day. I had just the thing to turn the evening around.

"Well," I said, standing a little taller, moving against the island so I could see his face. So he could see mine. I wanted him to see how sincere I was. I touched his arm, rubbing his skin with my thumb. "Baby, I think maybe it's time we just come out with it. I want to get engaged, you know, for real." I smiled at him, waiting for the relieved excited smile I'd been anticipating. There was a beat. Then another. No wide eyes. No big smile. All I got was silence. Why wasn't he responding?

"Dylan, this past week Hannah asked me to extend the New York trip for six months. She wanted me to run her business there while it gets off the ground."

His eyebrows raised a bit at this. "What did you say?"

"No. I said no. And you know why? Because I realized *this* is where I belong. It made me realize that I don't want to wait anymore." I stood on my tiptoes, grabbed his lapels, and tried to pull him towards me. "I want to be *here* with you, starting our life together. I'm ready, knighty. I want to get married. I want it all."

Dylan took another swig of his whisky. "Maybe you *should* go."

"What?" I asked, furrowing my brow. There was no way I'd heard him properly.

"It would probably be good for you to go."

My heels landed on the floor. I took a step back, and my heart slammed into my chest. "What are you saying?"

"We can't go public with our engagement right now. We can't get married yet." How could he be saying this?

"Dylan? I don't—what do you mean?" I tried to remain calm. It was late. He was mad, about what I still didn't know, and probably drunk. I was tired. We probably shouldn't be talking about this now, but we already were, and I needed to know what the hell was going on before I got on a plane in eight hours. He was supposed to be jumping for joy. He'd been begging me to say yes just yesterday. I took a deep breath, stood up, and went to the fridge for the wine. It was abundantly clear that this wasn't going to be the excited *we're-doing-this* conversation that ended in orgasms and disheveled sheets.

"Damsel, you should go for the six months—it's a great opportunity, and I won't be responsible for you giving it up." He ran his hand through his hair, took another swig of his drink, and landed his hands back on the island in front of him. "And I'm not throwing you into this life, opening you up to all the pressures of being with me. Not when I haven't got everything sorted myself. I need to get this MI6 nonsense behind me. I've got to get the board of bloody Hale Shipping off my back. And I've got to get Humboldt back in my name, before I can properly attend to a *wedding*, to guarding you against the unpleasantness that is my life, and from the absolutely heinous reality of socializing with this lot." He gestured to the picture of Beatrice again and huffed, "So, no. We're not announcing our engagement until I can figure out a way to shield you from all that, until I know this shite won't touch you." He stared at me, as though that were it, as though that made any sense at all, as though the conversation were anywhere close to over.

"Are you finished?" I asked him, feeling the anger in my voice and having a sip of my wine.

He nodded, wary. And he should have looked wary. My fury was rising, and I was barely keeping it in check. I felt my shoulders stiffen, and I found myself standing on the other side of the island, my own hands braced on the cold marble, mirroring his position opposite me.

"Dylan, do you realize how crazy you sound? First of all, I'm not giving up opportunities. I've opened a store. *In London.* The next step for me isn't going back to New York and doing it again. The next step for me is something bigger. I don't know what it is, but I want to figure it out *here* with *you*. I want my next career move to be something that will work for our life, for our *married* life. And do you honestly think that Humboldt and your mom aren't things I'm thinking about and dealing with *now*? The only thing that would change if the world knew we were engaged is that we wouldn't have to put up with this crap any-more." It was my turn to gesture towards the newspaper. I'd only meant to point to it, but somehow I'd ended up shoving it half-way across the island. "I mean, for fuck's sake, you *are* engaged. To *me*." I pointed to my bare chest, and Dylan's eyes went wide. He looked from the paper to me, finally taking in that I was get-ting pissed. Really pissed. He stood a little taller, running his hands through his hair, tilting his head to the ceiling, rolling his shoulders, searching for answers. His collar undone, his jacket hanging lose, he looked frustrated, angry, lost. His exhale practi-cally echoed across the room.

"Lydia, you have to trust me—"

I groaned, practically growled, in frustration. "No! No more 'trust me' crap. Dylan I *do* trust you—this isn't what that's about."

"So it's about a big fancy wedding then, is it?" He was will-fully misunderstanding me. He knew I didn't give a fuck about that shit. Leaning over the island, bracing himself on locked arms, looking right at me, his face was hard and cold, like he *wanted* to keep fighting, even if it was about all the wrong things. "You want the more flattering kind of paparazzi atten-tion now? Is that it? Think once we're engaged the press will all of a sudden treat you like a darling? Well, don't—"

"Fuck. You." I'd never said that to him. To anyone. But it was exactly what I felt in that moment.

"Excuse me?"

"You heard me. You know damn well I don't give a shit about that stuff. I don't know why you're pushing me away, Dylan, but I'm ready. I want to *do* this. *With you*." I gestured between us emphatically, and he stood there, his hands hanging at his sides, looking at me, half desperate, half mad, I wasn't even sure anymore. "I don't want to stand to the side anymore while you handle things alone. I hate that in the privacy of our home, I'm with you, I'm there, I'm part of our team, but once we step out that door, in the eyes of the entire country, you're on your own. I'm here, Dylan. I know that once we get engaged there is going to be more—there'll be expectations. Expectations we've avoided while we've kept our engagement a secret. I *get* that—that's *why* we were keeping it a secret. But I want to be in it together. Fully. You've been patient. You've waited for months for me to be ready to dive in. Well, I'm ready. So why are you fighting me? Why are we going to keep inviting *this crap*"—I pointed at the paper again and said it forcefully, more forcefully than it had even come out in my mind—"into our lives when we don't have to? I want the world to look at you and see the invincible team we are. Because we *are*. Together we can figure out the life we want. We can do anything. But the longer we let this go, the more we're going to allow them to break us down."

I was so frustrated. I needed him to hear me. I stood there, his robe falling open around my shoulders, my hair hanging loosely, and I willed my expression to say what my words were failing to communicate.

"Lydia," he sighed in a cold way, sounding frustrated himself, and put his hands in his pockets. "You don't understand. We get married now, before I've figured this out, and I'm walking right into my father's life. Overwhelmed by the duty of being duke and the rest of it, and I won't risk becoming the man he was, one who threw his *wife* under the bus to make it happen and let that life ruin him, ruin her."

"You're not your father!" I practically groaned the words. We'd been here before. I knew he knew he could be a better duke than his father had been—he already *was*.

His head snapped up and his narrowed eyes said I'd never understand. "You're right, and I never *will* be."

"And I'm not your mother!" I looked at him, placed my hand against my chest, pleading, trying one last time to cut through whatever was eating him. "Can't you see that? You told me once that we could do this our way. That as a team, we could take this on, that you wanted to be duke with me by your side. Has that changed? What happened to make you so skittish all of a sudden?"

"Christ." He ran his hands through his hair. "Of course nothing's changed. But now isn't the right time. There's too much…I just need to get this all sorted…once we announce our engagement, the floodgates will be open—"

"They're already open!" I screamed, hitting the marble countertop with my hand. "You think photos of me looking pathetic on the sidewalk, like some kind of naïve thing, are nothing? Because, they're not. *I* know it's not true, you know, but do you think it's easy to walk down the street with everyone out there thinking I'm some kind of sad desperate girl clinging to you? You think it's any easier helping you run Humboldt in secret than it would be to help you run it in public? You think any of this is easy *now*?"

"Baby—"

"Dylan, are we engaged or not?"

"Damsel, don't play that card. *Of course* we're bloody well engaged. You *know* that's not what this is about."

"Do I? I don't get it, Dylan. I've proven that I'm there, a thousand percent, when it comes to Humboldt. And I've told you I'm ready to take on the press. Even if I'm not eager for WedDyLy or whatever the press will call it, I'd rather the coverage be *true*, which is easier to handle than the lies. So, what?

Do you think I can't handle it? You think I'm not ready to be a duchess? Did you ever?"

"Lydia. Stop being ridiculous." His lips drew into a hard line. He was mad. Well, I was *furious*. I knew he *wanted* to marry me. I didn't doubt that. But I knew that didn't mean he was going to, and I was starting to believe he really didn't think I could handle anything.

"Dylan. Look, I love that you're protective. Or sometimes I do—I mean, sure, it's sexy. It's sweet that you want to give me this perfect easy life, but that's not *life*, Dylan. I don't *want* to be some quiet, kept woman, unaware of her husband's struggles. Fuck, I'm *not* unaware of your struggles. I'm living them right alongside you. Only instead of you owning that, instead of being able to proudly stand beside you and call them *our* struggles, I've been in the shadows, which was fine before. It was what we wanted, what I wanted, but I don't want that anymore. And you know what? I'm kicking ass at my own life too. We're already doing this together, and doing it well. So let's *really* do it, Dylan." I sighed, frustrated, knowing I wasn't getting anywhere. "It's like you want control over how all of this will play out, you want this pretty little risk-free version of life—"

"Goddamn right, I do."

"Well it doesn't exist, Dylan. That's not *life*. We're living life now, already, so why the hell can't we do it married?"

He pushed away from the island and his hands went flying into the air.

"Bloody hell! *You're* the one who wanted this engagement to be a secret!"

"And you *didn't*! And I don't anymore!"

"Well, you were right to want it to be a secret—I'm *not* going to drag you into this! I'm not!"

I stared at him. At his mussed hair. At the empty glass. At his loosened collar. And I realized this fight was over.

"Then I guess we're done here." I tightened my robe once again, noticing it had fallen loose at my chest, and stepped backwards, away from the island.

"What do you mean?" His eyes were narrowed.

"I mean, I have nothing else to say." I knew my expression must have looked void, empty. And it wasn't what I felt—I felt full, hot, powerless, and powerful in the same moment. Desperate and resigned. "I know what I want, Dylan. And you're not willing to give it to me. And as someone who loves you, loves you with everything, you can't imagine how painful it is to look at you, all of you, and see you holding up an epic stop sign that says 'no trespassing.'"

"What the fuck does that mean?"

"It means, how stupid am I that after everything, I'm right back where I started? Trying to convince you that we're worth fighting for. Maybe you're right, Dylan. Maybe it's time for me to go."

He stared at me, his expression morphing into one of desperation, but he said nothing. I looked at him, waiting, and with every passing second, the waiting turned into sadness. Why did it seem like I always found myself back at this same place?

I turned around and headed towards the stairs. My flight to New York was in less than eight hours, and instead of celebrating that we were going to make our engagement public, I wasn't even sure we were engaged anymore. I wished with everything that he'd say something, *anything*. That he'd call my name, say *damsel*, say *stop*, say he was sorry, snap the fuck out of it. But I was halfway up the stairs and all there was was silence.

Chapter 10

Lydia

In every wedding toast in every movie, I felt like the father of the bride or some great-aunt told the couple, "Never go to bed angry." Not only was I going to bed angry, I was falling asleep on a plane headed three thousand miles from my fiancé angry, and I wouldn't see him for a month, possibly six. I'd found an email in my inbox that morning from Hannah asking me to reconsider, practically begging, and instead of giving her the resounding *no* I wanted to, I'd said I'd think about it. All of a sudden everything was up in the air.

I'd woken that morning at four to go to the airport and Dylan was collapsed on our bed, still in his clothes from the night before. I didn't wake him. I didn't say goodbye. I didn't know what to say. I honestly didn't know where we stood. We didn't technically break up, but I didn't know if we had a future. There was a pit in my stomach, an ugly knot that scared me. Was I crazy to get on that plane? Was my relationship going to die on the vine because my fiancé, my "bloody fiancé," couldn't tell his perfect ass from his perfect eyelashes, couldn't pull that genius brain of his out of the sand for two seconds and realize that moving forward was the only way to move through?

I wanted to kill him. Except then he'd be gone, and I loved him too damn much for that. Even now, sitting in first class, I was annoyed. Initially I'd thought his upgrading my ticket without asking was sweet, but now it felt like a metaphor for our entire predicament. He was so preoccupied with keeping me safe and in the lap of luxury, so sure that he should be handling all of the enormous things on his plate by himself, that he didn't even consult me. Not that I was actually complaining, at least not about first class on a transatlantic flight. But about the rest of it? I was livid. I wanted to tear my hair out with frustration. Didn't he get it? We were a *team*. Or we were supposed to be. We'd promised to be.

Men and their *infuriating* need for independence. It was going to be the end of me. Only, I was actually afraid it was going to be the end of us. There was only so much more of this upper-crust stoic, "no, no, I mustn't be a nuisance" man-is-an-island crap I could take.

"Excuse me, madame?" I looked up to see a blond Nordic-looking flight attendant waiting patiently for me to hand her the once-warm-now-cool damp towel I'd been wringing in my hands. Then I looked down only to realize I was practically tearing the thing to shreds.

"Oh, um, sorry," I said, placing the towel in the basket she held.

Apparently this was getting to me. On the underside of my anger was sadness. I hated that I was going to be so far away, we weren't going to have the chance to resolve it. And on the underside of that was worry. I could avoid thinking about it as much as I wanted, but the top plan that British intelligence was working

with involved using Dylan for bait in a dangerous sting operation. I might have been angry with him, but I wasn't ready to
lose him to some stunt.

I closed my eyes and tried to push all of it aside, tried to find
some sliver of calm, normal happy thoughts. I only half noticed
that I was twisting my ring with my thumb as I drifted off, rhyth-
mically turning it as though the solution to all of this would be
unlocked.

* * *

Ten hours after I'd shut the door to the Belgravia house behind
me, I was setting foot on New York soil for the first time in eight
months.

I had packed light, just a roller bag with staples and a few
other items—I'd be doing laundry and collecting some of my
clothes from storage. So I felt oddly empty, just standing there
with my purse over my shoulder, my hand on the small suitcase.

The New York spring air—always colder than you wanted it
to be when you're hankering for spring—was kissing my cheeks.
The yellow cabs were lining up alongside those of us who were
lining up for them, both of us waiting to get paired off. The
American accents—*my* accent—filled my ears, and I caught
glimpses of everything: the way people moved, how the air
tasted on my tongue, the cars with their steering wheels on the
left. A thousand minuscule things told me I was away from
London.

In an instant I was taken back to the previous September
when I'd been arriving at that same airport on the departures
level, a crumbled notecard with Dylan's phone number on it in

my pocket. Luggage full of my best knockoff outfits. The keys to the Notting Hill house at the bottom of my tote. I'd been wearing my worn-in denim jacket. I'd been so excited to get to London. I'd been so eager to leave my grief behind. I'd had no idea what was coming.

Now I stood there, nearly eight months later. Inching forward in the taxi "queue"—and it was the word *queue* that rolled through my mind automatically, not *line*—in an Alexander McQueen black cashmere coat that *Dylan* had bought me in Greece. I stood there engaged to be married. I stood there completely changed by everything that had happened over the past months.

I'd had no idea that nearly a year after my father died, there would be a part of that grief that would clearly never waver, never fade. But I'd also had no idea just how effective leaving New York would be for pushing it to the side, avoiding it.

Standing on that bustling sidewalk, my luggage by my side, the smells of *home* woke up corners of my mind that had been lying dormant. Images of subway rides to Jackson Heights for Indian food flashed through me. The memory of when my father took me to the airport when I went visit a college in North Carolina (as if I'd ever have left New York back then) came to mind and was followed quickly by the memory of him being too sick to bring me anywhere just a couple of years later. I thought of our spring walks in the Brooklyn Botanic Garden, the taste of good coffee, the feeling of sitting on our stoop. For the first time in months, possibly years, I really thought of my life in New York, of who I was there, of what I'd lost there.

It wasn't until a taxi attendant tapped me on the shoulder that I realized my cheeks were wet. That my chin was quivering. That I was crying for my father for the very first time.

* * *

Dylan and I still weren't speaking, technically, so the silence was peppered only with the most minimal of texts, the first of which I sent when I got to the apartment.

> SATURDAY, 12:15 pm
> At the apartment. x

As I pressed SEND I could feel that there was something almost worse about that one *x* than nothing. Something perfunctory. But I didn't know what to say. The things I'd had to say couldn't be said over text. And all of the important things had already been said. But they'd never been heard, and maybe they never would be. I didn't know where we went from here. I wanted him. I wanted to *marry* him. But I wanted *him* to want to marry me, to have it be more important than his pride or his misguided ideas about separating us from the rest of his life.

He'd started and stopped returning my text for at least two minutes, the little dots appearing and disappearing, before his reply finally came through.

> SATURDAY, 12:17 pm
> Thanks for letting me know. Let me know if you need anything.

I'd sighed, sad, and tossed the phone on the bed, frustrated. *Let me know if you need anything.* Didn't he get that *that* was what I was mad at, or part of it? I *did* need something, and it wasn't a plane ticket upgrade. It was *him.*

I wished Daphne were there. Instead she was in Japan at some international law student conference. Figured. The one time I was actually *in* Brooklyn and needed her desperately, she was on the other side of the world and wouldn't be back for another week. I sank onto the bed and closed my eyes, just trying to be comforted by the familiar smells.

My father had owned the apartment. He'd bought it back when that part of Park Slope was considered dangerous, when no one lived there. Now I owned it, which was strange to think about. I'd avoided thinking about it for a year—it had been rented through a management company, and the lease had run out the month before. I'd decided not to renew it, thinking I'd stay here for these few weeks and then maybe rent it to Daphne or even consider selling. Now I honestly wasn't sure. Most of my father's belongings had been boxed and put into storage along with my own furniture and clothes, the few things I'd accumulated in my brief stint of New York adulthood before abandoning the continent altogether. But there were still several boxes in a locked closet. I stared at that closet door for about ten minutes before I managed to roll off the bed, open the door, and begin my search for one box in particular.

I removed the framed photographs one by one and placed them in their original homes—my high school graduation picture went on the upright piano in the living room. The photo of my father and me next to the roller coaster at Coney Island belonged on the bookshelf by the window looking out onto the tree-lined street. The photo of the lemonade stand I'd set up at Grand Army Plaza when I was eight went on a shelf in the kitchen—my father had always said that it should go in my office someday. "Evidence of your business savvy," he'd said. I'd have to remember to bring it back to London with me. Assuming I was going back to London. I put all the photos back in their places, and when I was done, I could somehow breathe easier.

* * *

I gave myself a buffer to settle in, to launder the sheets, buy fresh flowers and groceries, and take walks through my old neighborhood. I made the rounds, stopping to chat with the other people in our building and visiting my father's friends at his favorite bar, Great Lakes. I called the Franklins, the family I used to babysit for, and made plans to have dinner with them and see the children. I took those days to reassemble the threads of my New York life, breathe it back in.

Then I rolled up my sleeves and dove into work. It was the only way I could make the day go by, could keep my mind off the eerie silence that awaited me every time I looked at my phone. I needed the focus, the escape. I spent a day speccing out the new space with the decorator and contractor. I spent hours on the phone with the manufacturers, checking shipment statuses. We had two weeks to finalize the pop-up space in SoHo before we opened. And I still had the Madison Ave shop to think about—I spent hours sifting through résumés for eager potential sales clerks and store managers. And each night there'd be one empty "goodnight" text, but otherwise it was still silence on the transatlantic Dylan–Lydia wire.

I caught myself smirking at one point, when my mood had morphed into a slightly sardonic post-coffee "well, I guess this is my life" phase. I was literally on my hands and knees, on the floor of the shop space in SoHo, screwing in an outlet cover—when I realized that this time I had fled to New York to escape problems in London. How recently I had been fleeing New York. The irony.

The days were endless flows of checking things off of lists, and I began to fill my evenings with *I'm-back-in-town* dinners with friends. Anything to keep me busy, to try to reassert my New York self. I felt like I was digging around for evidence that pre-Dylan Lydia could be found here. I wanted to find her, to find something solid while so much in my life felt like liquid.

And it worked to some extent. I *did* love walking to and from the familiar subway stop on Fourth Avenue and Union. I loved the smells of walking through Chinatown. I loved being on *familiar* ground. I loved the old faces of college friends around dinner tables, and the reminiscing that came with it. But it wasn't complete. The dinners weren't just reunions, they were reminders of the man I was missing so much. Sitting in a friend's lounge—I meant living room (god, I really was becoming British)—in Greenpoint, someone asked me about my love life, and I'd had no idea what to say. I'd wanted to say I was engaged. I'd wanted to say, *Well, actually, it's kind of a crazy story*. I'd wanted them to know about it. Because them *not* knowing about it, about Dylan, about us, made it *all* feel like maybe it just had been a dream. Somehow Dylan had become part of me, half of me, and now, sitting in front of my Brooklyn friends, who had no idea about us, I felt like half of me was missing.

A week. This went on for over a *week*. One empty text a day, but no other communication. We should have talked, figured this out before I'd left. But I hadn't. We hadn't, and now I didn't know where we stood. I wasn't even sure what needed to be said, what could be said.

On the tenth day, as I walked from the subway to the shop at seven in the morning—I had only four more days to prepare the space before the shop opened for its two-week-long stint—my phone rang, and Dylan's face graced the screen.

"Hi," I said, stepping through the gate of the playground I'd been passing.

"I hate this," he said as I was sitting down on the swing, pushing myself back on my heels.

"Me too."

"Damsel, I..." He trailed off, never finishing his thought.

I don't know what I was waiting for, but it wasn't this. It wasn't an admission that this sucked. That we missed each other. The longer his silence went, the clearer it was that this wasn't going to be the conversation where we figured things out. Where we made up.

"Dylan, I have to get to the store," I finally said, leaning back and staring into the cloudy morning sky, as if it would provide me with the answers I wanted. The answers I'd been hoping he'd give.

He sighed audibly on the other end. "I miss you."

"I miss you too," I said, and I could feel the tears forming in my eyes. Because I did. I missed the crap out of him. I missed sleeping in his arms. I missed waking up next to him. I missed him touching me. I missed teasing him. I missed everything, and at that moment there was a part of me that was afraid we'd never get it back.

More silence. "I gotta go," I said and hung up the phone. I swung my tote over my shoulder, picked my coffee up from the ground, and walked towards the park exit.

My phone buzzed in my hand.

MONDAY, 7:03 am
I miss you like mad. I'm sorry.

MONDAY, 7:04 am
I'm sorry too.

Chapter 11

Lydia

After that phone call I zeroed in on work for eleven straight hours. Eleven hours of unpacking Hannah gowns, shopping bags, and accessories. Organizing. Reorganizing. Calling the design team who would hang the store sign for the two weeks we would be open. And finally, calling every local media outlet I could get in touch with to make sure the press for the pop-up shop was coming along. The style writer from the *New York Times* had been unavailable all day, and he was the last call I was going to try to make before packing it in and heading home.

"Hello?" The male voice on the other end sounded busy. I could hear the din of street noise in the background.

"Is this Eric Stuart?" I had my script memorized and was on total autopilot making these calls, just running down the list of contacts Fiona had prepared.

"It is," he said.

"This is Lydia Bell, calling from Hannah—"

"Lydia?" he asked, sounding surprised.

"Yes, I said my name is Lydia Bell, and I'm—"

"Lydia, it's *Eric*. From NYU? Intro to Journalism with Pro-fessor Mario?"

Suddenly, memories of my team project came flooding back—long nights of laughing our asses off in Bobst Library as we scrounged through articles so old they were still on micro-fiche. For about five minutes freshman year I'd thought I might be a journalism major—that class had cured me.

"Eric! Holy shit. You work at the *New York Times*? That's amazing!" I dropped the bags I had been sorting, and stopped to chat. "Sorry I didn't realize it was you I was calling—I've been making these calls off and on all day. I'm only here for a month—I'm hosting a pop-up store in SoHo for Hannah Ro-gan, and—"

"You're looking for press?" he asked, finishing my sentence, and I could hear the satisfaction in his voice.

"You got me. So what do you say? Can you help a girl out?" I asked.

"You said SoHo?"

"Yeah," I replied, resuming my cleaning up so I'd be able to leave once this call was over.

"You there now?" he asked.

"I am."

"I'm on Spring and Sullivan—why don't we catch up over drinks and you can give me your pitch?"

I looked at my watch—it was nearly eight. I was starving, and I could definitely use a drink. Eric had been fun to talk to during college, and suddenly there was something so appealing about just flopping down on a bar stool and catching up with a friend. Not to mention, I *really* needed the *New York Times* to cover the store.

"As long as they've got food too," I said.

"How about Raoul's in fifteen?"

At eight fifteen I walked into the small dimly lit SoHo institution and saw Eric sitting at the bar. He was broader than I'd remembered. And blonder. He had this scruffy five-o'clock shadow journalist thing going on, complete with a beat-up messenger bag and a pen he was twiddling between his fingers. As soon as he saw me, he rose from his seat and came over to give me a hug.

"How the hell are you?" he asked, giving me a once-over. "You look great!"

"You too," I said, following him back to the bar stools.

"So you work for Hannah Rogan now, huh?"

I nodded. "In London. I just opened her flagship store there."

"London. Wow. I can't believe you left New York. I didn't think you'd ever leave the city. And the flagship store. That's really impressive," he said, and I could tell he meant it. "So now a pop-up here, huh? Testing the waters?"

I nodded again. "Well, actually, she's moving into a permanent space in a couple of months on Madison—this is driving up the hype. So, you cover the fashion beat?"

And we were off. We laughed about the journalism class we'd taken together, about the horror of shadowing a television reporter through Queens the week there was a high-profile drug bust, about what we'd been up to since graduating. He told me about the *Times*, what it was like trying to climb the ladder from the inside of such an old established paper, how he wished he'd gone home to Vermont to make a name for himself, because at least there he'd have a fighting chance of getting on the front page. I told him about my job, about Fashion Week, and we caught up on our mutual friends.

It was two and a half hours, two burgers, and too many glasses of wine later by the time we exited the little restaurant. Eric stood by the curb looking to see if there were any cabs, but then he turned and walked back to me, his bag over his shoulder, his hands in his pockets.

"You'll get a car home, right?" he asked. The air was warm, a hint of spring in the air, and I could feel the heat of the restaurant rolling off of me.

"Yeah," I said, yawning. I rolled my head back, stretching my neck and rolling my shoulders.

"You're working hard, aren't you?"

"I am, but it's exciting," I said, and I held my phone in my hand, ready to open the app to summon a car. I was tired. I couldn't wait to get back to my bed. But then I felt Eric close. Too close.

"Eric, I—" I started to say, slightly stunned when suddenly his hand was on my hip, sitting at the crease where my jeans met my blouse.

"Lydia, I'm going to kiss you now," he said. And I could smell his breath, and it was so different. And he wasn't so tall, so his mouth was right there. It all just happened.

Maybe I'd had too much to drink. Maybe I was just too tired and too slow. Too confused. But suddenly his lips were on mine, warm and full and *wrong*. It was all wrong. I instantly pushed against his chest and pulled away, taking three steps back.

"Fiancé." I said the word instinctively, emphatically. It felt like the most important word to get out.

"What?"

"I'm engaged. I have a fiancé, Eric," I stuttered, and he looked back at me, staring, gaping. Suddenly I felt a cloud, thick and dark, settle over me.

"*Engaged*?" he asked. "You didn't say anything. I thought—"

"I thought we were just catching up. It was so nice to see an old friend…I…I should have said something earlier," I said, the panic welling up inside me. What had I done? Why didn't I tell him about Dylan? "I'm…I'm sorry. I have to go."

The next thing I knew I was practically running towards the subway entrance. I kept my head down, clinging my bag to my side. If I could just make myself small enough, fast enough, maybe I'd just disappear completely.

There was a train just pulling into the station when I entered the turnstile, and I ran onto it, grateful for the doors shutting behind me, separating me from what just happened. I slumped down on the hard plastic seat and immediately, instinctively reached for my phone, my hand gripping it in my bag. Dylan. I needed to call Dylan. He'd know what to do. He'd know what to say. But I couldn't call him. He couldn't help me. I was alone in this.

I pulled the phone out, and there was Dylan's nightly text sitting on the screen. It had come during dinner, and the pit of guilt in my stomach spread, thickened.

MONDAY, 9:05 pm
Our bed is so empty without you. Can't sleep. Are you awake?

I hadn't replied, and he probably thought I was giving him the silent treatment. Normally I would've said something, at least *goodnight*. I hovered over the reply, but I had no idea what to say. Anything was going to feel like a lie or an omission. Even if I hadn't meant to, I'd betrayed him. Even if I hadn't kissed Eric back, he'd be hurt. The anger I'd felt was now intricately swirled with guilt, reminders that I loved him. I put the phone down, and the tears started falling. In the mostly empty train car, I brought my knees to my chest, burrowing my face between them. What had I done?

Chapter 12

Dylan

Panic. Fucking panic. That was the only word for what I felt.

I'd texted her in the middle of the night, and it was an entire day later, and she still hadn't written me back. I wasn't even sure why I'd texted her what I had—I didn't know how to make up, how to go forward, and still protect her from the chaos being married to me would bring. All I knew was that I fucking *missed* her. So I'd texted, more than I had in days. And she hadn't written back. And now, well, now I was a bloody mess.

My girl was slipping through my fingers.

Emily came around the house at nine that morning, practically banging down my door when I failed to meet her for coffee. After she told me I looked like I'd been run over by a mountain lion, whatever the fuck that meant, I'd told her the highlights—that Lydia and I had had a row before she left for New York, that she finally wanted to go public with our engagement but that I'd put a stop to it.

"You're a first-class moron, you know that, right?" Emily said to me, flinging her takeaway latte cup around in exasperation so bits of milk foam were landing on the floor of my entry.

"Excuse me, dear sister, call me crazy, but the *last* thing I want to do is make Lydia's life more complicated. I need to sort all of this out—deal with Hale Shipping, figure out how I'm going to balance that and my own firm, et *cetera*. Then, maybe, I *hope* I'll be able to offer Lydia something less ridiculous by way of a life. But I'm not going to drag her any further into this until I'm certain. Does that really sound moronish to you?"

"'Moronish' isn't a word."

"Oh, sod off," I said, marching us back towards the kitchen.

"What happened anyway? You were all 'tallyho' and 'onward' about the engagement, practically begging her to put on a fluffy white gown. What happened?" I raised my eyebrow as I took a sip of my own cup of coffee, my third that morning. "Oh, fine, maybe I'm the only one who cares about the gown, but you know what I mean. What bloody well *happened*?"

"I had drinks with Mum—"

"You're not serious. *You* fell for one of Mum's manipulations?" The latte cup was abandoned, and Emily was now rooting around in my cupboards, digging around for biscuits or something.

"Did *you* know Mum nearly did a PhD in French literature?" I looked at her skeptically, rubbing my forehead. The lack of sleep was killing me.

"What? No she didn't."

"She did. It actually occurred to me this week that she might be lying, but I called Uncle Harold and he confirmed it."

"Blimey."

"Apparently she was rather brilliant at it. But she gave it up, to be with Dad." Learning this about my mother had convoluted everything I thought I'd understood about her and her marriage to my father. All I'd been able to think about was her potential, that she'd thrown it away without meaning to, that she resented my father and it had destroyed them. All I'd been able to think was that I was about to do the same thing to Lydia.

"Hmm," she said, sounding surprised. "That does rather challenge my belief that Mum is as dull as a lamppost, doesn't it?" She finally put down the biscuits, letting crumbs fly from the package onto the floor. "So did Lydia change her mind then? Say that she doesn't want to make those kinds of sacrifices?" she asked, chomping down into the snacks.

"No." I thought of Lydia standing before me in my robe, her hair twisted and laying over her shoulder, her bare feet on the kitchen floor. She'd come into that room so ready, so willing, so happy to see me, and I'd closed her off. She *hadn't* said she didn't want to make sacrifices or that she didn't want to be a duchess. In fact, she'd said the opposite, that she was ready to. That she had confidence in us, that we'd figure it out, even if it were messy. But all I could think, could still think, was *How could she know?* And *Isn't it my job, as the duke, to know for her?*

"Ah, so she doesn't trust *you* not to want her to make those sacrifices then—is that it? She thinks after you're married you'll turn into Dad and want her to give up her career?"

Again, I thought back to Lydia, her words, her petite frame stiffening with anger across the kitchen island from me, the very island where Emily and I were now standing. I'd never seen her so angry at me before, so downright furious, but all I'd been able to think, watching Lydia grit her teeth and search me with those big brown eyes, had been *She doesn't understand.* "No, she didn't change her *mind*, Emily. I didn't even tell her about that conversation with Mum. She actually said she believed we could figure anything out together, that we don't have to do it the way Mum and Dad did. She said that we already were figuring it out, that we might as well just do it married."

"But?" Emily looked at me as though I were possibly the most idiotic person on earth.

"*But*," I emphasized—apparently I needed to make Emily understand as well—"how could she possibly know any of that? I'm the one who's lived this life, who's seen it. Isn't it my responsibility to stop her? Isn't it my job to make sure she doesn't resent me the way Mum resented Dad?" Even as I said the words, I wasn't so sure anymore that they were true. "Actually, I would have thought—"

"Stop." I needed her to stop talking, because my chest was tightening, and there was no way I was going to let Emily take credit for kicking my ass into gear again.

"What?" She looked at me, confused.

"Stop. Because if you keep going, you're going to say something smart. And you don't need to. I'm a goddamn idiot, aren't I?" I ran my hand through my hair and exhaled, hearing Lydia's words echo through my mind: *How stupid am I that after everything, I'm right back where I started? Trying to convince you that we're worth fighting for.*

"I—" Emily tried to start in with her emphatic agreement of my self-assessment, but I held up my hand to stop her and then braced myself on the island, just as I'd done during my fight with Lydia. Only this time, I wasn't feeling defeated.

"I mean, bloody hell." I'd been sitting on my arse for over a week, like some kind of self-righteous arse, thinking that my life was too much for her, that being a duchess would be too hard for her, that she couldn't make up her own bleeding mind about her life. All because my mother hadn't known how to fight for hers.

Absurd is what that was. Fucking mental. And during our fight I'd been too fucking stubborn to see it, too fucking terrified that I was waltzing her into a life she'd resent. And I'd continued being stubborn for the entirety of the week that followed while she was away, convincing myself I was what? Doing the right thing? Bullshit.

Lydia was the strongest woman I knew. The only reason she was slipping through my fingers was because I was goddamn letting her. I hadn't been *listening*. I was a goddamn prat is what I was.

"Every reason I wanted us to get married, to make our engagement public, still stands, doesn't it? Mum will have to lay off. Lydia will be by my side. She's already doing most of the work of being a duchess *and* being bloody brilliant at work. She even said she wanted to think about her next career move, make sure it would work around the demands of our life. I'm a complete arse, aren't I?" Emily nodded. "And I should have trusted her, believed her, when she said she was ready, shouldn't I have?" Emily nodded again, mouth slightly agape. "Because, if I can't trust my bride on the day she says she wants to marry me, of *all* the days, I don't imagine I've got much of a shot, do I?" Emily shook her head. I never should have fought with Lydia. Never should have let my mother make me forget who Lydia was, how brilliant and strong, gorgeous and kind. I should have fucking swept her into my arms when she'd said she wanted to go public with our engagement. Should have kissed the ground she walked on for pushing us to do this, and do it well, do it together. *Goddammit.*

"I think," Emily said, "I think that what you're *meant* to say when your bride says she'd like to be publically engaged, in particular if you're *you*"—she pursed her lips, acknowledging that I was some sort of special case—"is say, 'Yes, please,' thank all that is holy that someone as sane and lovely as Lydia is willing to take you on, and march her on down the aisle. Preferably in a Vera Wang, but that's negotiable." Emily smiled, relieved, and oddly, maybe even proud of me?

I smiled at her, feeling the determination well up inside of me. No one was surprised more than I when I rounded the island and gave my sister a hug—or a side hug, which was still probably more of a hug than I'd given her in her entire life, which didn't last more than a second before she shoved me away and said, "Gross," making me laugh for the first time in over a week.

"Am I going to have to come in and set you straight every time you have a row with your fiancée? I can't recommend enough that you consider removing the middle man of this operation—far more efficient and all that—"

"Christ, you're annoying. You know that?" Emily just smirked smugly, and I couldn't do anything but smile at my kid sister.

I grabbed the car keys from the peg by the door and tossed them from one hand to the other as I grabbed my jacket.

"Where are you going?" Emily asked, digging back into the tin of biscuits.

"To get my girl—" Suddenly I remembered the day. "Ah, fuck. Shite! No, I'm going to a bloody meeting at MI6, *then* I'm going to get my girl."

"MI6? Who are you?" Emily now looked thoroughly confused and as though I might have possibly gone *completely* mad. I momentarily forgot she hadn't known about that operation.

"Your badass older brother." She harrumphed as I slipped on my shoes and opened the rear door. "I'll explain later, Em. Thanks for coming this morning—good chat!"

* * *

Because of that conversation I was late to the meeting with Jack, not that MI6 were the most efficient lot themselves, and not that I cared.

"My lord," he said, smirking. He was taking the piss using the formal address.

"Oh, sod off," I said, giving a half smile and sitting at the edge of my chair in his office. "I'm afraid I can't stay long, Jack. I have somewhere I need to be. So let's get to it, shall we?" I leaned back in the leather swiveling office chair and put my hands on my thighs.

His expression and his deep exhale said everything that needed to be said. "Right. Well, I'm afraid that the alternative plan won't work." I'd figured as much. "Our best option for apprehending King is what we discussed." I nodded. "Having you on the inside, someone who can serve as an actual witness to back up any recording, is really the best avenue, the most reliable."

"Right," I said, although this plan took on greater weight now that it was real, now that I knew how Lydia felt about it, that it worried her.

"You'll need to set up a meeting with him when the timing seems right, but the sooner the better. Our man on the ground in Moscow believes he's getting spooked, and all signs point to King going underground again, soon. We'll work with you on what you'll need to do, the strategies we've found effective in getting someone like King to say what we need him to say. Really, we just need him to admit to being who he is. And of course your security will be our highest priority. You'll be wired, we'll have armed agents nearby, at the ready, and they will intervene the moment you can confirm verbally that he's present."

"Indeed." I had a tingling sensation that told me none of this was going to be as easy as Jack thought, but I also trusted him.

"Tell Lydia she has nothing to worry about." Jack knew about Lydia, knew I lived with her. He had no idea she was my fiancée. I wondered if knowing I was going to be married would change his opinion about any of this, make it seem like less of a risk worth taking.

But the risk, if there even was one, *was* worth it. When this was sorted, I'd be one step closer to putting things right, to sorting out how the hell I was going to run Hale Shipping, to getting Humboldt back in my name, so I could focus on the firm. On Lydia, on us. "I understand," I said, leaning forward onto the desk. "I'll reach out to the Bresnovs and I'll let you know what I can accomplish. And then, when this is over, Jack, I'm counting on you to put those crooks behind bars where they belong."

Jack nodded in confirmation and nodded again. "Thanks, mate. Hopefully we'll pull this off as soon as possible, then you can officially tell that girlfriend of yours that you're a spy for MI6. Then maybe she won't be embarrassed to leave the house with you," he said, laughing slightly.

"You wanker."

He walked me through a stack of bureaucratic paperwork that would make anyone go blind, explained how the operation would work, and then I got the fuck out of there. I stopped by the house to grab a few things, and I swung by the firm to pick up what I needed. Then I told Thomas to cancel my next week.

Chapter 13

Lydia

It had been two endless days since I had possibly fucked up the best thing ever in my life, and I'd been torturing myself ever since. I needed to see Dylan, to talk to him, but the idea of starting this conversation when I didn't even know where we stood was paralyzing. I had picked up the phone and started to call him a dozen times, but I never let the call connect. I was being a coward, and I knew it, but all of our problems were still there, even without the Eric situation. Where would we even start? How would I even tell him?

I'd read about this kind of thing in *Cosmo* and heard it talked about on talk shows—was Dylan going to feel like I'd cheated on him even though Eric had just gone and kissed me without my permission? Would he believe me? Had I somehow allowed this to happen? I felt like a first-rate idiot for not realizing what Eric had been thinking, despised myself for not having told Eric about Dylan sooner.

These thoughts, this torture, had had me muttering to myself under my breath and generally acting like a crazy person as I put the finishing touches on the store that day. It was Wednesday and the store wouldn't open until Saturday. The team of contractors clearly thought I was insane enough to work double time to get away from me, and I'd been working twelve-hour days mainly to avoid my problems, so at least I was ahead of schedule.

I wearily climbed the subway steps on Union Street, exiting with all the others who were coming home from work, and made my way up the hill. I gave a halfhearted wave to Margaret, the woman who ran the taco stand, and tucked my bag under my shoulder. I was about halfway up the block when it started to rain. It had been clear it was coming—the clouds were heavy and the air was humid, thick with the impending drops—but its start was surprising all the same. The drops were full, the kind that soaked you instantly.

I should have run. I was only a half block from my door. But instead I stopped. My mind had been going at warp speed and my emotions were just a step behind. I was exhausted. I was weighted and felt foggy and dirty. I needed a moment. I needed to breathe. I needed to be caught, if not by Dylan, then by that rain. So I stood, not under an awning, but right there in the middle of the sidewalk and looked straight up into the drops hitting my face.

Rain always made New York smell fresh, for just a few moments before it smelled like wet city. It was cleansing. I stood there waiting for the familiarity to wash over me, the sense memories of New York in a torrential downpour. But they never quite came. And I realized that at no moment of this trip had I felt like I was truly home.

The raindrops started to bleed in with my tears as I realized that never again was the city I'd grown up in going to be home. Never again was New York, the city where I'd lived with my father, the city where I'd lost my father, going to be the one place that made me feel safe and cared for. I could never go back there. Never go back to before. No matter how many minutes away from Dylan, I was changed. He was part of me. My home was with *him*.

Maybe this is what people meant when they said *growing pains*, because fuck, it *did* hurt. I could feel my heart breaking all over again, losing a part of my innocence I hadn't realized I'd been holding on to.

I wasn't a girl just dating some guy. I was building a life with the man I was going to marry. We'd fought. We'd fought because we had baggage, and fears, responsibilities, and dreams. We'd fought because we needed each other. We'd fought because we were holding each other to a higher standard, the standard you hold someone to when you're going to spend your *life* with them. Getting kissed by a boy I'd once known wasn't going to break us. The only thing that could break us now was us.

How had I never known that loving someone so much was going to mean facing things you were afraid of? Why hadn't I realized that fighting for your relationship wasn't a onetime thing, but something you did every day?

Without realizing it I'd started walking towards my apartment, towards a dry place where I could call Dylan, because I may have lost a place, a city, that used to complete me, but it was clearer than ever where my home was now. I needed him. And if he needed time, I could give it. If he needed patience, I could wait.

Assuming, of course, he could forgive me after I told him about the kiss.

I rounded the corner and tucked my head down, walking straight towards my building. My jeans were soaked through, and my bangs were dripping their own steady stream onto my cheeks and nose. I tucked myself into the overhang of the doorway to my building and began digging through my tote for my keys. When I pulled them out to put the key in lock, I saw a notecard tucked into the doorframe.

Familiar cream-colored card stock with the four initials at the top, *DWLH. Dylan William Lucas Hale.* My breath caught in my chest as I took in the words.

Fancy a coffee?

I whipped around, feeling my heavy wet hair fling against my opposite cheek, and looked straight across the street into the coffee shop. There, sitting at the only table in the window, was a pair of high-end jeans, sexy-as-hell laced boots, a T-shirt, and a pair of impossibly blue eyes looking right at me. Standing, staring, meeting my gaze. I moved to cross the street, but before I even had a chance to look both ways, Dylan was a blur, the rain bouncing off his shoulders as he came for me.

His big warm hands moved me back into the doorframe, and I stared straight into those eyes, into my home. The rain was pounding at his back, and drips started to fall from his hair onto his face. He was looking right at me, and I saw everything. I saw how foolish we'd been for fighting, how even if the fight mattered, and it did, it was minor in the context of us, of the fact that we'd be together. Forever. No matter what.

He brought his hands to my damp cheeks and pushed aside the hair sticking there, clearing my face so he could look at me.

"Damsel," he said, then he closed his eyes for a just a second. "Lydia." The rainwater was cascading over his broad hand and dripping from his wrists to my chest. I couldn't believe he was there, in front of me, right where I needed him.

"Dylan, I…why are you here?"

"Why am I here? Baby, I'm here because I couldn't go another day not seeing you, not saying what we need to say."

"I need to tell you something," I started. I wanted this conversation to be everything, for us to get back to where we needed to be. I needed to tell him that someone else had kissed me. But before I could, he leaned down and pressed his lips against mine. Not with passion, but with purpose. So soft, so warm, so firm, so *right*.

"I love you," he said, leaning into me, so my back was pressed up against the door.

"I love you too," I said, looking up into those preposterously blue eyes, droplets of water gathering on his lashes.

Dylan once again brushed my wet hair from my face. "Open the door, damsel." His words were firm and loving as he whispered against my ear. "I want to talk to you, to see you, but let's do this inside, shall we?"

I realized the keys were still in my hands, but I couldn't move. I was so relieved, so warm, just beginning to ask myself how the hell he'd gotten here to my Brooklyn doorstep.

Eventually, he reached into my palm and took the keys, sliding the thick blue security key into the lock, and with his palm against my lower back he urged me through the doorway. I turned around, took his hand in mine, and led the way up the four flights of stairs to my apartment. I knew I was cold, I could hear my teeth chattering, but I didn't feel cold. I felt warm, relieved, stunned, so unbelievably happy to have my hand back in his.

We silently walked through my door, my bag dropping and

a puddle forming at our feet. Dylan shut the door behind us, locked it, and put his hands on my arms. He never took his eyes off mine.

"Dylan, I'm so glad you're here. There's so much to say. I want to tell you something," I started again and closed my eyes just for a beat.

"There's no rush, baby. I want to talk too. We need to. But you're positively soaked." I looked down and realized that he wasn't nearly as wet as I was. "I'll put on the kettle. Go change. I'm not going anywhere." He smiled again, and I kept turning back to look at him, to make sure he was really there as I walked to the bedroom.

By the time I emerged in my leggings and hoodie, my hair swept into a wet ponytail, Dylan was sitting on the old velvet sofa in my living room. One foot resting on the other knee, the window behind him, framing his muscular silhouette, his hair still wet from the rain. He looked calm, relaxed on that old sofa—Dylan was *here* in my apartment. Months ago I would have felt so odd about him, the 17th Duke of Abingdon, on my couch, but now it was just *him*, and it was perfect. Or it would be.

He held his arms out, inviting me, and I walked towards that couch knowing that this was going to be one of those moments that worked its way into the story of us.

"Come here." He hauled me onto the couch, pulling my legs over his lap, and handing me a mug of tea. "I'm sorry, damsel," he said.

"No. I'm sorry—" I started.

"Let me say this, Lydia." I nodded, and slid just a little closer to him. "I was wrong to let you just go. That night my mother told me how much she'd sacrificed to be with my father, and

I…you know, it doesn't matter what she said. What matters is that I didn't trust you to know what you wanted. I was terrified that you didn't know what you were getting into with me. But you deserve more from me. I promised that to you last year. If we're going to repave this godforsaken road I've been on, and we are, we will, I must trust *you*, trust *us*, and I didn't. I wish I could go back and do it again."

"It's okay, Dylan. I get it. I do. You're unlearning everything you'd convinced yourself of for years. And I'm learning it all for the first time. But I do know—I do—that you're it for me." I put down my tea on the coffee table, shifted to sit on my heels, and I kissed him gently on the cheek. "I love you. So much." I gulped, because I knew that the rockiest parts of this conversation were yet to come, but the way he was looking at me in that moment—I wanted it for just a second longer before I said what I needed to say.

Our fingers were interlaced, and he was stroking the back of my hand. Suddenly, I felt him fiddle with my left hand, felt him slide something onto my finger.

"I think it's time you wore this, don't you?" he asked, smiling only slightly.

I looked down and gasped. I saw the most stunning ring on my finger, and every thought I'd just had emptied from my head. A brilliant canary diamond, four not-so-tiny white diamonds, a classically beautiful antique setting. I would never have known to imagine that ring. It was perfect. I wasn't sure I was breathing. Not sure I was seeing or hearing or feeling anything other than the sparkling testament on my hand. Just like it had the first time we touched, the world zoomed out into a fog, and he zoomed in.

"Dylan," I said. His name coming out as a breath. "It's beautiful. I…" I couldn't finish the thought. I was entranced, not believing this was happening, suddenly feeling like the engagement was real in a way it hadn't been before.

"It's the ring my grandfather gave my grandmother. She never took it off. There are others—a sapphire or an emerald if you'd pref—"

"It's perfect," I said, shaking my head already feeling fiercely possessive of the symbol on my hand.

"You're perfect."

"No, I'm not. But I love you so much."

Dylan pulled me against his body, our damp skin melting together.

"You're mine, damsel. Forever. It's time the world knows we're in this together. Not just for a night, but for life."

I nodded, crying for the second time in an hour, and crawled over his lap and into his arms. "And you're mine." I buried my face in his shoulder, and he held me so tightly against him, as though wrapping ourselves in each other could undo days of silence, of absence. Slowly he began stroking my hair, and I found myself mindlessly drawing circles on the back of his neck with my finger. I smiled like a fool when I saw the hundreds of tiny diamond rainbows dancing on the wall, the light shining through the stones in my ring.

"I hate to ruin this moment, damsel, but I've had nothing but coffee for the last six hours as I waited for you in that coffee shop. How do you feel about dinner?"

I laughed, imagining Dylan sitting there among the Park Slope work-from-home crowd, the college students who fancy themselves poets, and all the others who turned that coffee shop into their office all day, much to the baristas' chagrin. He must have stuck out like a sore thumb. "Famished," I replied, and grabbed my phone from my bag to call up the takeout options.

We were going through the menu of the sushi place on the corner when a text flashed across the top of my phone screen.

From Eric.

Only the first few words were visible, but those few words were enough.

WEDNESDAY 8:55 pm
Lydia, I'm sorry about the kiss. I didn't…

No. No. No. This wasn't how this was supposed to happen.

My hands stilled. I couldn't take my eyes off the phone, and I could feel the weight of Dylan's stare on my cheeks. A beat passed. Then another. Both of us frozen.

Finally, because I knew I had to speak first, I said, still staring at my phone, "Dylan, this is what I needed to tell you. It's not what you think—" God, I knew how that sounded. So cliché.

"Look at me, Lydia," he said, all the warmth gone from his voice. I turned to look into those blue eyes, now steely, vacant. He had the outward appearance of total calm, but I knew that rigidity, that impassiveness. He was lowering the curtain on me, and I couldn't let him.

"Fuck." The word just came out of me. I didn't know how to get the rest out.

"Fuck?" His eyebrows were raised, declaring what a stupid thing that was for me to have said. He pulled away from me and sat perched on the edge of the couch, as though he were ready to launch himself away from me.

"No, listen. Please. Two nights ago I ran into a friend from college, a writer from the *Times*, from the style section. He was going to write something up about the store." I gulped. I kept waiting for him to be enraged, for him to stand, to stomp, to slam something, but instead he kept his eyes on me, testing, gauging. "I was exhausted from the day, and we went out for drinks, which turned into dinner. We were just chatting and catching up. We just drank and ate, and talked about college and friends. That was it. Then when we got outside, and I was waiting for a car, he kissed me. He just did it. And it was horrible. It was *horrible*. And I broke away. I swear I did. And I told him immediately I was engaged, but—"

"But it was too bloody late at that point, wasn't it?" It wasn't a question. His facade was cracking—there was the anger I'd been waiting for. The hurt. "You couldn't have bloody well just said you were dating someone, could you? You obviously didn't appear unavailable." He was furious. He was standing now. Pacing the room.

"Dylan, we hadn't talked in over a *week*. When I left I wasn't even sure what you were thinking. I've spent every second of every day thinking about you, about us, about our fight. I've been drowning in thoughts about us. I wasn't not telling him because I wanted him to think I was single. I'm so used to *not* talking about us, to anyone, so I just didn't tell him anything. It's not like he asked if I had a boyfriend and I said no. I was nervous to tell you about it, afraid of this reaction, but I knew I needed to, wanted to. I was going to tell you tonight but then you put the ring on me and I got distracted. I had no intention of hiding this—there's nothing *to* hide. He kissed *me*, not the other way around. And the second it happened I stopped it and told him I was engaged."

His face became calm again, and I realized my phone was in his hand. He looked down at it, and then a look of sheer determination came over him. He reached for his shoes.

"Where are you going?" I asked, and I saw him pocket my

phone as he reached for my keys with his other hand.

"I'll be back. I need to think, Lydia. Don't leave this apartment," he said. It wasn't threatening. It was efficient. And I hated it. I wasn't supposed to be about efficiency. I was his person, the part of him that freed him from that, and now he was treating me like a board meeting. And I probably deserved it.

"Dylan!" I shouted as the door closed behind him. I was sitting on the couch, in my leggings, a sweatshirt, and a priceless engagement ring on my finger, and once again I was crying. What had I done?

* * *

Two hours had passed, but it felt like two days. I was curled up in my bed, in the fetal position, all thoughts of dinner forgotten, staring at my engagement ring and running the entire scenario through my head. I needed Dylan to understand that it had meant nothing. He couldn't be so rash as to throw us away over this. This stupid, stupid thing.

The door finally clicked open, but my back was to him, and I was too afraid to turn around. I heard the rustling of clothes, and the sound of crinkling plastic, and then I felt his hand on my shoulder.

"Look at me, Lydia," he said.

I turned to look at him, and could feel how red-rimmed my eyes must have been.

"Dylan, I—"

"No, listen."

I nodded in compliance—I had to let him lead this show.

"I know it meant nothing. I know it wasn't your fault."

I nodded again, almost not believing what I was hearing, but so grateful to hear the truth come from his lips.

"It doesn't mean I'm okay with what happened, but I'm not angry, baby. Eric said you hadn't been flirting, that it was on him—"

"What?" I sat up in the bed. "You called him? You didn't believe me?" A flash of surprise crept over my skin.

"Are you going to try to convince me that I didn't have the right to confront the man who kissed my fiancée? Of course I believe you. I trust you. I was just so furious that someone else thought they had a right to touch you like that. I had to set him straight—he needed to know with zero uncertainty that you were *not* available." That made me feel better, knowing he believed in me, in us. "It was rather enlightening, actually. You know he tried to call you seven times since Monday night?"

"I know. I didn't want to talk to him. I'd already felt like I'd betrayed you enough by allowing him to kiss me. I couldn't bear to face it. I needed to talk to *you* before I would ever talk to him again, but we weren't talking, and…I just couldn't—" My words were flying out of me a mile a minute, and I could feel my breathing start to pick up, go into panic mode. Dylan wrapped his large hand around my shoulder, not quite soothing me, but wanting me to stay with him.

"Yes, well, you probably should have answered. He'd Googled you as soon as you'd left him at the curb—'ran away like a house afire' were his words"—and he actually flashed a minuscule smile as he said that. "And it had taken him all of three seconds to put together that you were engaged to *me*. He was doing you a favor—trying to either warn you, give you time, or get you to comment before he broke the story."

Oh god—it hadn't even occurred to me that Eric posed that

kind of threat. I'd been so preoccupied by the personal betrayal of the whole thing, I'd momentarily somehow forgotten that he could hold that over me, that he was *press*. "Fuck, I've made an ever bigger fuckup than I fucking realized," I yelled at myself and threw my head into my waiting palms. I'd been so caught off guard that he didn't know, I didn't think about what it meant if he *did*. "And I told him we were engaged. Not just dating but engaged. Everyone will know." The words were muffled by my hands.

"Yes, well, I've taken care of that aspect."

"How?" I sniffled.

"Well, for starters, the guy clearly cares about you, and I told him you'd be devastated if this is how the news was released. He's not going to say anything. I also, *unfortunately*, had to promise the man that kissed my *fiancée* that we'd provide him with at least one exclusive detail at some point. Can't say I'm eager to keep that promise."

"I'm so sorry, Dylan."

"Yes, well, more importantly, we *are* engaged aren't we?" He took the hand and held the ring that rested there. "Even if we don't make an official announcement, the reality is, as soon as we walk out that door tomorrow, there's no keeping it a secret anymore. And if it's not Eric Stuart"—he made a look of disgust as he said his name—"it will be someone else who breaks the news."

I nodded, because it was true. It wouldn't happen tomorrow—there were no Brooklyn paparazzi stalking us here, but it *would* happen. The ring *was* our announcement.

"Also, damsel, this was one of the consequences of being a secret. While this was never one of the reasons you cited when arguing for us to make our engagement public—I don't believe 'it will stop men from trying to kiss me' was ever mentioned—it is undeniably true that while our engagement went unannounced, men would presume to have a chance with you." He sat closer to me on the bed and wrapped his large hands around my face, forcing me to look up into his eyes. "And really," he whispered, "how can I blame them when I can't keep my hands off you either?"

"Dylan, can you really look past this? I'd want to crawl out of my skin if someone had kissed you."

"I didn't say I didn't want to fucking throttle that fucker. I did. I do. But, baby, the truth is that this very nearly happened to me—not under the same circumstances, but the night of that party at the palace, Beatrice and Amelia tried to bloody mount me."

"*What?*" I asked, taken aback.

"Baby. They *didn't* kiss me. I assure you—I didn't let them. I understand your panic though—the fact that it *nearly* happened had me out of my mind. I didn't tell you because nothing happened. But if it had...the thought of losing you kills me, baby."

"You should have told me." I looked at him, disappointed, sad, jealous in retrospect.

"I should have." I just stared down at him, wishing none of this had happened.

Dylan took my hand in front of him and twisted the ring around my finger. Then he slid my other ring, the placeholder ring, from my right hand. "No need for this anymore." He put it on my nightstand. I looked at it sitting there and was sad for moment—it meant something to me, but I was happy, so happy to be feeling like we were edging our way out of a near miss. Together.

"Now," he said, exhaling as if to say, *I'm glad that's all over with*, "what have you eaten over the last two days? If I know my girl, you've been so absorbed by this that you've probably had a latte, full stop."

I shrugged my shoulders.

"As I thought. Let's remedy that. I can't have you wasting away on me." Dylan went back to the entryway and returned with a large takeout bag. "How does sushi sound?"

"Yes!" I groaned with longing and practically leaped over the edge of the bed and ran towards the kitchen to get out plates and chopsticks. It was after eleven, and we were finally sitting down to dinner.

Chapter 14

Dylan

I watched Lydia inhale two sushi rolls and a serving of Japanese dumplings in under ten minutes. Her relief was palpable.

There was no denying it. Knowing another man's hands and lips had been on her made me want to crush something. And I nearly did. When I left her apartment, I turned the corner and rammed my fist into the brick facade. She hadn't noticed, thankfully, but I could feel my knuckles swelling as I sat there beside her.

The evening hadn't gone exactly as I'd thought. The first part had—getting that ring on her finger made me feel like king of the goddamn world. But fucking Christ, when that text came in, it was like the earth froze over. I'd been thrust out of perfection with the kind of force you can't predict, a goddamn tsunami with the scraps of happiness I'd found in my life its only target. I had to get the fuck out of there. I left with the intent of calling the fucker journalist and telling him I was giving him exactly an hour to disappear from the planet before I hunted his ass down. Then I listened to his voicemails and realized I needed to actually deal with the wanker. I also realized he really hadn't known about me when he kissed her.

What I wouldn't tell her is that when I called, I made that fuckwit detail every second of his interaction with her. I needed to know everything if I was going to put this to bed. I did trust her, but I needed to hear it all from him. And I couldn't ask her to do that for me. And I also wouldn't tell her how pure my satisfaction was when he'd answered the phone expecting her and I heard his gasp when I said, "Dylan Hale here. If it's not a convenient time to speak, I suggest you make it one."

I wasn't trying to be a prick. Or that wasn't my sole purpose. But he needed to know in no uncertain terms that just because we hadn't gone public—*yet*—did not mean there was anything undecided.

The only thing that kept me calm was the look of sheer panic and loss in Lydia's eyes. Her look expressed everything I needed to know—utter terror that we could be over. If she felt that way, then there was no way she'd willingly cheated on me.

Lydia fell back in her chair, resting her hand on her belly, as though she were full, and smiled a tiny content smile that brought me back to the moment.

"I'm glad you're here," she said sleepily, sated.

"As am I." She looked fucking beautiful—her hair messed from having been caught in the rain, wearing those leggings of hers that drove me bloody insane. "Lydia, you can tell me anything. You know that, right?"

"Of course. I did *try*. You really would have wanted me to?"

"Honesty. Always honesty."

She nodded, her lithe little legs sitting cross-legged in the wooden dining chair. Then she surprised me. She stood up from that chair and sauntered over to me. She was about to crawl into my lap, but I put my hands at her hips, halting her. She tilted her head, curious, just a little wary, her ponytail falling over her shoulder. I gripped the fabric clinging to her thighs and pulled those bloody pants down her lean legs, tapping the back of her thigh to prompt her to step out of them. The lovely girl obliged, and my dick responded predictably. I wanted my hands on her.

Now, clad only in a sweatshirt, she crawled over, straddled me, and rested her arms on my shoulders. Her eyelids had gone heavy. No matter what had happened over the past week, she fucking belonged to me, and there was no denying she owned me as well.

"Always," she said. Then she took my injured hand and brought it to her lips, kissing each knuckle. Apparently I hadn't fooled the little foal sitting on me. And she kissed me. She kissed my hand, the inside of my wrist, my shoulder, my cheek, and finally she placed those plump perfect-as-fuck lips on mine. "Thank you for being you," she said. "Thank you for my ring." She kissed me again. "Thank you for coming for me." She must have caught my lips' twitch at her last comment, because she immediately followed up with "Don't worry. You will."

"Oh, I wasn't worried, damsel. Now let's get you to bed before I lose my bleeding mind." My voice came out like a goddamn growl. I looked at the ring on her finger again, and I knew there was a smile wrapping clear around my face. *Christ*, I was a possessive wanker. "I fucking missed you so much, baby."

By the time we made it to her bed, I had her wearing nothing at all. And by the time I had worked her up, had her little wrists pinned above her head so I could feel it when her hips tilted to beg more of me, so I could see all of her, so I could feel her tightening around me, I was desperate for her. "I love you," she said as we came. "I love you." The words became a faint chant against my skin, and I chanted them right back to her.

* * *

When I woke in the morning, I forgot for a moment where I was. I stared up at high ceilings, crown molding, and the feeling of sheets wrapped around my legs. And something else wrapped around me. Lydia. Her light-as-a-feather arm draped over my abdomen, her soft breathing on my chest, her hair falling against my arm. The sunlight poured through the tall windows, and I could hear the incessant honking outside, perhaps a block away, but close enough. Every time I'd been in New York, I'd stayed in high-rise hotels in Midtown, safely tucked away from all the noise.

This was Lydia's New York—these sounds, the street right outside her door. The apartment was simple, but bigger than her father would have been able to afford were he buying today. She had told me that when he'd bought it, when she was five, the neighborhood wasn't considered safe. For the first time since arriving, I took in the furnishings, and I could see Lydia everywhere. Slightly bohemian. Creative tweaks to make the place hers. She'd done a good job. Even as a teenager it was probably she who decorated and took care of this place, and the thought made my chest sink a little.

Along the far wall of the bedroom were her father's guitars, each on a rack affixed to the wall, better than an expensive piece of art. My girl was talented, and she'd worked hard to get where she was. Christ, it made me want to make her life easier, to give her the fucking world.

But I also loved seeing this side of her. I hadn't realized how much of her I was missing. She'd come to me fresh, having left this behind, but this was *her*. I could see her everywhere. Her scrappiness was there in the inexpensive dresser she'd lacquered and affixed new knobs to. Her beauty and gentleness were there in the long gauzy curtains spilling into the room. And her love for the people in her life was in every single photo placed around the apartment. I couldn't see them from the bed, but I'd need to savor each one.

She started to stir against me. Her little waking moans paired with the way her nails curled into my skin gave me a fucking hard-on. She thought I woke up hard, but the truth was her waking up fucking *made* me hard.

"Good morning, damsel." I ran my fingers through her hair and lifted her body against mine, bring her lips into kissing distance.

Another luscious little moan. I blanketed her atop me, and she burrowed her face into my shoulder. Oh no. She wasn't going back to sleep on me. I gave her ass the *swack* it deserved, and she jolted against my dick like her body knew that was exactly what I'd been hoping for.

It earned me a little shriek and her eyes met mine, challenging.

"What time is it?" she asked groggily.

"Half eight."

"What day is it?" She groaned, sliding back against my body.

"Thursday, baby. You must need to be at the store," I said, stroking where I'd spanked her a moment ago.

"Nope," she replied, clearly more awake, and I could feel her lips curl into a smile against my shoulder blade. "I finished prep early—the upside to all that trying to avoid thinking about things. We don't open until Saturday." She climbed atop me and sat straddling my stomach—fuck me, her bare tits were just sitting there, pert and high, her hair tumbling over her shoulders. Fucking *Christ*, she was gorgeous. I gripped her hips to stop my hands from attacking her like some kind of feral animal.

"And…" She resumed leaning forward, bracing her weight on my chest with her small hands and leaning down to kiss me. "I'm showing you New York today."

"I do hate to disappoint you, darling, but I *have* been here before."

"No you haven't. Not with me. You, Dylan Hale, seventeenth Duke of Abingdon, architectural genius, are going to learn to be a Brooklyn boy today. You're going to find out what it would have been like to date me had we met here, in my world."

She had a delightfully mischievous grin and was biting her lower lip. I'd do anything for her, to keep that spark of delight in my life.

"Am I?" I raised an eyebrow at her.

"Mmm hmm. Think you can handle it?"

"You sassy Brooklyn thing." I pulled her down on top of me and flipped us over, so her pert little arse was in the air, and I was standing on my knees above her. I stroked that perfect creamy ass, rounding it out in my palm, not fucking believing how lucky I was that she was mine. "I'll let you show me this town. I *want* you to show me your town," I said, and I knelt over her and interlaced my fingers with her own. "But don't forget for a second whose ring you wear."

Her breathing had shallowed and there was a pink flush spreading across her back, a telltale sign she was ready for me. I ran my palm down her back and resumed my kneeling position behind her. Reaching between her legs, I felt her waiting, ready, so fucking wet, and I sank a finger into her, pressing down into that spot I knew made her crazy. She rewarded me with one of her perfect sighs, her eyes closing just a little tighter, her cheek hitting the mattress just a little harder.

"So fucking perfect, damsel." I slid my finger up to her rear and pressed gently, loving the way her buttocks clenched around me, her body struggling between submitting and resisting. Christ, that turned me on—I was going to fucking lose it.

I gripped her ass cheeks and spread them, wanting to see her perfectly as I entered her, as I felt her pussy squeeze around me.

We'd ended the previous night with our hands and mouths all over each other—we'd bloody well consumed each other after everything we'd said, but we hadn't fucked. And now, with my dick inside her, I could feel her impending release, her total submission to *us*. Each of her little breaths was a response to this, to me, and the way she offered herself was like she was so fucking pleased to be back in my arms. This was her forgiving me. It was me forgiving her. She was going to spend her life slowly dominating me—I knew that—but in this moment she was mine.

The sweat built between us and I could feel those involuntary quivers, the tiny contractions, pick up pace. "You're close, damsel. I want you to come for me, baby. Come for me," I whispered, and she did. She convulsed around me, and my dick gave it all right back to her.

I thrust into her at a powerful rhythm, my body showing her exactly how much I approved of those little convulsions, how much I needed them.

My own groans filled the room, and I collapsed to the mattress still inside her, bringing her body with mine, onto our sides, so her back clung to my front. We were catching our breath, our chests heaving. I grabbed her breast—my whole palm covering her, and slid out of her. I felt her wince.

"Did I hurt you?"

"No, it's just intense."

"It is." I kissed her back, and she gripped my hand to her chest, pulling me tighter around her.

Chapter 15

Lydia

So where to first?" Dylan rubbed his hands together outside my front door, scanning the street, taking in the little shops and bodegas. After we'd made love that morning, he'd had his bags delivered—they'd been held by his hired driver so he wouldn't have to drag them around. He was now standing before me, being his most low-key self. For Dylan that meant designer jeans and a T-shirt that may have made him look like a living version of the *David*, but could not be accurately described as casual.

He gripped my hand and tried to move us towards the black sedan parked outside my door, and a driver emerged. He didn't get far though—I stood my ground.

"Nope. Sorry, mister. There will be no town cars today."

He turned questioning, but a look of acceptance crossed his brow. "Right. Well…then let me just get my jumper," he started, but I pulled him back. His sweater would be the absolutely gorgeous designer cream cable knit I loved so much.

"No, that will be our first stop. If you're going to date me like a Brooklyn boy, you need to dress like one. This way," I said, practically giddy, and pulled him towards Union Street. I was wearing a loosely fitting floral dress, a pair of flats, and a denim jacket, with a messenger bag slung across my body. He couldn't be in one of his *I-regularly-talk-to-sheiks* outfits.

"Do tell, what does *that* involve?" he asked, part laughing and part skeptical as he enveloped my body from behind.

"Trust me," I said, leaning into him and gleefully throwing the words he said to me so frequently right back at him.

We walked the three blocks to the Brooklyn Industries shop, its windows lined with mannequins sporting various Brooklyn T-shirts and hipster garb, and he laughed heartily as we entered the store.

"Lydia." The pierced blue-haired woman folding T-shirts waved at me as soon as I was inside, and Dylan gave me a side-glance. I used to come into the store weekly when I lived there, and the woman had been working there for years. I caught up with her while Dylan perused, and then I did what I usually did in that store—bounced from table to table and longingly held up cute witty T-shirts and tried on the jackets and bags they had on display. When I looked back at Dylan, whom I hoped would be trying on sweatshirts, he was just staring at me.

"What?"

"Nothing," he said, but he was definitely thinking something. I put down the shirt I was holding and went up to him.

"What?" I asked again.

"It's silly."

"What?"

"You. I love seeing you here. I love you. Let's go back to your apartment"—his voice fell to a whisper—"and I'll do that thing to you—"

I interrupted him with my laughter. "You can't stand not knowing where we're going or what we're doing, can you?"

He shrugged and smiled sheepishly.

"No. This is going to be great," I said as I reached behind him and grabbed a navy-blue hoodie that said BROOKLYN across it in orange letters. "And I'm getting you this."

He leaned down to kiss me and tried to grab the sweatshirt out of my hands. "I'll be buying the sweatshirt, you saucy little thing."

"Nope," I said, pulling it back. "Today is my treat." He reached to try to grab it back, but I walked straight to the register and gave the clerk, who'd been watching us, a *help-a-girl-out-and-don't-let-that-guy-pay* look. Meanwhile, Dylan's body was pressed against my back, his arms trying to reach past me, but I reached behind me and playfully pushed him away with one arm as I handed the clerk my credit card with the other. Finally, he shook his head in defeat.

As we left the store, Dylan looked down at his new sweatshirt while I ripped the tag off the sleeve with my teeth. He stared at me, horrified, and I couldn't help but laugh and shake my head. This was going to be fun.

"Trust me, babe, if you were one of the guys I dated before you, you'd have been jumping for joy that I was willing to pay for the sweatshirt." I was still laughing, knowing how frustrated the whole thing would make him, wanting to egg him on.

"Prats," he muttered under his breath as he took my hand firmly in his own.

Once we were a block away, he stopped in front of an upscale children's shop. He stood in front of me, put his palm to my chin, and forced my gaze up to his. "Are you really going to fight me on paying for things the whole day?"

"No."

He sighed satisfactorily. "Good."

"Because we're not going to do things that cost money. Or not much anyway."

He gave me a skeptical raised eyebrow, and I stood on my tiptoes to kiss him.

"You know, you're just as much trouble as I thought you'd be when I met you in Canada," he said while he shook his head in mock disapproval.

"I'm as much trouble as you'd *hoped* I'd be," I corrected him, and once again I had my fiancé laughing in the middle of the street. "Now come on, fancy boy, I have a park to show you."

We walked past the brownstones on President Street and headed towards Grand Army Plaza and Prospect Park. "See," I said, pointing to the gas lamps still in use in front of some of the houses, "we have old-fashioned things here in Brooklyn too."

"I can see that," he said. "You know, these brownstones are from the Victorian era," he started, and even though this was my neighborhood, I found myself getting the local architecture tour from Dylan. He waxed on about how he could tell things about the sourcing of the stones, and why people had a parlor level and a ground entrance. I could see his love for architecture written so plainly on him. Stripped away of all of the business and the firm politics, and what was left was his true love for what he did.

We ambled into Grand Army Plaza and stopped in front of my favorite coffee cart, set up every weekday morning for the people running to catch their subway.

"Lydia!" said Charlie, the roaster and owner behind the little cart. "Where has my favorite customer been?"

"Hiya, Charlie," I said, walking around the side of the cart to give him a hug. "I've been in London. I'm just back for a bit. This is my fiancé, Dylan," I said, introducing the two men. I could see

Charlie wince, ever so slightly, as they shook hands. Dylan must have been engaging in the handshake version of a dick-measuring contest. My future husband, the Neanderthal.

"Dylan," I said in a slightly scolding tone. "Charlie and his *wife* are old friends and have been making the best coffee in Brooklyn for years." I couldn't exactly blame him for his jealous tendencies after the Eric thing, but I knew he caught my tone. His arm loosened around me, very slightly. "Charlie, can we have two of your exquisite lattes, please?"

"You got it, kid," he said and got to work behind the little single-shot espresso thingy. "I've been hoping to see you for a while, you know. I never got to say how sorry we were about your dad." He looked kind and sincere as he said it, and I nodded. "He was a like a neighborhood institution."

Dylan and I chatted with Charlie for a few more minutes. When he handed us our coffees, I went to hand him the money, but Dylan grabbed my arm to stop me at the same time that Charlie shook his head. "On the house, kid. Don't stay away so long, next time, okay?"

"Thanks, Charlie," I said, depositing my cash into his tip jar.

As we stepped away, Dylan's grip around my waist tightened again, not out of jealousy, but out of that lunatic-like desire we both apparently had to be touching each other all the time. "Do you know *everyone* in this town?" he asked.

"No," I said. "Don't be silly. I just grew up here."

But I looked up at him, and it was as though I could see him seeing me differently. Like he was realizing I had once been a part of somewhere else.

We walked around the park, and I pointed out my running route, the meadow where Daphne and I used to come on summer afternoons and make up stories about the couples and families we'd see and sometimes try to do the *New York Times* crossword puzzle, or at least see how far we could get before we started cheating. It reminded me that she was due back that day from Japan, and when I saw her, as I surely would the next day or the one after, it was going to be with Dylan. I looked down at the ring, and had my first giddy *oh-my-god-this-is-happening* moment of the day.

* * *

"There's a suggested donation," Dylan said with a frown.

After our leisurely lie-down in Prospect Park, we'd walked over the Brooklyn Bridge. He'd kissed me in the middle and held my hand as we reached Manhattan soil. We meandered through SoHo, and I showed him where the pop-up store would be, and the West Village, where we tried to inconspicuously spy into the magnificent brownstones that lined those precious streets. We watched waves crash against the pilings along the west side, and people watched along the High Line. And eventually we'd made our way onto the subway and up to the Metropolitan Museum of Art.

"*Suggested* being the operative word," I replied, pulling him past the membership desk.

"But we can afford to pay." Dylan held his ground, his hands firmly in his pockets.

"Next time, we can pay double. Today is 'what it would have been like to date Lydia if Dylan weren't a duke' day, and on *that* day we experience New York the way I did before I met you."

Dylan grimaced and followed me reluctantly past the membership desk.

It was near closing time, and the museum was thinning out. All day we'd been talking. He asked so many questions, it was as though he was retracing my steps, learning my life backwards, exploring every corner of my experiences. But then, in the museum, he was quiet.

I caught him looking at paintings, getting lost in the photos of buildings in the architecture gallery. He was absorbed, but contemplative. So I let him contemplate, and I wandered on my own. I drifted from room to room, pausing when something caught my eye, letting time drift away.

I finally sat down in a tiny back room of the impressionist wing, with only a couple of paintings and one of those long narrow backless benches, waiting for weary visitors like me. I tipped my feet on my heels in front of me, looking at my flats and noting how scuffed up they were. I was alone in the gallery and slid my arms back behind me, locking them in place, tipping my head back, lengthening my body, stretching. This place was eerily empty—most people were probably gone or at one of the more popular exhibits, so I indulged in the private moment. When I opened my eyes and looked ahead, I found myself lost in a painting I hadn't even noticed at first, a picture of a woman sitting on a window seat. Her features were clear as day, and even though they were painted with broad rough strokes, the concern and care in her expression were unmistakable. Even though there were shades of green and blue used to round out her cheeks, she looked so real, like I was intruding on her private moment.

I found myself wondering what or whom she was looking at, imagining she was in a window at Humboldt Park, that she was looking out into those vast wild spaces from the curated refinement of the grand hall. Maybe that's what life had been like for Duchesses of Abingdon from the past.

That's where my mind was when I felt Dylan's hands on my shoulders from behind. They were firm, steadying, warm, and I sat up straighter for him, relieved to have him back. I was about to rise and turn around to face him, ready to go on to our next destination, when he slid onto the bench behind me, his long legs on either side of mine, my back flush against his front, and he wrapped his arm around my stomach, pulling me against him.

"What are you looking at, damsel?" he whispered in my ear, his chin resting on my shoulder.

"The museum's about to close," I said, but he seemed intent on ignoring that fact.

He nudged just a little closer, and my breathing hitched at his touch, his nearness and warmth.

"What do you see?" he asked again when I didn't answer. My eyes were closed, and I tipped my head back, letting it fall into the crook of his neck as his hand spread across my abdomen, his thumb brushing against the underside of my breast. "Tell me." His voice was getting firmer, more commanding, and I found myself opening my eyes for him.

"I want to know what she's looking at," I said, not believing how soft my voice was.

Dylan's hands drifted down my body and edged between my thighs. "What do you think she's looking at?" he whispered, and he gripped my inner thighs and pulled slowly, forcing my legs apart.

"Dylan." I exhaled the words and resisted, trying to urge my legs back together. I looked up and around the room, worried about others seeing us. The intimacy of the moment spooked me. But I'd been trained to trust him, to believe he'd know when the risk was too great for these kinds of shenanigans.

"You're breaking character," I said on a broken exhale. "No Brooklyn boy would have the nerve…" I couldn't finish the thought. I was too lost to him already.

"Don't care. Open for me. We're alone." He pulled harder, and my legs separated between his. His hands were hidden beneath the light skirt of my dress, and his frame was hunched over mine enough that it would be hard to see, but we were still in a public place, and his soft fingers were still moving dangerously close to my center. My breathing picked up, becoming shallower. I couldn't escape the sensations, the promises in those skilled fingers. "What do you see?" he asked again.

"I'm her," I breathed and closed my eyes. Dylan was drawing circles on my inner thigh, and every other second his fingers would brush against the cotton panties I was wearing beneath my dress.

"Did I say you could wear knickers?" he asked, but I could hear him smiling.

"No," I said, barely able to hear my own word as he slipped a finger beneath the elastic and found me slick for him.

"Tsk tsk." Dylan slipped his finger inside me, and I gripped his thighs next to my legs, digging my fingernails into his legs. I could hear my shamelessly shallow breaths pick up. "Good girl." He slowly developed a rhythm, slowly fucking me with one finger, then two. "You are her."

I moaned quietly, begging, unsure if I wanted him to stop because this was absurd, or keep going so I could come on his hand right there in the Metropolitan Museum of Art.

"And what are you looking for, sitting at that window, damsel?" He continued his strokes, and I heard myself let a moan go into the cool air-conditioned air. "What do you see? What do you want?"

He hooked his finger inside me, and I gasped as I spoke. "You. I see you. I'm looking for you."

"That's right, baby. And I'm looking at you. For you, too. Always." His strokes went deeper, harder, faster. Oh my god, I was going to come right there, on a bench in a far corner of one of Manhattan's great institutions.

"I can't," I exhaled. "Not here," I protested.

"You can. Quietly. Nice and quiet for me, baby." His voice brimmed with confidence in my ability to do this, as though his commanding it would make me capable of coming in his hand without making a sound.

"No," I whimpered. I couldn't come in public. I wouldn't, would I?

"Yes." He picked up his pace again, and I tried to press my legs together to stop him, to control it, but he wouldn't let me. It was agony. It was perfection. And then it was there. I clenched around him involuntarily and my mouth flew open, ready to moan, but he clamped his hand over it, allowing my legs to cross over his hand, as though I could stop him at this point. I was utterly gone.

"Shhhh, my sweet girl," he said between kisses along my shoulder.

Slowly, I came down, back to earth. He released his hold on me, let my legs fall naturally together, let my damp panties fall back into place.

My body was shivering. I wasn't even sure I could stand in my current state. Dylan must have anticipated my predicament, because as he stood he held out his hand and grabbed my elbow with his other, helping me up. He pulled me into a tight hug, our chests melting into each other. "I hope you know I'm furious with you," I said, my cheek against his chest. "You can't just go around making girls come without their permission."

"A couple weeks away from me, and you've become decidedly too independent. Have you forgotten who makes the rules around here?" I could feel him smiling above my head, the smug jerk. I hit him in the chest, and he laughed, making my cheek bounce against his chest. "You can get me back later."

"I will."

"I know."

Chapter 16

Dylan

I could still smell her on my fingers.

Fuck, that was hot, wasn't it? I don't know what came over me. Each hour that passed without someone pointing me out, without a photographer angling for a shot, without the subtle but powerful need to keep my guard up, I felt just a bit unleashed. A bit more reckless. And with each hour that passed with Lydia adorably and enthusiastically dragging me around Brooklyn and Manhattan, proudly showing me her stomping grounds, I felt a growing urge to bring her to heel, to show her that any other little prick that took her out before me was a goddamn imbecile, and never again in her life would she feel anything less than completely taken care of.

So by early evening, when I saw her sitting on that museum bench, mesmerized, open, ready for me, I couldn't fucking help myself.

I understood why she hadn't wanted to pay the admission fee for the museum, but I felt the place deserved something. Not just for giving me a memory I was going to be having a wank to for the rest of my life, but for making Lydia's life better for all those years before I came into it. For being a place she could afford to go, that had given texture to her life. While she'd used the loo before leaving, I texted Thomas and had him make a generous donation. If it had been up to me, it would have been used to designate that entire impressionist wing for our private use.

I'd wanted to get her back to her apartment after that—I was hard as a rock and wanted her under me, and soon. But the girl had her heart set on an outdoor movie. So there we sat. Or I sat. In Brooklyn Bridge Park. On a blanket I'd bought at a shop in Dumbo an hour before. The sun had set, the air was cool but not cold. The bridge lit up in front of the perfect view of Manhattan, and Lady Liberty stood regally to the south. On the mammoth screen in front of us played *Singin' in the Rain*. Now clad in a sweater and jeans she'd had stashed in that bag of hers, with her gorgeous head in my lap, the girl I was going to marry lay laughing at the slapstick comedy.

She was so beautiful.

The day had been perfect. She'd been perfect. I respected her wanting me to understand that her life was rich, even if she hadn't had money before me. I loved seeing how her passion had made her world expansive and lush. Even if part of me had wanted to punch the coffee chap for knowing her, for caring about her, I was mostly grateful to him for looking out for her. Fuck grateful, I was in awe. My girl was loved, and not just by me. I'd never met anyone like her—who cultivated love the way she did? Who drew people in like that? Her world was incredible, and money had nothing to do with it.

She laughed again and looked up to see if I was laughing too, or maybe because she wondered why I wasn't. I stroked the soft skin of her cheek, and fuck me if it didn't feel like satin under my thumb. What the ever-loving fuck had I been thinking not putting that ring on her finger the second she'd asked me to. I was some kind of first-rate arsehole, apparently.

I looked at the screen and smiled for her behalf, but I really just wanted to stare at her like some kind of pathetic git.

When Donald O'Connor did his "Make 'Em Laugh" routine on the screen, Lydia was laughing so hard she was shaking in my lap, which inconveniently made my dick hard. I had to get fucking a grip. I pulled her up to sitting across my legs, which were stretched out before me. She settled in, still staring at the screen, and grabbed some of the gummy bears from the bag she'd bought at the grocery store before coming into the park. She'd also snuck in a bottle of cheap wine. It should have been horrible, but coming from her I enjoyed it. Every sip.

Grocery store candy, cheap wine, and free movies in the park. Where had this been my whole life? We were surrounded by people who felt free. Who'd come out to watch film stars from another era dance on-screen. It was part of the reason I'd become an architect—to bring people together in spaces the way we were at that moment. And it was Lydia who had dragged me in, showed me. I was the goddamn 17th Duke of Abingdon, and it had taken this wee lass from Brooklyn to make my life worth a cent.

I took the candies from her hand, and she stared at me, wondering what I was up to. I plucked one plump gummy bear from the bag and fed it to her. She rolled her eyes for good measure, making sure I knew she thought I was being ridiculous, but then she indulged me, happily, greedily, plucked it from my fingers with her lips, and I fed her another. After another, she leaned in and kissed me.

"I love you," she whispered into my ear. How did she do that?

How did she know exactly when to say those words? Words my own family hadn't uttered to me once in my life. She kissed me again and looked back to the screen.

This was it. *This* is what I wanted for my life. This fearless girl who made the world fall in love with her, who brought me out of Humboldt Park and into a world that made joy seem like an everyday occurrence. This woman who made me want to crawl out of my skin with desire and who crawled into me in a way that fucking terrified me.

"Marry me," I said before fully realizing what I was saying.

"What?" she asked, laughing at what was on the screen, throwing me a quick glance.

"Marry me," I said again, louder. I felt more certain of what I was doing. More certain than I had about anything.

"I already said yes, silly," she said, looking at me intently, starting to see what I meant.

"Tomorrow. Now. Marry me, now. I don't want to wait anymore. I want you to be my wife." I spun her around so she was straddling me. We were surrounded by people. Families. Couples. Friends. Everyone laughing. Everyone absorbed in the screen in front of them. But I couldn't hear or see any of it. Only her.

She stared at me, looked hard to see if I was serious. I was serious.

"Tomorrow?" She looked at me, searching.

"Tomorrow."

"Okay," she said, and the corners of her mouth slowly started to perk up.

"Okay?"

She nodded and bit her lip in that way that made me want to take her to bed immediately.

I wrapped my hands around her perfect face and kissed her. I slid my tongue between those generous pink lips, and she welcomed me. I threaded my hands through her hair, and she relaxed into me, leaned in, so we fell towards each other. She offered herself completely, joined me in not giving one shite about the people around us. This wasn't dominance or bossiness. It wasn't coyness or shyness from her. It wasn't playful. No banter. It was just us, and not a thread of anything else. "Tomorrow. You'll be my wife tomorrow."

To any one of those moviegoers, we must have looked like any other normal couple in the throes of early love…Actually, I had no idea what we looked like, and I didn't care. All I cared about was her.

"Can I take you home now, sweet girl?"

* * *

Lydia snuggled into my side in the town car. I'd texted the driver our location when we'd arrived at the park. He was there in a moment, and I was grateful Lydia allowed me to take her home in privacy.

"How do we get married? *Can* we even get married tomorrow? Is that even legal?" she asked, keeping her head against my shoulder. She looked relaxed, but I could feel her wheels turning. The wee thing was constantly in director mode, trying to iron out kinks before they existed.

"I honestly don't know. I'll have my lawyer look into it," I said and reached for my phone with my free hand to shoot him a text. My other hand was wrapped around Lydia's thin middle and holding her hand. I found myself twiddling her engagement ring between my thumb and forefinger, silently loving the symbol of my possession like some kind of caveman.

My phone rang within a minute of having sent the text, and I reluctantly answered. I didn't want to talk to anyone, but this phone call with my lawyer was going to have to happen at some point, and the sooner we spoke, the sooner he'd have the details for me about getting married. It was after two in the morning in London, but I guess that's why I paid him what I did.

"Evening, Trevor." I braced myself for the onslaught of questions from my friend, who also happened to be my lawyer, and sure enough they came flying at me, beginning with "Are you sure you know what the bloody hell you're doing?" and "What are you? A lad with your first hard-on?" If the questions from my foulmouthed lawyer hadn't been peppered with actual law-related questions including requests for Lydia's full name, social security number, her parents' names, city of birth, and what county we were in, he'd have seen a different side of me.

"You're an absolute nob, you know that, don't you? Just get me the bleeding information, so I can get married tomorrow. We'll fly to Vegas if need be." He laughed into the phone, uttered a profanity or two, and I hung up on him. I knew I could count on him to deliver.

"So? Is your lawyer going to help you find some excuse to get out of this cockamamie plan of yours?" Lydia smiled at me as we pulled up in front of her apartment, but I could tell there was some part of her that was worried I'd been impulsive, some part of her that still didn't believe that I intended to make her my wife as soon as fucking possible. Fair enough, we were fresh on the heels of an epic row and hadn't been speaking to each other because I'd refused to announce our engagement—the girl had a right to be skeptical.

I'd have to fix that.

I flung the car door shut and pulled her close to me, taking her under my arm as I took her keys with my free hand. I kissed the top of her head and pulled her through the door as efficiently as I could. When we were safely inside the building, and she was thoroughly confused, I lifted my darling girl over my shoulder. Her sweet laughter filled the hallway as I carried her up the stairs.

"Dylan!" she shouted, and she tried to hit my ass but couldn't quite get the angle. Didn't matter. I could. The sound of my palm meeting her rear echoed through the stairwell.

"Quiet, you cheeky thing. You think I mean to start my marriage off with my wife questioning my every decision?" I spanked her ass again as I rounded the stairs onto her floor, and I found myself laughing with her as I put her down. The idea of Lydia ever being a submissive little stay-at-home-wife was laughable, to both of us. She was ambitious as all hell, and I loved that about her. I mean, fuck, she could do as she pleased. I hoped she knew that. If not I'd make it very clear—my only concern was her happiness, whether she was CEO of her own company or did yoga all day, I couldn't give a fuck.

"Intend to make me your sex slave, do you? As soon as I sign on the dotted line?" Her words reminded me of our first real fight, when she'd called herself my fuck buddy, and I'd flown off the handle, hating that she thought of herself in such crude terms when she meant so much more. I knew now that even then she'd probably known I loved her. Somewhere, somehow, she knew. Even before I did.

"My wife, the comedian." I kissed her nose as I backed her against the closed apartment door. "Let's get a few things straight, shall we?"

She looked up at me in that way she did whenever I took charge—ready, willing, but with fire right there at the ready to put me in my place if I stepped too far. I took her hands in my own and raised them above her head, effectively pinning her in place.

"First, I'm marrying you tomorrow. I've never wanted anything more. So no more doubting it."

God, she looked so petite standing beneath my frame, with my forearm on the door above her head. She nodded.

"Good. Brings me to the second item. You must tell me if this isn't what *you* want, damsel. Will you regret not getting married with a big white wedding and all that?"

She shook her head. "Couldn't care less."

"Are you sure?" She nodded vigorously, and I kissed her again.

"I'll give you whatever party you want when we get back to England. Or here. Fuck, I don't care. But tomorrow is for you and me."

She nodded again, her eyes never leaving mine.

"And third, you will never call yourself my sex slave, my fuck buddy, or any other demeaning ridiculous pile of horse shite again—got it, my sweet girl?" I stroked her cheek with the back of my hand, and let it drift down the front of her chest and up the inside of her sweater. "Because tomorrow, Lydia, you will be my wife." She nodded slowly, her eyes never leaving mine. "You'll also be a duchess."

Chapter 17

Lydia

Duchess.

Holy shit.

I was going to be a *duchess*.

For some reason, somehow, even though I'd thought about it before, even if I'd been pondering the practicalities of "what does that job entail?" for months, even if I'd had flashes of lowercase "holy shit," and "won't that be weird," this was different. This was Holy. Shit.

I was looking up into Dylan's blue eyes, those blue eyes that had kept me centered through countless new experiences, and I pleaded with them to center me now. I could feel my breathing pick up, like the hugeness of this decision was propelling me out of the warmth and making me zone into my own head and all the anxieties that lay there. All the unknowns.

"Shhh." I heard Dylan's voice soothing, matching the stroking of my cheek with the back of his hand. "Baby, just us, remember?"

"A duchess." I closed my eyes tightly, trying to digest this thing that suddenly felt so big.

I felt his finger under my chin, tilting my face up towards his.

"Hey, look at me. Show me those brown eyes." His tone turned back to the commanding bossy one that always got my attention, and my eyes snapped open. "Good girl. Now let's go inside, and I'll make that overwhelmed look of yours go away."

He reached down by my hip and unlocked the door, moving me out of the hall and into the apartment with him. I was about to go to the kitchen to put on the kettle for tea when he pulled me into the overstuffed armchair in the living room. My legs draped over his lap, and his strong arms encompassed me, held me close to him by wrapping his arm fully around my hip.

"Damsel," he started, sifting his fingers through my hair with his free hand and holding my head against his body. "This marriage of ours is going to be about you and me, got that?" The tightness of his hold echoed his words and calmed me. I breathed into his chest, and reveled in the closeness. "It's not about the media or about *HELLO!* magazine. It's not about anything bigger than us. We will have to deal with all of it, but first and foremost, this is about us."

I nodded, looking at him to continue. "I know."

"It's time, damsel. You were right about being public. I have no intention of letting our marriage be a secret. And I won't sugarcoat it for you—it will be trying at first, the press *will* go mad. But, I promise you, we'll handle it all: the media, my mother and sister, who will likely want to slaughter us when they've discovered we've gone and gotten married without them."

I laughed a little into his chest just imagining Emily's look of horror when she realized she'd missed out on the real affair, not to mention his mother's, whose horror would be about the fact he'd married *me*. "Oh, we're having a wedding," I said with purpose. "I have a feeling it won't fly for the Duke of Abingdon to tie the knot without some fanfare." I'd be happy to indulge Emily's whims, and his mother needed to know this was for real.

Dylan chuckled back. "Probably, but we won't do anything we don't want to do." He leaned down and kissed the top of my head. "But, baby, I, better than anyone, understand why the title feels overwhelming. We'll figure this out together. We'll break new ground together. I can't be a duke without you. And I'll never ask more of you than you want to give when it comes to being a duchess."

I could actually feel, beneath his skin, in his bones, his posture, the truth in his words. And suddenly I couldn't remember why I'd been worried. Yes, it was big. Yes, it felt grand and new. Yes, it was going to be my life's work to be a duchess but also to be me, to pursue my dreams. I'd been serious when I'd said that I didn't want to open another store, that I was ready for the next big thing. And now, I realized, that whatever that next big thing was, it was going to have to work with the gowns, the events, the duties of being the Duchess of Abingdon. Much in the same way his architecture firm would have to work with all of his duties. But we could do it. Together.

I wriggled out of his hold and shifted to straddle him. He never took his eyes off my face as I adjusted and rested my elbows on his shoulders and wrapped my hands into his hair. "We got this, don't we?"

"We do." He smiled as he said it and surely would have dived in to kiss me if I hadn't beat him to it. I stroked his lips with my tongue and kissed and kissed.

"Make me your wife, then, already," I whispered, and he chuckled. "What's taking you so long?"

Dylan laughed heartily and moved his hands to my ass, which he squeezed just to the brink of pain. "You cheeky thing."

He rose from the chair, and I wrapped my legs tightly around him. I broke the kiss for only a moment. "Don't we have details to figure out?" We couldn't get lost in each other if there were things to plan.

"Nothing can be accomplished at ten in the evening, damsel. Not where legalities are concerned." He nipped my neck, and a shiver shot down my spine, settling right at my quickly dampening center. "Nothing except to remind you, my saucy little fiancée, that no previous date with any Brooklyn boy ever had a chance of ending the way this one will."

He slapped my ass before he dropped me on the wide low bed. I grabbed the hood of his sweatshirt on the way down, making him topple over me. And he showed me, as he promised, that no guy I'd ever dated had even stood a chance.

* * *

I woke up to three distinct sensations—the smell of coffee, the sound of Dylan's bossy business-tone barking into the phone but shifting to a whisper as he got closer, and the pulling of the sheet away from my bare chest.

I opened my eyes and saw Dylan, clad only in a towel wrapped around his waist, cover the base of the phone with his palm and focus those impossibly blue eyes on me.

"Happy marriage day, damsel." He leaned over, clearly intending to give me a quick kiss on the lips but was unable to go away once he'd started. He kissed my neck. My clavicle. He groaned, started to pull away, and then came back to kiss my breast. I laughed as I ran my hands through his hair, and he groaned again, frustrated that he was still on the phone, which just made me laugh harder.

He retreated towards the living room but gave me a quick desperate look before leaving the room.

I rolled back into the bed and closed my eyes again for a moment. Assuming we could pull it off, I was getting married that day. *Married.*

I slid further into the sheets, and what started as a daydream of he and I walking into city hall that day—him in a suit, me in a simple white dress—slowly churned into details of the day running through my mind. What *was* I going to wear? Did we need a witness? Should we go out to eat afterwards? Should we invite anyone? How do people *get* married anyway? How many forms of ID was I going to need? Where was my birth certificate? Where was city hall anyway? Wait, was city hall where people actually got married or was that just on TV?

Within a minute, I was sitting up in the bed, clinging the sheet to my chest. I took a big gulp of my coffee, winced at the hot liquid burning my throat, and dialed the one person who could help me figure all this out. Well, the one person besides Dylan, that is.

Daphne.

As the phone was ringing I began to realize how crazy this was going to sound to her, but I didn't have a chance to dwell on it.

"This better be good," she said groggily into the phone. I could hear her sheets rustling. Hell, I could practically still hear her dreaming.

"I'm getting married."

"I know. You told me," she said, yawning. "You woke me up at…What time is it? I'm so fucking jet-lagged. You woke me up at…" I could hear her rustling around. "Eight in the evening to tell me you're engaged?"

"It's six in the morning."

"Not in my brain, it's not."

"Well, tell your brain it's Friday at six a.m., because I'm getting married, Daphne. *Today*," I said. "And I need you."

"Wait, what?"

"Dylan surprised me yesterday. Wait, was it yesterday? No. Crap, sorry, I've lost track of time. He surprised me by coming to the apartment. To New York. On Wednesday. We had this kind of fight about Eric—"

"Eric?"

"Eric Stuart? From that journalism class I took college? Keep up, lady."

"Wait, what does he have to do with anything?" I had her attention now, and I could hear her making coffee in the background.

"It doesn't matter. I'll explain later. The important thing is that Dylan and I are good. And we've decided to get married. Today."

"What the? Um, okay. Lydia, are you sure? Wait, what is happening?" I heard her yawn again. I felt like I was talking to someone on another planet. I'd forgotten how *not* a morning person Daphne was, which seemed to be seriously exacerbated by jet lag.

"Yes. I know it was fast before, but weirdly, now it's not. It's right, Daphne. I promise it's right. I'll explain everything. But I need you. Can you take the day off?"

"Wait. Hold on. The coffee maker is going now. Let me make sure I understand—you're getting married?"

"Yes."

"Today?"

"Yes."

"And Dylan is there? At your apartment?"

"Yes."

"I'm on my way over. Give me twenty-five minutes."

"Bring—"

"I'll bring everything."

"I love you!" But she was already hanging up. I had activated the Daphne machine, and I could feel my shoulders sink with relief.

When Dylan came back into the bedroom a few minutes later, I was standing in front of my closet, the sheet wrapped around my body and my coffee cup in my hand. I was staring into the cramped overstuffed space as though maybe it would magically produce the perfect dress to wear to one's spur-of-the-moment wedding. I could hear him coming but hadn't yet turned around.

"Was that your lawyer? What did he say? Do you have your birth certificate? Daphne's coming over." I clung the sheet to my body with my coffee and went to move some clothes aside, but I stilled when I felt Dylan's chest against my back. His arms sliding over my shoulders, trying to settle me.

"I want to buy you a dress." I turned around to look at him for a moment, and he kissed my forehead. "May I do that?"

"Yes." For some reason, buying something new hadn't even occurred to me. In spite of having gotten the better part of one cup of coffee down, I still was trying to grasp how we were going to accomplish this.

"Trevor pulled some strings and secured us an actual appointment at the city clerk's office for four this afternoon. Does that give you enough time?"

"Plenty." I sighed and leaned back into him. His presence

calmed me, even if my mind was still buzzing, slowly building a to-do list.

"Daphne's coming?"

"She is."

"Do you want her to be our witness?"

I turned around completely, swallowing the remainder of my coffee and wrapping my arms around him while the empty mug dangled off my finger at his back. "Is that okay with you? She's the closest thing I have to family."

"Damsel, I want her there. For you. We'll get a chance to do this all over again, and I'm afraid it will very much be about my family and fanfare. I want this day to be ours. Yours."

"Thank you," I said and landed my forehead against his firm bare chest. "You're still only wearing a towel."

He stroked his hands up my back, and started to pull the sheet down from my body. "I didn't much see the point in getting dressed." I could hear the seduction in his voice, the hunger, and it awoke every cell, set each one afire, but I pulled the sheet back and resecured it around my chest.

"Oh no, you don't," I said. "No more sex until after we're married. You'll have to make an honest woman out of me first." I gave him a coy gaze and moved back, making a show of keeping a distance between us.

"Baby," he said, pulling me back against him and making my refusal nearly impossible. His skin was so warm, and he smelled so good—that earthy scent humming in the air around us. "That's a mere ten hours from now. Surely you can overlook the technicality."

"Sorry, Hale. Rules are rules." I squirmed free and moved behind the standing screen in the corner of the room. I took the robe hanging from its corner and slipped it on out of his sight.

He groaned in frustration for the second time that morning. "You're maddening, you know that, right?"

I smirked as I reemerged.

"And speaking of rules," he added, marching back towards me. "I'll be buying you a dress. But: No. Knickers."

"Who does he think he is?" I grumbled to myself while laughing as I headed into the kitchen for more coffee.

"I heard that," he said firmly. "And the answer is: your husband."

"I know you did!" I shouted back. "And the nineteen fifties called and they want their bossy man back!"

We continued the banter as we ate breakfast but quickly turned back to the practical issues at hand.

"So are you going to tell your mother?"

"That we're getting married?"

I nodded.

"Well, it would kind of defeat the purpose of some of this if we never told anyone, don't you think?"

I groaned, not being able to bear the idea of that conversation.

"Look, I know she's made this about as difficult as she possibly could have. She's bloody impossible. And I don't want to call her. Or Emily. Anyone. We'll tell them when we get back and take it from there. We should decide what we want—or don't want—in advance, but I promise we won't agree to anything until we've had a chance to consider it all together. Is that all right by you?"

"That seems fine. I just hate that it's a thing."

"It was always going to be a thing. I'm sorry for that. Me getting married…The best way I can describe it is that it impacts everyone, and not just in the ways a wedding normally impacts others. It's—"

"It's about the future of your family, of the name, of Humboldt. I get it. It's just hard to reconcile that with the idea that it's also just about us."

He nodded and pulled me into his lap—he'd sat down on one of the old colonial chairs at the kitchen table. "Think of it this way: Our marriage is just about us—we're the ones who decide everything about it. But we have to be thoughtful about those decisions, maybe think a bit harder than the average couple about what we decide to do. It will always be what *we* decide, but it would be unfair to ignore that the repercussions extend beyond us."

I stared thoughtfully into my empty mug.

"Baby," he said. "Don't let this put a damper on this day—"

"I'm not. I actually feel lucky. And not because of the title, but because you're a part of something that pushes you to be a better man."

"And now you're a part of it too. Or you will be by quarter past four today." He smiled as he said the words. Then he reached across the table to grab his phone, which had started vibrating, his lawyer's name flashing on its screen. "Hale," he said sternly into the phone, all businesslike. "Well done. Thank you, mate." Silence, and he began pouring himself another cup of coffee. "What's the first thing?…I did, and the answer is still no." He walked across to the fridge to get the milk. "I think I've made myself clear on this point." He listened intently into the phone and actually rolled his eyes. I didn't think I'd ever seen him do that before. "Bloody hell, fine! I'll ask her." He pressed a button on the screen of his phone. "Trevor, you're on speaker. Lydia, say something so he can hear you."

"Hi," I said warily.

"Hello, Lydia." Trevor's voice crackled from the speakerphone.

"Now." Dylan interrupted and looked at me purposefully. "Lydia."

"Um, yes?"

"Do you want a prenuptial agreement?"

Oh, fuck. I hadn't even thought about anything along those lines. Of course Trevor, as his lawyer, would be concerned. He should be. We'd met a few times, but regardless of that, he should of course advise his client not to marry a girl he'd known less than a year without a prenup.

"Lydia?" I hadn't said a word, and Dylan was obviously starting to worry.

"Um. I think you should do whatever Trevor advises." I tried to say it with as much warmth as I could. I didn't care. I really didn't, and I didn't want Dylan to think I was being defensive.

He looked at me for a moment, searching, making sure I was being honest. Then he spoke back into the phone. "Well, you heard her. She says it's up to me. And I don't want one. It's a bloody waste of your time. And mine."

He looked at me with so much warmth. Not a hint of challenge. He put the phone off speaker and brought it back to his ear.

"What you fail to understand is that if Lydia leaves me, I'll be worthless anyway, and I'd happily give her every cent I had. And there's no way in hell I'd ever leave her. And Humboldt, as you know, is locked up in Hale Shipping anyway. So like I said, waste of time. And ink." He looked at me the entire time he was speaking, and I nodded back, hoping to convey that I felt the same way. Not that I had anything to give, but that I loved him that much as well.

"Sure, I'll let you know," he continued. "So what's the second thing?" He spoke more calmly into the phone and came around to stand behind me as he spoke. He was running his hand along my robe-clad shoulder, and leaning down to kiss my head when he said, "What? Well, what can we do about it?" I turned quickly to look at him when I heard him speak. His voice had gone down an octave, and he was running his fingers through his hair.

He put the hand over the receiver end of the phone again, and spoke softly to me on the side. "Trevor got the marriage license squared away—we'll just need to sign it when it's delivered—but there's a twenty-four-hour waiting period. One needs a judicial waiver—"

At that moment, the door to the apartment swung open—I could hear it from the kitchen, and I'd know those footsteps anywhere. Daphne came barreling into the kitchen just as Dylan was filling me in. "Did he just figure out about the judicial waiver issue?" she asked.

"Yeah, what can we do about it?" I asked her.

"So I was looking into this on the way over, and it's really simple. It's just a signature. I think I know someone who will sign it for you—the judge I interned for last semester. She loves me. I've got you covered."

"I'll call you back…No, call him anyway, but Lydia's friend, Daphne, apparently knows a judge. I'll call if I need you to call Senator Hampson."

Dylan hung up the phone, marched over to Daphne, and put his arm around her, giving her the most emotive hug I'd ever seen from him. I mean to someone other than me.

"Well, hi there, Your Royal Highness." Daphne patted his back.

"Minister." I laughed at their ridiculous ribbing of each other.

I laughed at both of them, and enjoyed this moment of all us just standing in my kitchen. The two people I cared most about in the world.

"So," she said, grabbing a cup of coffee and looking at Dylan. "Once I forgive you for not asking for my blessing—"

"Sorry for that," he said.

"Noted." She reached into the fridge for milk. "Now we can get down to business. Lydia, you need to get dressed. We have errands to run. While you do that, I'll call Judge Fogel." I nodded, relieved to have our wedding planner in-house. "And, Dylan, you and I have some other details to discuss."

"Indeed."

I stood there, waiting to hear what they had to say, but they both just looked at me. Obviously they wanted to chat in secret. The nerve.

Chapter 18

Dylan

Six hours later, and I was eating lunch in Midtown. I took a room at the Yale Club, with whom Cambridge had a reciprocal relationship, and set up office. Trevor had sent me a prenup, which I'd promptly tossed to the side. I understood the risks and the ramifications, but I'd also meant what I said. If anything ever happened, I'd *want* Lydia to have half. Fuck it—she could have it all. And I wanted to be making that decision while I felt this way, not if or when I was angry with her about something. That woman was the love of my fucking life, and I knew in my goddamn bones that she was a good person, the best kind of person. And I already owed her my fucking life. So fuck that. No prenup.

I couldn't help but laugh at the thought of how hard a time she'd have adjusting to having money though. Christ, as it was I'd already gotten several texts from Daphne about my girl's asinine stubbornness. I'd sent them to Barneys and arranged for Lydia to see a personal shopper. I'd called ahead, given them my credit card, and instructed them not to let her know the price of any of the dresses or accessories. I wanted her to pick the clothes she wanted to wear. I knew she'd tried to weasel it out of them, and at one point she texted me from Daphne's phone trying to suss out if I'd set a price limit. I hadn't, and I saw right through her. I loved this side of her, but I also loved the idea of taking away the worry that lay beneath all that stubbornness.

I thought of that apartment, of our Brooklyn day and how she'd been so conscious of saving, giving, and it thrilled me to know she'd never have to worry about money again. She had no idea, but I'd tasked Thomas with arranging for a joint bank account and second credit cards to be rushed in her name. Now that we were going to be a team, I wanted her to understand as quickly as possible that we were in all of this together. But I still couldn't wait for the moment she called me because she saw her bank balance—it made me smile every time. She'd have a complete fit. She'd get sassy and fight me. Then I'd bring her right back to me. It was going to be fucking adorable, and sexy as hell.

In the meantime I just had to make it until four. I'd also arranged for her and Daphne to go to the spa and booked a room at the Pierre, where they could get ready. And Daphne was supposed to text me about anything else they needed.

The fax machine started to hum, and I saw the signed waiver slide through the printer. I couldn't believe we still used these archaic things, but at the moment I was completely grateful. That judicial waiver was the one thing standing between me and making Lydia my wife.

I had one more thing I needed to do before slipping into my own newly purchased clothes—the suit I'd bought at Barneys had been delivered and was hanging in the closet, waiting.

The phone rang several times before anyone answered. Unsurprising for a bar at one in the afternoon.

"Great Lakes," said the man on the other end in a gruff well-worn New York accent.

"May I speak with Jake Ritter please."

"Speaking."

"Jake, my name is Dylan Hale, and this afternoon I'm intending to marry someone I understand you know well. Lydia Bell."

"Hey, Rhodes!" the voice excitedly shouted into the room on the other end of the line. "Get your sorry ass in here. I have an Englishman on the phone who says he's marrying Rick's daughter."

"Sir—"

"Hold your horses, fancy pants. This is a family matter," Jake said into the phone before shouting back into the room. "You heard me…Lydia, you sorry ass. What other daughter did Rick have? Get over here!"

I was immediately glad I'd called, and when both men were on the phone, I told them exactly what I had planned.

* * *

At three thirty I sat in the lobby of the Pierre. I'd settled the tab, given instructions to have the girls' belongings brought from the room to the car, and now I was waiting. I was waiting for my *bride*. How this had happened, I'd never fully understand. It's not like I'd sat around imagining my wedding day. Fuck, a year ago I didn't even think I'd have a wedding. Ever. For a decade I'd seen relationships as an impossibility, hadn't even entertained the possibility of building anything with anyone. And now, here I was. It was monumental, bizarre if you knew me. And there was only one person, other than Lydia, who truly knew me, and suddenly I was sad he wasn't there. I picked up my phone and texted Will.

FRIDAY, 3:32 pm
I'm getting married, mate.

FRIDAY, 3:32 pm
I know, you sad wanker. Fancy a game of billiards? Come round the club. The new sous chef is on duty, and I'm getting obliterated.

FRIDAY, 3:33 pm
Can't. I'm bloody getting married, you arse.

My phone immediately started ringing.

"What in the bloody hell?" Will did not sound drunk. He liked to talk a big game, but I had no doubt he would actually be home by eleven. Lately he'd been acting even more like an old man.

"You heard me." I was enjoying this already. "I'm in New York."

"And you two are getting married today?"

"We are." Just saying it out loud to my best mate made it real.

"Fucking hell. Were you going to invite me, you daft prick?"

"It was a bit spur-of-the-moment idea. We'll have a proper do when we get back, after we deal with the wrath of the dowager."

"Aww, shite. I'd pay to see that conversation." I winced, recognizing just how miserable that was going to be. "Well look, mate, happy wishes. Lydia's perfect for you. Not to mention hotter than hell."

"Hey—"

"Aww, come on. She is. You're going to have to get used to men talking about how gorgeous your *wife* is."

At that moment, the elevator dinged, and I knew it would be her.

"Gotta go, Will. I'll kick your ass for that comment when I get back." I could hear him speaking into the phone but I hung up. All of my attention was now on Lydia.

Christ. She was wearing a dress that somehow made her look both conservative and sweet and so insanely sexy I didn't think I could get through the next few hours. It was all ivory and silk and made her look a fucking dream. There were tulips, peonies, an entire English garden crawling up the silken fabric, gathering at the tiny tailored waist and somehow emphasizing her breasts hidden behind the scooped neckline. She was wearing a sweet navy jacket on top and wild blue heels that made her legs look fucking endless. Her hair was down, soft, perfect. Elegant and traditional with just a hint of rebellion. She was my girl.

She looked around and then her eyes landed on me, and I knew I was smiling like a goddamn virgin. This woman. How did she render me so fucking defenseless?

I rose, buttoned my jacket, and went to her. I took her hands in mine, and my finger grazed her bracelet. I looked down to see the diamond cuff I'd bought her the night everything went to shite the previous year at the palace.

"It's my favorite," she whispered, and only then did I realize I was thumbing it, shifting up her wrist.

"You're stunning." I looked into her brown eyes and watched as the blush spread from her chest to her cheeks, like I knew it would. It always did when I made her realize how I looked at her. How I saw her.

I broke the moment to kiss Daphne on the cheeks. "Thank you, Daphne." Even Daphne blushed. Christ—we hadn't even left the hotel, and these girls were already on the edge of tears.

We rode down Broadway in the car, and I kept Lydia's hand in mine the whole time. Daphne prattled on about their day, but I couldn't process a word. If I wasn't looking at Lydia's legs, crossed demurely in the footwell next to mine, then I was looking at her face. Fuck, I loved this woman. She caught me looking at her and squeezed my hand, lacing her fingers with my own.

When the car pulled up in front of the stately building downtown, I let Daphne exit the car, but I pulled Lydia all the way onto my lap.

"You ready for this, baby?"

She bit her lip, and it was then I noticed her eyes were glassy. "Damsel, what is it?" She shook her head, but I caught a tear slip past. I brushed it away with my thumb and took her face in my hands. She needed to look at me. "Lydia, talk to me."

She took a deep inhale. "I just wish...I wish my dad could have met you. I wish he could know that I am getting married. That I love you. That you love me. That...that I'm so happy."

Her eyes cast down into her lap again. "Look at me." I tilted her chin with my finger. "Are you sure you want to do this? Do you want to wait?"

She shook her head without hesitation. "No. No more waiting."

I nodded and held her against me. "You're brave, beautiful, and absolutely brilliant. I'm sure he wished he could have been here too. But I've no doubt in my mind that he knew you'd find your way."

She nodded into my shoulder, and I kissed the top of her head. I sighed deeply as the reality of that moment sank into me. For the rest of my life I'd do anything in my power to make sure Rick Bell's daughter was the most loved woman on earth.

Chapter 19

Lydia

Dylan exited the car, then reached in to take my hand. Even though we were outside a municipal building downtown on a Friday afternoon, this moment was more romantic than the all the times we'd exited a fancy Mercedes and were headed into party filled with members of the royal family. This moment was better.

I smoothed my gown and gripped the lapels of my cropped tailored jacket, centering myself.

Daphne and I had had a blast trying on gowns. I considered everything from a traditional white gown to a little black dress, but this one had felt right. The perfect compromise. It was tea length in front and ankle length in the back. It was white, but covered in an array of spring flowers. It was structured taffeta and silk, tailored but whimsical and summery with its spaghetti straps and simple scooped neckline. I could have worn it to a ball, but with a jacket, I could wear it to a dinner.

I loved it. I felt beautiful. I felt bridal. I felt like me.

Dylan, wearing a slim new navy suit, tucked me into his side and gripped my waist, ushering me up the stone steps. Daphne, decked out in a slim red dress, walked beside us. We were doing this.

When we got inside, Dylan turned into his efficient business-man self, and within a moment had us headed into the clerk's chambers. He introduced us all and laid our paperwork on the table, all while never letting go of my hand.

"Shall we begin?" the judge asked.

"Yes," I said, before Dylan had a chance to answer. Then I leaned up and pressed my lips to his ear. "Let's do this, knighty," I whispered.

Dylan smiled and took my hands in his own.

When the judge got to the part with the rings, I looked over at Daphne, and she handed me the ring that I'd gotten polished earlier that day. Dylan's eyes widened. I knew he didn't expect me to have thought of this part.

"It belonged to my father's father," I whispered. "And now it's yours."

Dylan smiled and looked at me with narrowed eyes, as though he couldn't believe I'd managed to surprise him. Then he removed something from his pocket. Before I could process what was happening, the thin diamond band I'd been wearing for months was slid onto my ring finger. Now it was my wedding band.

* * *

Dylan still hadn't told me where we were going when we emerged from the restaurant and were walking towards the car. We'd had a quiet dinner at Gramercy Tavern and talked about every aspect of the ceremony, burning it into our memory, crafting the story of our day.

Wherever we were going now, he assured me that Daphne would meet us there, and he said that he "hoped" I'd be pleased. I'd told him I wanted to spend our wedding night in the apartment. Our life in London was our future, and of course I loved it—his luxurious house in Belgravia, Humboldt Park, the hideaway house he'd built in the country, the house on Ikaria in Greece where we'd vacationed the previous fall. Holy crap—*four* houses, and all of them state of the art and with nine-million-thread-count everything. But this night was the one night when I was really going to bring my side of the story to our marriage. In the absence of any real family to bring into the picture, I wanted all of the things that spoke for my past, even if they were the humble Park Slope apartment and a bodega breakfast in the morning. Dylan, to his credit, hadn't even hesitated. And to my credit, I didn't attempt to make us take the subway back to Brooklyn.

"So where are we going?" I asked as he pulled me onto his lap in the back of the black sedan.

He moved the hair off my shoulder, and used both hands to slip my navy-blue jacket off my shoulders. He laid a kiss on my exposed arm, and took my hand in his own. He reverently stared down at the rings and moved them between his fingers.

"I don't think I'll ever tire of seeing these on you," he said and kissed my hand. Then he looked down to his own ring. "And I love this. Thank you."

I smiled for a moment. "I'm glad. But stop deflecting. Where are we going?"

"Baby, it will be so much better for you to just find out. Patience."

I groaned and lay my head against his shoulder, letting go a sigh.

"I'll take the Manhattan Bridge, sir, if that's all right. Less construction," the driver piped up from the front seat.

"Sounds fine." Dylan's voice was authoritative but softened by all the emotion of the evening.

"And might I add, congratulations to you both."

"Thank you," we said in unison, and I looked out the window as we crossed the bridge.

"I love this view," I said. "Leaving Manhattan behind and seeing the Statue of Liberty in the distance always makes me feel like I'm going home."

"You are."

I nuzzled into him and watched the familiar streets pass us by until we pulled up in in front of one of the most familiar bars on one of the most familiar streets. I sat up straight and looked right into Dylan's eyes, taking his face in my hands. "You didn't." I asked, already feeling the smile spread across my face.

I looked out the window at Great Lakes, my father's favorite dive bar, the place I'd practically grown up. The home of the dart record I held. The home of my father's best friends, and the one place where he still took refuge and managed to get to even in his last days. The lights were dim inside, as they always were, but there was something different about it. I looked at the door, and they'd strung twinkly lights around the entrance. Unless Jake and Rhodes had suddenly decided to get fancy, something was definitely up.

"What's going on?" I asked, but the car door swung open, and Dylan stepped out, smiling and reaching his hand inside to help me. As soon as I stepped out, I grabbed his hand and pulled him to the entrance. "Oh my god. I can't wait to show you this place!"

I was about to pull the door open when I saw a piece of white paper taped to the door with electrical tape—just Jake's style. It read, in big block letters:

A WEDDING HAPPENED. WE'RE CELEBRATING.
COME IN IF YOU HAVE TO, BUT IF YOU FUCK IT UP
YOU'RE OUT.

I started laughing and looked at Dylan. "And *that* is why my dad loved these guys. Loyal to an insane degree." Dylan laughed and looked at me with so much love I thought I'd choke. He looked at me in a way that said that while he may have thought the sign was entertaining, it was the fact it meant something to me that he cared about. "Come on," I said and practically dragged him through the doorway.

I was buoyant and giggling when I stepped through the door, but as soon as we were in the room, I felt a rush of emotion. My fingers threaded through Dylan's, and I just stood still. Everyone was there. Jake, Rhodes, their wives. My dad's other friends from the bar—a group of surly Brooklyn guys—artists, bar owners, musicians, cooks, and shop owners. Daphne and her parents, Charlie and Karen. All the people that had loved him, and me. It was almost as if my dad *were* there, and I felt a tear fall.

I also felt Dylan's hard chest against my back, and his strong hands gripped my waist and pulled me close to him. He leaned over my shoulder and whispered into my ear, "Okay there, damsel?"

I nodded and leaned back into him. "Thank you," I whispered back.

And then they were there.

Jake picked me up and twirled me around, giving me an insane bear hug and then depositing me on a twirling bar stool and giving it a spin. "Get this girl some of our finest bubbly!" he said, and a pint of beer quickly landed in front of me.

One by one the guys came up to me. Hugged me. Told me how much they missed my dad, how happy they were for me, how much they knew he'd want to have been there. And while they talked to me, they also took turns talking to Dylan. I knew they were all giving him the third degree. I saw arms crossed over chests, standoffs, and once-overs. But in each case, the conversations quickly settled into laughter, pats on the shoulder, and in the case of Rhodes, an actual hug. They were all doing what my dad couldn't do—watching over me, giving their blessing, and letting Dylan know that each one of these men was my father.

At some point, Daphne pulled me aside. She was giggly and drunk and had been flirting with one of the other bartenders.

"Are you okay?" she asked with a look that somehow conveyed excitement for me as well as concern. She knew exactly the wave of mixed emotions running through me.

I nodded, and gave her a hug. "Was this your idea?"

"Nope. Well, I mean, Dylan ran it by me, asked me if I thought it would be what you'd want, but really he did the whole thing on his own. I thought about inviting the other girls, but I figured you guys might not be quite ready to enter into the gossip mill yet."

"Thank you. I'm glad it's just you and the guys. Thank you, Daph, for everything today. I didn't need much to make today perfect, but I needed you." I pulled her into another longer, firmer hug. "I miss you, ya know."

"I know. I miss you too. Come back more, okay?"

"I'll try."

"So what's the plan now that you guys are hitched? Do you have to go to like Duchess School or something?"

I laughed, so giddy from this night. "You're so weird. No," I started, and she shrugged her shoulders as though it weren't a ridiculous possibility that Duchess School existed. "For now, nothing. I don't know how long having a normal full-time job for a company will work—Dylan has to go to events all the time, and now that we're married I'll go with him."

"Aww, poor Lydia, having to go to all the balls." She mocked me lovingly, otherwise I would have smacked her.

"Very funny. But seriously, I can't very well be coming to New York for a month at a time for Hannah if Dylan and I are taking care of Humboldt or attending events. So, I really don't know. But you know, I think I want to work for myself. I'm not sure exactly what or how, but I think I could do what I've done for Fiona with her jewelry business and Hannah with her store for other designers." I shrugged my shoulders, not ready to delve into my career options at my wedding reception, but also feeling oddly calm in that something like that, something independent, *was* where I was headed. "Dylan and I will figure it out."

"Plus, you're going to have like a dozen little aristocratic babies, right?"

"Daphne!" I shoved her in the shoulder with as much love as I could while it could still be considered a shove.

"What?! Aren't you? Don't you have to like line up the next duke or whatever?"

"I'm only twenty-five!"

"Tell me you've at least talked about it," Daphne said, interrupting my train of thought. I was still silent. "Lydia!"

"Of course we've talked about it, but we're not in any rush." She was such a pill.

"What are you two up to?" Dylan's hands landed on my hips, and his lips landed in my hair. "You look like mischief."

"Who, me?" Daphne asked, playing the innocent.

Dylan lovingly glared at her. "All I know is that she was laughing, and now my darling wife looks far too serious." He kissed me again, this time leaning around to the front to kiss me on the lips. There were hollers and whistles from the bar area. "Dance with me," he instructed, and I turned around into his guiding arms.

I was pulled out to a small area where Dylan had pushed some tables aside. There was no real dance floor at Great Lakes. Ella Fitzgerald started to play from the jukebox, and Dylan pulled me close against him. We barely moved. Instead he swayed me in his arms.

"At the wedding, we'll waltz. But that will be for everyone else. This is for us," Dylan whispered into my hair and pulled my head beneath his chin.

"You don't mind that our wedding night is being spent at a Brooklyn dive bar?" I asked him. It had nagged at me a little, just how different this was from anything in Dylan's world.

"It's perfect. I've had luxury and exclusivity all my life. Now I have you. And you have this. And it's perfect."

"But it's so different from your world."

"Our world. These are both our world now. One place."

I nodded into his chest. Our world. It didn't feel that way yet. Technically, I was now a duchess. And it still felt foreign, like not quite a part of who I was.

"These people love you," Dylan said, gesturing to the bar around us. "And they loved your father. I think they consider you one of their own."

"They do. I can't believe you thought of it. Thank you. Thank you, Dylan, for everything."

He stopped our dancing and moved his hands to frame my face. His eyes held mine for a moment before he started speaking. "No, baby. No 'thanks.' You're a part of me. There's not a thing I wouldn't do for you, and this? Bringing the people who love you together? It's a given."

I reached up—I didn't need to go too far in the heels I was wearing—and pressed my lips to his. "I love you, Dylan William Lucas Hale, seventeenth Duke of Abingdon, architectural prodigy, and the hottest non-eligible non-bachelor in London."

He laughed and pulled me against him, his hands moving to grip my waist firmly. "Cheeky thing, let's—"

He was interrupted by the sound of silverware on glass. "Okay, good-for-nothings, scoundrels, and everyone else in here. And you two"—Jake pointed at us—"the *lady* and *gentleman* of the evening. Daphne's a lady too, I suppose."

"Hey!" Daphne shouted.

"Yeah, yeah, Miss D., fancy attorney." He appeased her and we all laughed at their banter. Daphne was almost as much family here as I was. "Now shut your yappers. I need to say a few words. Because we know if Rick were here he'd say at least a few." The crowd laughed, and Dylan held me just a little harder in his arms. "Your dad, Lydia, was also a gentleman. He was, without question, the smartest, kindest, classiest guy I knew. Lord knows what he was doing hanging around with the likes of us." There was an "all right all right" from behind me, and a gentle laugh rippled through the crowd. "The first time he brought you in here, you were a tiny little thing. You couldn't have been more than five. He perched you right here on this bar," he said, knocking the mahogany ledge with his free hand, "and ordered you a Shirley Temple. And from that moment on you were family."

Dylan wrapped his arm around my waist and pulled me further into him. I smiled up at Jake, feeling safer and warmer and more whole than I'd felt possibly ever. "You know most of our stories, Lydia. You probably knew more than you should have at too young an age. But there are probably a few things you don't know. When you started at NYU. Your first day. Your dad came here at noon and sat on that stool right there. He always felt sorry that you were stuck with him, but we all knew you two were the luckiest pair that ever walked this planet." I nodded in agreement. "But he sat there and my god, until the day you graduated, I'd never seen a man prouder. And the day you did graduate? Well, you know. He was pretty sick by then. You were there giving your speech, and your dad was in the hospital. Me and Rhodes over there went to the hospital to sit with him. He had a transfusion that day." I gasped slightly. The transfusions were always hard on him. He'd told me his doctor's visit that day was routine but couldn't be rescheduled because of the clinical trial rules. "He knew that if you knew, you'd skip your graduation without a second thought. But, and here's what you may not know, your dad always knew what you were giving up for him, and it broke his heart every day. But he wasn't worried. Just like the rest of us, he could see how special you were. You are. He had to accept early on he'd have to miss some of the big days, so he told us he tried to look at you like every day was graduation day. Like every day was your wedding day. He said that was the only way to get through. He didn't avoid thinking about the things he'd miss. Instead, he said he thought of them every day. He imagined you finding a fella. He imagined you having kids and buying your first house. He said he imagined all of it. Every day. He said it made him feel like he wasn't missing things. So, baby girl, he didn't miss today. He saw it. Every day."

I wiped a tear from my eye, and Dylan threaded his fingers

through mine as our hands rested against my stomach. He kissed the top of my head, and I submitted to it. I submitted to it all. To all of the love in that room, to being taken care of, to missing my dad, to being part of something new. I smiled at Jake, trying to convey the tidal wave of gratitude rolling through me.

"The one thing I know he'd never have seen coming though, is that mister there." He smiled and pointed at Dylan with his beer cup. "You've got yourself a class act there, Lydia. And if he has half a brain, which I'm pretty sure he does, he'll treat you the way you deserve to be treated." Everyone cheered, but Jake raised his glass again and shushed them. "And. *And*. He'll bring you back here every now and again."

"As if he could keep me away!" I shouted, another tear falling, and Dylan laughed with me and the rest of the room.

"That's our girl!" Jake raised his cup into the air, and the whole room, many of whom were strangers, just the standard dive bar audience, followed suit. "To Lydia and Dylan! Definitely too good for this place but ours all the same! You're family now, Dylan, so drink up!"

Someone shoved shots into our hands. Dylan looked at me with a huge smile on his face and barely containing a crazy mix of emotions—I saw laughter and reverence and love all over him. We slung back the burning liquid, and then he curled me into him.

"Time to go home, Duchess. Time to make you my wife." He spoke only to me, and I could feel the heat spreading, beginning in my cheeks and reaching into the far corners of my body.

Chapter 20

Lydia

My first morning as Mrs. Dylan Hale. Wait, was it Mrs? Lady? Oh lord, I was going to have to figure this shit out. Could I even say *oh lord* anymore if I was actually married to a lord?

My first morning as Dylan's *wife*, and I woke to the smell of coffee and toast. My favorite toast—seeded rye with lots of butter. I fluttered my eyes open and saw the delicious breakfast on my nightstand. Then I felt Dylan's hand stroke my back.

"Baby," Dylan said. "It's nearly eight. Do you have to work?" He looked slightly pleading as he asked the question. "Let me rephrase: Can you get out of working?"

I smiled, because there was nothing I wanted more than to get out of working. Technically, it was our honeymoon. But technically it was also the opening day of the pop-up store. My shoulders sank, and he knew as well as I did that I had to go.

"I have to go to the store, and I committed to a month, but then I want to go home, to London, with you. Can you stay? Work from here for another two weeks?"

"Damsel." He looked at me like he was explaining something

to a child. "Don't you understand? I never want to be apart from you again. Of course I'll work from here for the next two weeks. Just promise to get your arse home to me every night."

And I did.

For two weeks we lived our New York life. Dylan worked from an office at the Yale Club, working on the final touches for the Olympic Stadium, checking in on Humboldt from afar, and conducting preparations for the MI6 operation of some kind—apparently, against all my hopes, he was going to have to go through with it after all. I went to SoHo for the pop-up shop, and the days were a blur with sales and press exceeding all of our expectations. And I found myself daydreaming about what exactly my career might look like when we got back.

We just went about our days. One night we hosted a dinner party for Daphne and the rest of my college friends. Other nights we went back to Great Lakes and had a drink with the guys before coming home and ordering takeout. And other nights we walked to Prospect Park, went to the movies, and made our own version of Brooklyn life—not the one I'd known before him—the one we made together.

We were married, and we felt it. It was as though our little world, the one that consisted of Dylan and Lydia and all of our wants and needs and inside jokes and annoyances and private gestures, grew. That world expanded, made its mark. And the rest of the world felt like it was falling away. I was pretty sure this is what a honeymoon was supposed to be, even if ours was happening on the fourth floor of a Brooklyn brownstone. And there were nights we just stayed in. Dylan made sure we took our marriage consummation duties very seriously; by the end of the two weeks, I seriously doubted there was any part of me he hadn't consumed.

* * *

We decided to fly back to London late on a Saturday afternoon. So that morning I woke early to pack and try to put the apartment back together for the management company. A tenant would likely be moving in the next month, and I needed to make sure all of my personal belongings were put back in the storage closet.

"I think we should keep this place, use it," Dylan said, while I was taping up a box of my dad's stuff that I planned on bringing by the bar for the guys.

"What do you mean?" I finished that box and started moving the boxes that would stay here back into the closet. Otherwise we were ready to go.

"This is your home, I want it to be our home. Or, one of them, rather." Dylan held up the framed photograph of my father and me at my high school graduation, and then turned it back so he could look at it. "You were adorable. I love this picture."

"It was a good day." I smiled back at him as he approached me and wrapped his strong arms around me. "But, Dylan, this is New York. We live in London."

"I come here for work. So do you. There are people here who love you. We should come back more and stay here. I love this side of you. And I love this place. This will always be the place where we were first married, baby. I don't want other people staying here. It's yours. It's ours."

I thought about it and immediately wondered why I hadn't thought about it myself. He was right. It was perfect, it was me.

"Okay," I said. "Deal."

Dylan reached behind me into one of the open boxes and picked up a photo of me and a bunch of high school girlfriends before prom. "If you'd been at my school, you would have had a boyfriend."

"If I'd been at your school, I would have been twelve when you were a senior."

Dylan chuckled above me. "You know what I meant." He swatted my behind. "Now we're taking some of these. I want your pictures in our London house."

"Our London house."

"That's what I said."

"Feels different now, doesn't it? Like before it felt like we were playing pretend when I called it our house. Now it feels real."

"It's always been real." Dylan looked around the apartment. "So does that mean we're done here then?" He looked around, and he was right. Especially if no tenants were going to come in, we were ready to leave.

"Yeah, I guess we are." It was going to be strange reinhabiting this place, reclaiming it, even from afar.

"Good. Then let's get going." Dylan grabbed my bag and handed it to me.

"Where are we going?" I looked at Dylan's watch—we still had a few hours before we'd planned on heading to the airport.

"To meet your father."

* * *

When Dylan said he wanted to see my father's grave, I felt guilty. Like I should have thought of that myself. But the truth was I still wasn't used to the idea that I could visit him like that. That his grave was someplace I could go.

We rode in the car in silence. No tension, just quiet. My hand was in Dylan's and he twisted my rings between my fingers. They still felt so new to me. I hadn't even had a chance to get used to the engagement ring before Dylan had fixed it there with a wedding band. When we got to the cemetery, I realized I hadn't been there since the funeral. And in that moment, I realized just how avoidant my grieving had been. I was looking out the window, passing the uniform grave markers, flowers adorning some, others long abandoned, and I realized that I hadn't been ready before. Ready to talk to him while still acknowledging he was gone.

Dylan leaned against the edge of the car and nodded, indicating that I should go ahead. He obviously realized I might need time alone with my dad before introducing him to my husband.

I walked slowly to the grave, noticing how odd it was that grass grew there now. The fresh pile of dirt long gone. I laid the bouquet of flowers we'd stopped for at the base of the marble stone, and waited. I waited for the tears. But the funny thing was that they didn't come.

"I'm sorry I haven't been before, Dad." I looked down at the grass, as though he could see me through it. "I know. I know you didn't expect me to. You told me to go live life to the fullest, and well, boy did I take that directive seriously." I actually found myself laughing, thinking about how he'd be laughing right along with me. I looked back to Dylan, who smiled at me. "See that guy? You're not going to believe it, but we got married two weeks ago. That's right, *married*. Your straitlaced, careful, responsible daughter married a man she's known for less than a year. Can you believe it? Yes, he's good enough for me. I promise. He's kind and funny and generous, and so talented. And he's helped me, Dad. The way he loves me, it's like I can see myself more clearly. It's like just by loving me, he's helping me become who I want to be. You'd really like him." I paused for a minute imagining an alternate universe in which they could shake hands and have conversations. "Our life is back in London, so I won't be able to visit as much as I want, okay?" There was the first tear; I wiped it from my cheek. "But, Dad, I love you. And I miss you. And I think about you every day. I'm doing really well over there, with work, with Dylan. I think I understand why you loved living there so much." I sighed and looked to the sky.

I looked back to my father's grave, and whispered to him. "I'm happy, Dad. I want you to know that. So wherever you are, you can rest easy. There is someone here taking care of me."

"And your daughter takes care of me."

Dylan had approached so quietly, I couldn't be sure how long he'd been there. He placed his hands on my hips from behind and pulled me against him. I took his hands and wrapped them around my body, hugging him to me. "Dad, this is Dylan."

Dylan turned me around and placed his fingers beneath my chin, prompting me to look into his eyes. He wiped away a tear I didn't even know was there.

"Can I have a minute with your father?" he asked, both with his words and his eyes.

I nodded and kissed him slowly on the lips before walking away.

I took up his spot by the car and watched him. This tall, imposing figure looking down at my father's grave. His broad shoulders and lean waist. He actually wore his hoodie with his fancy jeans. Somehow even with a hoodie he looked like a duke. Some things couldn't be helped. I had no idea what he was saying, or if he was even speaking at all. But somehow, this moment, maybe even more than standing before a clerk and ex- changing rings, made me feel like he was my family.

And thinking of family, I knew we had one more stop to make before we went to the airport.

* * *

"Thanks for doing this with me. I know you don't really know them." We were standing outside the Franklins' apartment. I'd had dinner with them the first week I was back in New York, but we hadn't discussed Dylan. I was sure this was going to be a shock.

"They're important to you. Of course I want to see them."

I leaned up to kiss him, our hands intertwined, and my lips were still on his when the door to the loft swung open. I could feel the blush spread across my face as I turned to see Charles and Maddy at the door, quickly followed by Kate and Cole.

"Mommy! That man was kissing Lydia!" Dylan started laughing, and I covered my face with my free hand, a little less mortified than I had been in Canada when Maddy asked Dylan if he loved me after I'd known him for about ten minutes, but mortified all the same.

"Maddy. What did we say about saying everything that comes to our mind?" Kate asked her seven-year-old daughter.

"Sometimes it's not appropriate," Maddy recited back as though bored by the entire concept of appropriateness.

"Yes, I was kissing her," Dylan said, looking at Maddy. "What do you think of that?" I noticed Cole couldn't have been more bored by this topic, and just drifted over to me, hugging my leg.

"You're just like Anna and Kristoff," she said. "So I guess that's okay."

Dylan looked at me, confused.

"Disney characters," I explained quietly, and he nodded in understanding.

"Glad to have your approval, Maddy, because I intend to kiss your friend Lydia here often. For the rest of my life in fact."

My eyes shot to his. I hadn't exactly thought we'd get to this place in the conversation before we'd even gotten past the front door. He was smiling. The man couldn't help himself. I looked to Kate and Charles, who were looking at each other. Then at me. Then at our hands, where our rings were still shiny and new. Then back to me.

I shrugged my shoulders and found that I couldn't keep the smile from my face. "Surprise," I said softly.

"You're *engaged*?" said Kate, eyes wider than I'd ever seen them.

"Married, actually," said Dylan before I could respond.

Eyes even wider.

A slightly awkward moment passed before Charles clapped his hands, grew his own big smile, and said, "This calls for Champagne!"

"Oh my goodness! This is so exciting. Come in. Come in. I want to hear everything."

"You're married?!" Maddy screeched as she grabbed Cole's arm and twirled him into the room. The poor boy was slightly confused by all the fuss.

Over the next hour, Dylan and I told them our story. While I braided Maddy's hair "like a mermaid," we told them about the run-ins we'd had with the media, about how we'd decided to lay low with the engagement, and about our very small spontaneous wedding. Eventually Cole and Maddy decided they'd had enough of sharing me with the grown-ups and dragged me into their playroom. I looked back to Dylan, who smiled at me, and to Kate and Charles, who were riveted by Dylan. They'd met him a few times before, in Canada, where we'd met, but I had a feeling it was different seeing him as my husband rather than a friend's nephew. He was just starting to proudly tell them about the store and everything I'd been doing in London, when I disappeared down the hall with the children.

Even in just the nine months I'd been gone, they'd grown so much. They showed me their new toys, and Maddy showed off how much her reading had improved by reading aloud a chapter book. Meanwhile, Cole sat in my lap with a deck of cards, patiently waiting to explain the rules of a game he'd learned. And it was heaven.

Chapter 21

Dylan

Christ, her ass is perfect.

I admit that was my first thought as I watched her saunter away from me with those two children. She was wearing her black leggings, wanting to be comfortable for our flight, and fuck me, but those leggings killed me every time. I couldn't wait to bite into that ass, pry her apart, sink into her. *Fuck, fuck, fuck.* I could *not* have a hard-on in front of these people.

That thought, thankfully, was interrupted by one that was more difficult to define. I tried to work it out as I bragged shamelessly to Kate and Charles about Lydia's work. I wanted them to know that I loved her for everything she was. I was probably overcompensating for the filthy thoughts about her ass. But that second feeling. It was bigger, warmer. Her hair was hanging down her back, the light from the enormous loft windows was making her face glow, and in each hand was the small hand of a child. I found myself gulping. It was beautiful. Pure. Grand in some weird way. What the ever-loving hell was going through my mind?

I gave Kate and Charles my attention.

"It sounds like you two have quite a lot going on over there!" Kate spoke with a maternal concern. It had a hint of awe, but I could see her worry for Lydia right at the surface.

"Dylan." Charles cleared his throat. "Eloise told me about your father. I'm very sorry for your loss." The man was genuine, but there was something in his tone that made me suspect that my aunt had probably aired her own feelings about my father. They hadn't exactly been close.

"Thank you," I said, as one should. I hated when people said they were sorry. I never knew what to say to that.

"I can't imagine the responsibility of taking on Humboldt Park and those responsibilities on top of your architecture career. That's quite a lot—"

"He's really kicking ass at it." Lydia's voice all of sudden filled the room, and I looked at her reentering. She now had a ribbon in her hair and a toy police belt around her waist.

"Lydia! You said the A word!" Cole stood and gawked at her, indignant, and I found myself laughing. Her eyes met mine, and I laughed harder.

"You're right, Cole. I shouldn't have said that." Lydia was trying not to laugh as she spoke, which had the unfortunate effect of making me laugh harder, which in turn earned me a glare.

I tried to cough down my laugh. "Thanks. Um." I cleared my throat again. "Lydia is helping a lot with the estate. I couldn't do it without her." And I realized at that moment just how true that was. There was no way I'd have been able to think through all of those decisions without her. Or I could, but I didn't want to. I knew, instinctively, that we were making better decisions together than I would alone.

"Will you two be back in Canada at all on this trip?" Kate asked, looking between us. It made me realize how much Lydia and I had to talk about. Did she even realize that she now co-owned La Belle Reve, the Canadian estate where we'd met?

"Unfortunately not. We have to get back, I'm afraid. As you know, Lydia's been here for a month. I joined her two weeks ago, but we both have to return to London. In fact, baby," I said, looking to Lydia, who was now trapped on a love seat between the children. "We should probably think about heading to the airport."

"Oh, you're leaving now? What airport are you flying out of?"

I was about to say "New Jersey" or something else vague. If I told them Teterboro, which only serviced charters and private flights, they'd know we were flying private, and in general I tried to avoid sharing that information. It made one sound like a douche bag. Thankfully the shrieks of the children didn't give me a chance to respond. Maddy and Cole were folding over Lydia's body.

"You can't go! We don't want you to go!" they were saying in harmony. And Lydia was calmly holding them close to her, telling them she'd be back soon, she'd send more postcards.

She looked beautiful sitting there, even with the chaos and shrieks around her. She looked *peaceful*. And suddenly I felt like an idiot, like a total bloody cliché. Everyone said the second you were married you'd want children, which I'd found idiotic. But apparently it wasn't. I looked at her, and there was zero doubt in my mind that Lydia would make an incredible mother, and suddenly I wanted nothing more than to make her one. I wanted to see her there with *our* children.

Fuck.

Fuck, fuck, fuck. I wasn't supposed to want children. I couldn't be a fucking father. Look at the example I'd had, and I'd vowed not to thrust the life I'd had upon a child. But, Christ, this woman made me want to be better than that, to *do* better. A child of mine wasn't destined for the life I'd had. I wanted to see her pregnant with our child. I wanted to see her love that child. And I wanted to see myself through her eyes when I was a father. It wasn't long ago that I'd told her I wasn't sure I'd ever want kids, and she'd said, in no uncertain terms, that she wasn't ready. And now I knew with certainty, as though the idea had taken roots in my bones, that there was nothing I wanted more. But what if she decided she *didn't* want to be a mother? What if she was never ready?

"Dylan?"

I looked up and Lydia must have said my name more than once, because everyone was looking at me as though I'd been catatonic.

"Which airport are we flying out of?" she asked.

"Teterboro," I said mindlessly. Oh, well. I just hoped they didn't think I was douche bag.

The next several minutes were a blur of hugs, well-wishes, reminders that no, we *hadn't* told my family about the marriage yet and *yes*, please keep it under wraps for now, and *of course* they'd be invited to the big reception when we had it. I did my thing. I held Lydia's hand and went into social mode. No one, except for Lydia, I'm sure, knew anything was off. And nothing really *was* off. It wasn't as though I'd just started considering completely changing my outlook on a major life decision or anything.

Fuck.

* * *

My phone rang as we boarded the plane, Jack trying to get a hold of me for the fourth time in two days. We'd been playing phone tag, and I wanted to get this over with. It was after midnight in London—I had to give him credit for persistence.

"Jack," I said.

"Dylan," he said, having the nerve to sound irritated. "Bloody finally. Your assistant tells me you're in America?"

"Have been, yes. I'm boarding a plane to return to London now. What's up?" I followed Lydia on board and sank into the cream leather seat beside her. She was curled into the chair, looking out the window, contemplative. We were about to embark on our last eight hours of having any sense of privacy—I had no doubt that within hours of Lydia leaving our house with that ring on, the papers would be flying through the printer—and I wanted to be off this bloody phone call and back with her as soon as possible. Which reminded me: I had to tell my mother and sister before they found out through the gossip mill.

"Do you have any other intercontinental trips planned?" Jack asked, sounding slightly stressed.

"No, although this trip wasn't planned. What's the problem, Jack?"

"The higher-ups are getting antsy, and everyone's a bit concerned with the time sensitivity of all this. The last thing we'd want is to get word that King was in London and then not be able to isolate him. We think he may be planning a UK trip soon, although we're still trying to confirm that."

"Of course—sorry, mate. As fate would have it, I can ease your mind on one count. I've successfully been in touch with the

Bresnovs, who mentioned the UK trip. They've also confirmed that King will be there and agreed to the meeting—"

I heard what sounded like a grunting fist bump on the other end of the line. "Thank fucking Christ. That's exactly what we needed to hear—"

"I'm glad. I'll be back by morning, and I'll have my assistant set something up, and we can discuss details. We don't have a date yet but should soon." I stood and walked to the galley to get a water as I finished my conversation. I looked at Lydia settling into her seat and heard myself sigh. "I'm looking forward to this being over, mate."

"Aww, fuck, as am I. We can't thank you enough for your help, Dylan."

"Sure you can—"

"I know. You have my word—the Bresnovs will be taken care of immediately."

"Thanks, Jack." As I hung up the phone, I downed the water and looked back to Lydia. I couldn't wait for this operation to be over. I looked at the woman in front of me, and I wanted to show her, tell her, that I was ready to put everything stressful about my past and present behind us, that I wanted us to be a *family*.

Chapter 22

Lydia

I'd flown with Dylan only once before. On our trip to Greece, and the whole thing had felt like a fantasy. My aristocratic boyfriend whisking me off for an exotic holiday. It had been fitting somehow that the trip involved a small private jet and a helicopter ride.

This was different.

It was nearly six when we settled into our seats, and the server brought us drinks. Dylan had taken his phone call, and I had my legging-clad legs curled beneath me and felt a little like I was settling into a living room for a seven-hour duration. It didn't feel normal—I doubted it ever would—but it felt comfortable, which was weird in itself.

Dylan was also different. He was staring at me. More than usual. When I ignored the instructions to fasten my seat belt—I was waiting until the last minute—Dylan reached over and fastened it for me. He was quiet, attentive, even while talking to whom I guessed was his friend Jack from MI6.

"Is this the same plane we went on to Greece?" I asked when he got off. It looked bigger.

"No. I charter them. Easier than owning. Less fuss. More efficient." He leaned in and kissed my ear. "Plus," he whispered, "this one has a bedroom in the back."

"You think of everything, don't you?" I said, scolding him. Did the man think of nothing but sex? But his only response was to slide his large hand between my folded legs, right above the knee, and lovingly stroke my leg with his thumb.

We were both quiet as we took off, letting the last few days settle over us. I had no idea what was on Dylan's mind, but I was fixated on the view outside the window. Downtown, the Manhattan and Brooklyn Bridges, the Statue of Liberty. The symbols of the city I'd grown up in. The city that had been my home would always be home a little. But now I felt like I was *going* home. So leaving New York was odd.

I looked down and saw a patch of green deep into Brooklyn. It could have been any park, but maybe it was the cemetery. The cemetery where my father would live forever. I looked back towards downtown, where the Franklins lived, where just hours before those children, whom I adored, had been clamoring over me, how that had felt like family too. Dylan had been sweet to put up with that—I knew he still wasn't sure if he even wanted children. He and I were going to have to have that conversation again eventually. But not yet. We'd been married for two weeks, the world didn't know it yet—we barely knew it yet.

I looked down at New York and saw Daphne, NYU, Great Lakes, my internships, my primary school, the hospitals where I'd spent days and nights with my father. But I also saw the city where Dylan had put a ring on my finger. Rings on *our* fingers. Where I'd become his wife.

As if reading my mind, Dylan leaned over me to look out the window too and squeezed my leg, stroking it just a little more affectionately. "I love New York." He looked down at his hand and twisted the shiny new band that lay there. "Even more now."

We were high enough now that seat belts didn't matter. Or if they did, Dylan decided he didn't care. He flicked his open and did the same with mine. Without saying a word, he laced his fingers through mine, tugged me from my seat, and led me back towards the polished wooden door at the rear of the plane.

When he pushed it open, the small room opened up onto a bed stretching from one side to the other. Plush and inviting. He pulled me in and shut the door behind us, closing us in the small space.

Suddenly the air was gone from the room, and I felt like I couldn't breathe, in the best possible way. His smell—that familiar combination of wood and salt and fire—filled the air around me, and the warmth from his body reached mine, heating me up from the inside. I felt the familiar spread of electric anticipation reaching through my limbs, leaving my fingers tingling.

"Lydia," he said, firmly but with so much desire. In these moments I became putty, liquid, elastic, ready. His fingers pressed my chin up and I looked into his preposterously blue eyes. I gulped, waiting. "I want to see you."

I nodded, and moved my hands to the hem of my shirt. But he gripped my wrists to stop me and just shook his head. I stilled and waited.

He slid his knuckle under my shirt and ran it along the waistband of my leggings. Slowly, his skin, that gentle touch, heated me, trailed along my skin, until it was two knuckles, two hands, ten fingers wrapping around my waist beneath my shirt. He glanced at me expectantly and I understood to lift my arms above my head. Within a drawn-out fluid moment, like he was moving to a long note in a symphony, my shirt was off of my body, somewhere on the floor.

I closed my eyes and looked to the ceiling as Dylan sank to the floor in front of me and made the same leisurely moves to remove my leggings, leaving me in nothing but my bra.

Infinitesimal sparkles lit and crackled on my skin, making every touch feel like it could be the one to tilt me over my axis, knock me into the abyss. Dylan's hands never left my body—they were slow, worshipful, and without effort he lifted me onto the bed and hovered above me.

Words had ended somewhere in the beginning, and this seemed too big for them. This was different. Something had changed in him. The way he touched me was like he was touching our marriage, our future, our entire life together. This was celebratory but reverent. Thick with hot emotion, but steady. It was a wedding.

When we were done making love, I put my hand to his cheek, and he stilled and looked at me. "Why are you so quiet?" I asked, searching for answers in his eyes. He sighed for a moment, and then lay back in the bed pulling me against him.

"I want…" But he wouldn't finish his thought.

"You want what?"

He waited another moment, and I saw a question pass through his eyes. "I want to marry you again."

* * *

Seven hours later it felt like three in the morning, but it was already eight in the morning London time, and we were sleepily leaning against each other in the backseat of the Mercedes as Lloyd drove us home.

"I trust you had a good trip, Your Grace," Lloyd had said when he saw me. I yawned, barely able to keep my eyes open. I knew I was supposed to stay awake to deal with the jet lag, but there was no way that was going to happen.

Dylan leaned down and whispered in my ear, "He's talking to you."

I probably looked like a scared rabbit in that moment and suddenly felt very awake. "No, Lloyd, you are not allowed to call me that. I'm not ready."

Dylan chuckled. "You can see why I married her," he said to Lloyd, whom I actually caught smiling.

"Excuse me then, Mrs. Hale, did you have a good trip?"

"Ack! That's even crazier!"

"Hey, don't you want be called Mrs. Hale?" Dylan had pulled me towards him, smiling at me in a teasing way. "I think you'd be the first of the duchesses to *not* take their husband's name."

"I'm taking your name. I'm just not used to being Mrs. Anything. I'm only twenty-five. It feels weird," I said as I yawned again.

Dylan turned towards Lloyd. "I think I'd better let the wife nap—she's obviously not thinking clearly." He stood behind me, and I thought he was going to grab my hand, but instead he swung me into his arms.

"*Another* threshold?" I said, yawning again and remembering when he'd carried me over our threshold in the Brooklyn apartment.

"Only a few more to go," Dylan said.

My eyes were closing, and I rested my head against his chest.

"Caveman," I whispered on an exhale.

"Lloyd," Dylan said over his shoulder, "could you please let Molly know we'll be having my mother and sister for lunch at noon?"

On a subconscious level I knew that if I heard those words, I would wake right the hell up, so I let them glide past me and pretended they didn't exist. Because one thing I was definitely not ready for was telling Charlotte that I was already Mrs. Hale, Her Grace, the new Duchess of Abingdon.

Chapter 23

Dylan

Lydia was in the shower when the doorbell rang, trying to wake herself up after a nap. Of course my mother was early.

"Hello, darling," she said in her saccharine way, waltzing in with a newspaper tucked under her arm and her sunglasses still on. It meant the shield was firmly back in place.

"This better be good," said Emily, traipsing in behind her, looking like she'd been out all night.

"Did you just come in from Cambridge?" I asked.

She shrugged and yawned, even though it was midday.

"I stayed at a friend's in town last night."

Friend in town? I gave her a look that suggested she'd better fess the bloody hell up if there was a sodding male around. *Spent the night?*

She rolled her eyes dismissively. My mother was already in the kitchen talking sternly to Molly about the proper way to make Yorkshire pudding, which was a joke since I doubted my mother had ever even used an oven. I'd have to apologize to Molly later, although she was used to my mother by now. Emily glanced towards the kitchen and then back to me. "Like I said, this had better be good."

She started to walk past but I grabbed her arm, and she turned to me. I flashed her my wedding band surreptitiously before sliding my hand back in my pocket. Her eyes widened. Bloody enormous. Then her jaw dropped. I loved shocking my sister. I so rarely got to do it. In fact I couldn't remember the last time I'd genuinely surprised her.

She got a huge smile on her face and then charged passed me, up the stairs, presumably to find Lydia.

"I'm going to kill you two, you know," she shouted over her shoulder, but she didn't sound the slightest bit mad.

I chuckled as I walked into the now silent kitchen, but I stopped when I saw my mother staring at me.

"I can't imagine you'll defend her now, Dylan."

What?

"She's finally showing her true colors. It was only a matter of time." At that moment too many things happened at once. My mother held up the newspaper she'd come in with, the morning edition, and Lydia and Emily came bounding down the stairs, chattering and laughing. "And I can't imagine what business you had in New York—I'd hate to think you ignored business here for weeks for some kind of pleasure trip."

It was as though the images in the paper were glowing. Two large color photos, side by side in the society section. In the first, Lydia and me, in New York, outside the museum, kissing. And in the other, Lydia and Eric, *kissing*.

Fuck.

"Oh god." Lydia's voice was fragile, muffled as her hand went to her mouth.

"What do you have to say for yourself, dear? You've successfully made my son look like a fool. No small, feat, I assure you. He managed to keep an impeccable public image before you came along, and now, well, I can't imagine how you'll justify this."

"Oh god," Lydia said again, and began to turn. She was going to run.

"No," I said firmly, and I marched over to where Lydia stood and held her hand firmly in my own. "Mother, you'll stop right now. Not another word. You want the story, you ask us the story. You should know better than anyone that newspaper articles don't reflect reality. Your own efforts last year with Amelia should tell you that—only that time the papers said what you wished had been true. That lie hurt me, hurt Lydia, and you don't appear to have lost a wink of sleep over it. So get off your high horse and listen to me." Emily stood by the kitchen door, attentive, probably ready to launch into one of her speeches should it be called for.

I was furious. I was gripping Lydia's hand so tightly, I hoped I wasn't hurting her. I couldn't look at her, because if I did, I knew I would just wrap her in my arms, sweep her up the stairs, and protect her from this preposterous cruelty. And I needed to do this—my mother needed to know that she was done. I would no longer allow her to be an emotional terrorist in my life. I would no longer allow her to use her grief and the years of being mistreated by my father as an excuse to forget who she was: *my mother*.

She was staring at me, mouth hanging open just slightly.

"It ends now. Do you understand? You will no longer be anything other than polite and kind to Lydia."

"And why on earth should I do that, Dylan?"

Emily stood behind me, Lydia to my side, and I could feel them frozen in anticipation.

"Because she's the woman your son loves, Mum. Because she's my *wife*."

My mother froze, and I took it as my cue to bring Lydia into the hug I'd been longing to give her. She let me kiss the top of her head, but then she pulled away. She continued to hold my hand, but she stood on her own.

"Charlotte," she said, and I knew she used my mother's name not out of disrespect but because they were technically family, and to Lydia that meant something. "I don't have a mother. I never have. And even if I had had one, I wasn't raised in your family, or with the responsibilities or privilege of Humboldt Park. So I won't pretend to know what your relationship with Dylan is or should be. But I know how much I love him. I know how much he loves me. And I know how important you and Emily are to him. I know you don't think much of me. But I assure you," she said, pointing at the newspaper, "that I have never and would never be unfaithful to your son. Dylan knows the story behind that picture, and *he* knows that while it's unfortunate, it's not what it looks like. The one of Dylan and me, however, is *exactly* what it looks like."

Emily scoffed behind us—I could practically hear her making fun of me for the public display of affection. It turns out that we hadn't been as safe from the press as we thought—I couldn't believe the photos had been leaked almost three weeks after the fact. It probably took that long for someone to realize what they had.

She sighed next to me, and I could feel her shaking slightly in my hand.

"We did get married without you, and without you," she said, turning to Emily, "and I'm sorry for that. It was what was right for us, and it allowed me to say 'I do' to the love of my life in the place where my father had raised me and was laid to rest. And even though my father wasn't alive to be there himself, your son made sure he was as present as he could be. He did that for me." She squeezed my hand. Fuck, she was stunning right then. In her jeans, bare feet, and a loose sweater, her damp hair in a braid over her shoulder. Not a lick of makeup. She was perfect. She was herself, and she was defending us, with all of herself. "And I will be forever grateful. And I'm so grateful to you." That caused my mother's brow to crinkle—Lydia's generous honesty was disarming her. I could see it happening. "You raised a good man, Charlotte. You raised the person I want to spend the rest of my life with. I hope one day, you'll be able to accept me as your son's choice. We want a wedding here in England, and of course we want you there."

Christ, I loved her. But fuck all, at this moment, I wanted my mother as far away from her as possible. It took everything I had not to physically protect Lydia from my mother, but I knew she could hold her own. My mother remained silent for a moment longer, until Emily spoke up. "Mum, don't be ridiculous. I don't know what—"

My mother held up her hand, and Emily stopped speaking. Mum stood and walked towards the door. She paused for only a moment. "Of course I'll be there. You haven't given me much choice, have you? What's done is done. Plus, what on earth would people think if I wasn't?" And then she was gone, sunglasses in place, the door shutting firmly behind her.

I looked down at Lydia, and I caught the tear rolling down her cheek before she wiped it away.

At first, I didn't know which part had upset her the most, but that question was soon answered. Lydia grabbed the newspaper from the kitchen island, and sighed.

"I've really done it this time, haven't I?" She wiped another tear away from her cheek. "Emily, I swear this isn't what it looks like," she said, holding the paper up. Then she looked back to me. "And I guess there goes any hope of your mother ever liking me."

I tried to pull her into me, comfort her, but she pulled away. She silently poured herself some coffee and retreated upstairs. Fuck, this was not what I wanted her homecoming to be like. *Our* homecoming. How had that gone even worse than I'd expected?

Emily stood there staring at me as though I'd lost my bleeding mind and like she didn't know where to start when it came to handing me my arse.

"You know she's already up there reading every sodding wanker on the Internet right now, don't you?" Emily had her hands on her hips. I was still rather stunned by everything that had happened this morning, and we hadn't even had lunch yet. "And you know they're calling her horrible things, right?"

Oh, fuck.

I bolted up the stairs behind Lydia.

"Exactly, you idiot!" Emily called behind me.

* * *

Lydia hadn't been reading the Internet, thankfully. Or she had, but she said she'd stopped when she saw that there were as many people who claimed to disbelieve the story as there were calling horrible names. It "gave her hope," she'd said and then sighed, regrouped, and we'd decided to try to pick up the scraps of the morning.

By three in the afternoon we were sitting back at the kitchen island, eating a quiche Molly had made and attempting to make sense of everything. We'd filled Emily in on the story about Eric, the wedding, all of it. Lydia even managed to get lost in the moment enough to recount Jake's toast from our informal reception, but within a minute her somber frown was back. We had to fix this.

Emily slapped her hands on the counter and slid her plate away from her. "Okay. I have a plan."

"You do?" Lydia asked, looking up hopefully.

"You do?" I asked, incredulous. "I was thinking I would just give my PR team a call—they can a release a statement about this all being hog's wallop, per usual."

Emily rolled her eyes and looked at me as though I were a moron.

"You moron," she said, rolling her eyes. "That won't work this time. There is an actual *photograph*. Of *Lydia. Kissing another man*. And they are vicious. They called her a whore, Dylan." I fumed and Lydia cringed. I fucking hated what they were saying about her on the Internet. And "whore" had been the least of it.

Emily looked to Lydia apologetically. "Sorry, but it won't help to ignore it. And it's bloody obvious by the picture of you two that you're not just "casually dating" or whatever it is you've been trying to pull off for the last six months. Look, you two need to come clean. And not after a wedding. Not with some quiet private ceremony. Not with a fake engagement leading up to a fake wedding. You need to come out, and big-time." Lydia and I looked at each other, bracing ourselves. This wasn't exactly what we'd been imagining. "Instead of avoiding the press, you need to get them on your side. First, you need to announce that you're already married. Come out and say that this bloke Evan—"

"Eric," Lydia corrected her. "I believe him when he said he didn't leak this." I looked at her skeptically. We'd called him—he was the most obvious source—but he'd claimed he hadn't, and what motivation would he have had for planting a photographer to catch him kissing her? It didn't make sense. I admitted there was a part of me that would have been happy to have another reason to despise that nitwit, but I had to agree with Lydia that it didn't seem like he'd been behind this. Bad luck is what this was. The only good thing to come of this was that we didn't have to give him an exclusive anything anymore—he'd gotten his own bit of fame by association, and at this point it would just look odd if he were reporting on our wedding.

"Whatever. Eric," Emily continued, waving her hands about. "So come out—and Dylan *you* should say this—come out and say Eric didn't know Lydia was engaged, and how you set him straight, and how Lydia was taken off guard. Tell everyone how you romantically eloped. People will love it. They'll fall in love with you two."

"Really?" Lydia asked. "I feel like it's going to take more than an elopement to win people over. Your mother, in particular."

"First," Emily continued, "you're right. Which is why you also have to give them a big, lavish wedding to anticipate. And you'll have to leak the best details leading up to it—people will go absolutely mad. They're hammering for more of Richard and Jemma, but in the absence of that they'll take you two." Prince Richard and Jemma were getting married at the end of the summer, and the public was insatiable for anything about the "wedding-of-the-century." After a debacle in which a wedding atelier had been broken into by some clearly insane people looking for sketches of Jemma's dress, the palace had become an inviolable vault when it came to details about their impending nuptials. Emily was right—we could fill that void, and people were primed to forgive when a wedding was on the table. "And as for my mother—she'll follow the public, unfortunately. All she cares about right now is herself. She's not in a good place. If Dylan looks good, if the Abingdon name looks good, she'll be pleased. Plus—"

I cut her off. "Plus, I don't give a rat's arse if she never comes around." I pulled Lydia onto my lap, balancing us on the bar stool. "You and me, remember?" I whispered into her ear. I tucked my hand between her crossed legs and gripped her thigh under the counter.

"Dylan, don't be daft. It's sweet that you don't care, but that's a horrible position for Lydia to be in, for about eight billion reasons."

Lydia giggled, actually giggled, for the first time that day. It wasn't a long giggle, mind you, but it was there.

"Fine," I said, exhaling. "So, what do we do, if you're so smart?"

Emily beamed, so fucking pleased to have me deferring to her.

"You," she said, pointing to me, "call that chap at the *Guardian* and fix this bleeding mess," she said, pointing to the paper. "No PR people—they'll want it from you. Don't forget the part where you tell them you already swept her off her feet and married her. Everyone's going to think you've gotten her pregnant, but who cares."

My heart beat out of my chest. I looked to Lydia immediately and saw she was pale as a ghost, and her eyes were wide. Fuck, she really wasn't ready to have babies with me, was she?

"Christ," I muttered under my breath and rubbed my forehead with my fingers.

"And you," Emily said, directing her attention towards Lydia, "are going to plan a wedding." This time Emily was practically giddy, jumping up and down. "And get that boss of yours on the phone. You'll need a proper dress this time."

Chapter 24

Lydia

The morning Dylan's mother had come over was terrifying. Before Emily took over and gave us hope, I'd been sure I would be too mortified to leave the house, terrified that everyone who saw me was thinking that I was unfaithful to Dylan, that I was some kind of slut, that I should have a scarlet letter tattooed to my chest.

A few days later, I was terrified to leave the house for an entirely different reason. Emily's planned had worked. Well. Too well.

The very next day a front-page story ran in the *Guardian* about our elopement, complete with quotes from Dylan about him surprising me in New York, about how we'd met, how we'd actually been engaged for months but had wanted it to be private, about the ring I wore and our plans for a big English wedding. He'd explained about Eric, albeit briefly, and even said, on record, that I was the love of his life. And people ate it up. The public seemed to love that we'd been hiding away our commitment—it seemed romantic and dramatic. They loved that I was an American but had been born here. They seemed to love all of it. Of course there were snide Twitter posts and comments on the articles, but all in all, Emily's plan had gone off without a hitch, and people were going mad.

My public perception problem may have been largely fixed, but I don't think I could have imagined the spotlight being quite so bright if I'd tried. The day after the article ran, I'd opened the front door to leave for work, and there was an enormous man dressed in black and khaki with a camera at the ready and a flash exploding, blurring my vision. He was firing off questions at me, but all I heard was my name, "duchess," "eloped," and things like "the other guy," and "are you sure the baby is his?"

I was never leaving the house again.

Dylan had somehow snuck out the back door that morning before I'd woken—he'd called from the office around seven thirty to wake me up. I had gotten dressed, had coffee, and opened the door thinking I was actually going to go to work when Rambo paparazzi had attacked me.

So right, apparently I was a hermit now, because there was no way I was going to go through that again. I mean, I knew I'd have to leave the house eventually, but maybe later?

I'd called Hannah and asked if someone else could watch the store until I could figure things out. She'd agreed, but "only because you're allowing me to make the wedding gown, and I'm sure you're going to quit on me soon anyway," and then she'd hung up on me in a flurry—I could hear her barking orders at her apprentice before she'd even gotten off the phone. There were so many things about that phone call that had bothered me. For one, "allowing" her to make the gown? Since when was I someone who "allowed" Hannah to do anything? I cringed thinking about how being Dylan's wife had already started to change everything that had been familiar about my life. And second, she thought I was going to quit? Anxiety rose like poison, making me feel queasy. I knew that Dylan and I would come up with our plan, that I'd figure out what I wanted to do with my career and how it fit into being a duchess, but the idea that the whole of England would continue to think I was a horrible wife, or woman, or aristocrat or whatever just because I kept my job was exhausting. It all made me want to dive back into bed and stay there. I figured every good restaurant delivered, and there was really no reason why I'd ever have to leave the house again.

Unfortunately there was apparently no way Dylan or Emily was going to allow me to do that.

Emily had called four times that morning already, urging me out the door and already asking me if Dylan and I had set a date. And at that moment I heard a commotion on the street outside, shouts of Dylan's name. Crap, that meant he'd come home. He was definitely going to try to coax me out the door.

I hid even deeper under the covers.

It was only a few minutes later when I felt the bed dip where he must have been sitting. Then I felt his hand intertwine with my own—my treacherous fingers must have been peeking out from the duvet.

"Baby," he said, pulling back the covers.

I opened one eye and looked at him warily. He smiled and pulled the covers back further.

"What on earth are you wearing?"

After I'd retreated from the door, I'd shimmied out of my pencil skirt, but I was still in thigh highs, a bra, and a silk blouse.

"Not that I'm complaining," he continued, running his warm hand over my bare backside and up the inside of my blouse, rubbing my back.

I groaned and buried my head back in the pillow. Dylan chuckled and stood. I could hear him removing his jacket and shoes, the telltale zip of his trousers. Within a minute, I felt the heat of his bare chest hovering above me.

"Baby," he whispered, and he moved the hair from my back and over my shoulder. "Listen to me." His tone was soothing but firm. So in control. And already his control was making me feel better, making feel like at least one of us had some ideas as to how to steer us through this chaos.

He kneeled up on the bed behind me, his legs on either side of my own. And in a flash he had effortlessly lifted me so my knees were tucked beneath me, my backside in the air. His fingers tickled my chest as they unfastened the buttons of my blouse, and he pulled it from my back and arms. My bra followed in quick succession, and the fabric was replaced with his wandering hands.

"I know," he said. "Those vultures are bloody terrifying." Kisses were placed on my back, his warm mouth making a trail over my body in concert with his hands. "But you are my wife. And I won't have my wife feeling like she has to hide away in our house. Understand?"

His words were loving, understanding, but he wasn't going to let me go around this problem—we were going to have to dive in. Dylan had been this way on our first date, not letting me play coy or dumb, and he was going to be this way forever. He'd never let me hide, and I knew, even if it was terrifying, that he was right.

He kissed my ass cheek, and suddenly I was on my back looking up into my eyes. "Understand?"

I nodded, the heat spreading so fast, pulsing in my limbs, pooling at my core.

"Good girl." He kissed my breast. "This is what is going to happen." His words were echoed by his hands, his fingers previewing his words. At that moment, his fingers sank into me, and my back arched off the bed, my eyes closing, so happy for this escape.

"Look at me, Lydia." Damn him and his never letting me hide. "Open those gorgeous eyes for me and look." I did, and I saw the most loving face, those ocean-blue eyes, staring down at me. "I won't let anything bad happen to you." He kissed me again.

"I'm going to fuck you, darling. So hard, and so well, that you won't even remember what had you hiding." My chest was rising and falling off the bed, anticipation crawling all over me. His fingers pressing inside of me, summoning every cell, lining every vein of desire up like a soldier, ready to be commanded. I nodded again.

"You're going to remember that you are my girl, my brilliant wife, my gorgeous duchess, a woman no one should reckon with. Then you're going to get this fine ass to work." He slapped the side of my ass for emphasis, and my breathing hitched. Shit, that felt good. The heat that remained in the wake of his hand added a sweet sting to the wave threatening to crest against his fingers, now strumming my clit in sync with their thrusts.

"Dylan," I moaned.

"That's right, my sweet girl. That's right." He lifted my ass onto his thighs and slid into me, his cock so much thicker than his fingers that I gasped and rolled as my body tried to accept him. As though he didn't do this to me all the time, as though my body shouldn't know exactly what was coming.

Within a moment, I was pulsing around him, crying his name as he took me with complete control. His hands held my waist, keeping me steady, and it was as though my anxiety, my fatigue, my feelings of being so small in the face of the world outside the door writhed out of me as the orgasm took me over, as I gripped his forearms with my hands and felt his strength beneath my palms.

"Dylan," I exhaled and took him, took everything he did to me. I heard his own heavy breathing, his own shuddering chest as he came inside me, and in that moment he had succumbed as much as I had.

The broad daylight settled over our naked limbs, and I found myself sitting up, my stocking-clad thighs wrapped around his waist as he leaned against the headboard. His hand pulled one of the sheer black stockings down to my knee, and he rubbed the skin of my thigh.

"I love these," he said, looking down appreciatively.

"Thank you," I said, smiling. Then I looked at him, caught his attention so he understood that I needed him to look right back at me. "Thank you," I said again, this time for shaking me loose.

He nodded, and kissed me again on the lips.

"Time to face the music. You're stronger than they are."

I nodded.

"And fucking gorgeous to boot."

I laughed and collapsed against his chest.

"No, up. I have to go too, damsel. I came right from a lunch with a client and I have another meeting."

"You squeezed rescuing your pathetic wife between important business meetings?"

"Not pathetic," he said sternly, giving me that warning look he gave when I said things about myself he knew not to be true. "And yes. Hannah called me when you didn't come in."

"She did?" I asked, crawling off of him and heading to the closet. I could hear him rustling out of the bed himself.

"Mmm. I know you think she's cold, but she cares about you." He came up behind me, zipping his trousers, and reached over me into the closet to pull out a fitted dress with a short pleated skirt. "You look so bloody fit in this—makes every one who sees you go mental."

He handed me the hanger, and I began pulling myself together. I couldn't believe Hannah had called him.

"Fiona called as well. Apparently you two were supposed to have lunch."

"Oh, fuck." I put my hand to my mouth. "I completely forgot. I emailed her and Josh when we got back and told her we got married, but I still haven't seen them. I was going to catch her up, and we were going to look at branding options for her jewelry line. Shiiiiit." I hurriedly chose a pair of red suede booties to go with the dress.

His hand slid down my arms from behind soothingly, and he kissed the top of my head. "I think she understands. They were both just worried about you. I think they are also excited for you, baby. They wanted to chew *my* ear off about our wedding."

"Which one?"

"Which what?" he asked, buttoning his shirt and straightening the cuff links.

"Which wedding?"

"Oh, Fiona wanted to know all about the real one. Hannah was fishing for design details about the fake one."

"Figures."

"Speaking of, my mother called."

I paused completely, my dress half zipped, and stared at him. Did I really want to hear this?

"How do you feel about a wedding at Humboldt?"

"Great?" I said, wondering what the catch was. "I mean, great. I assumed that's where this shindig would be. Why? What did your mother say?"

"Well, I asked her about it, and she was rather pleased. I don't know what to do about her, darling, honestly. And I want to throttle her for saying everything she's said—"

"Dylan, I'm not worried about your mother. I mean I was, but I know she's still grieving. I know I'm not what she envisioned for you. But I have faith in us. We'll earn her blessing." I almost believed the words I was saying. "Somehow."

He turned me towards him and kissed me again. "I don't deserve you."

"Tell me about it," I said, and in a flash, he'd turned me, lifted up the hem of my dress, and smacked me on the ass. I jumped three feet and laughed, put my hands on my hips, giving him a playful glare of death. "There'll be no more of that. I need to get to work."

Dylan said he'd drop me at work and pick me up—I agreed it was time to get back to my office at the store, but I honestly did feel safer with him. As we rode in the Mercedes, he held my hand firmly in his own and played with my rings, which was quickly becoming his new mindless habit.

"What's your meeting this afternoon?" I asked as I caught him turning our hands to look at his watch.

He sighed, which couldn't be a good sign. "MI6."

We'd both been avoiding this particular subject lately. It made me nervous. I knew it was going to be dangerous, and now more than ever I didn't want that. It gave me a pit in my stomach. I couldn't lose him. Maybe I was being ridiculous, but it physically hurt to think about him going into danger. Just thinking about how he'd been able to pull me out of my bad mood, how he knew me so intimately to do that. How could I ever again be in the world without that person, without him?

Dylan squeezed my hand, sensing my anxiety. "It will be fine."

* * *

Once at the shop, as long as I didn't look outside where there was a throng of bored-looking photographers hanging around, I could mostly forget the chaos of the marriage announcement. And when Fiona and Josh came barreling in an hour before closing, I was able to forget it completely.

Josh flung open the door dramatically, held it open for Fiona, who struggled her way with some giant box, and then he turned in the doorway, and actually curtsied for the photographers. I could hear the flashbulbs eating up his show, and when he came fully inside, he had a huge smile on his face and promptly locked the shop door behind him.

I could barely speak through my laughter. "What are you doing? We don't close for an hour!" Before I even finished the thought, I was deep in a hug with both of them. I hadn't even seen them since I'd returned from New York.

Josh flicked his hand dismissively. "Oh, whatever, any customers can wait till tomorrow. We need our Lydia time, and we *have* to hear *everything*. An elopement? A possible pregnancy? A scandalous kiss on the side?" I had my face in my hands as he spoke, part mortified but mostly laughing. Josh had a way of deflating the situation of all of its seriousness and finding the fun in it. "I mean *hello*, you're the best thing that's ever happened to office gossip anywhere."

Fiona shoved him aside and brought me into a hug all her own. "Ignore him. I think it's insanely romantic, and I loved what Dylan had to say in that article, and I want every detail."

I looked at them both and my chest just filled with love. These were my friends, and I hadn't realized until that moment how much I needed to bring them into this, to share this whole craziness with them.

"Also, we brought you this," Fiona said, opening the large white box on the counter. Josh was jumping up and down with excitement, and I looked at them both warily. Fiona stepped aside to reveal a three-tier bright red wedding cake with a cardboard-cutout picture of Dylan and me on top, and around the top layer it said in very nonprofessional-looking frosting writing:

Royal Congratulations to Lydia and London's Most
Shaggable Man Who Probably Has a Huge Nob

"The writing was Josh's idea!" Fiona held up her hands in self-defense as I gripped my stomach in laughter. "Now tell us everything."

"Thank you, guys. I will," I said, still laughing and clearing my throat. "And said shaggable man will be here to pick me up in an hour, so you can congratulate him in person."

"Oh, for Christ's sake," said Josh, digging through his man bag and pulling out a knife. "We have to eat this bit before he gets here." He immediately started to cut into the word *nob* on the cake.

I turned down the shop lights, we moved to my office, and for the next forty-five minutes, we ate cake and I walked them through everything. I told them about the Eric kiss, about Dylan showing up, about all of it. Josh got up to bounce or exclaim something barely intelligible at least three times, and Fiona seemed genuinely thrilled. Their impromptu celebration was the perfect antidote to the paparazzi horror show that had started the day.

* * *

"That was rather remarkable," Dylan said once we were seated at dinner. He'd come to pick me up at the shop only to find Fiona and Josh and me full of cake and still laughing. "I'll never cease to find it amazing how quickly you make people fall in love with you." I gave him a roll of my eyes. "I should know," he responded defensively. "I fell harder and faster than anyone else."

"I love you too," I said, taking a sip of my water just as the waiter arrived with our steaming plates of Indian food. Dylan had wanted to take us to a fancy restaurant in Covent Garden, but I'd felt like comfort food instead. So we'd ended up at a tiny hole-in-the-wall restaurant Will had shown us one freezing February night.

"So what was the news from your meeting this afternoon?" I asked. After the first time I'd brought up Dylan's association with MI6 in a public place and he had stopped everything, turned around 360 degrees to make sure no one was listening, and then proceeded to call his security people to do something in reaction, I'd learned quickly that one does not say *MI6* in public, at least not if you're *actually* involved with them.

Dylan paused as he was sweeping up creamy sauce with his naan and didn't look at me when he gave his reply. "The date is set for a week from Friday."

When I dropped my own fork he finally looked up. He knew I didn't want this happen. He also knew that I was proud of him, that I understood why he was doing it, and that there was no way I'd say anything to get in the way of it.

"Okay," I said. "So can you tell me more? Do you know more?"

He reached across the table and grabbed my hand, stroking the top side with his thumb. "Baby, I know this is the last thing we need, but at least it will be over with. And, damsel, I got this."

Alpha-male idiot.

Didn't he understand that's what all men who fancied themselves to be Thomas Crown or James Bond or Batman or whoever all thought: *I got this.* The good news was that I was an optimist, and even if I thought he was being at least partially a moron, I believed in statistics, and I figured the odds of this not going well were low. MI6 wasn't going to put one of Britain's most beloved aristocrats in *real* danger, right? I mean, they wouldn't risk it. So it would be fine. Not because Dylan thought he could karate chop his way out of anything—let's be honest, even if a decade of private kickboxing classes in a Knightsbridge studio gave him a sculpted body, it probably didn't offer much in the way of any real self-defense skills—but because I'd had enough crap in my life already, there was no way I could lose him. At least that's what I was telling myself.

"I know," I said, and squeezed his hand back. "Let's just get it over with—one less thing on our plate."

"Also, how would you feel about hiring Frank again? Just for a bit?"

"Frank?" I asked, remembering the burly man Dylan hired last year while I was being harassed.

"Just until the wedding is over, until things settle down. I never want you to feel afraid to leave our house." He looked at me seriously as he said this. "The paparazzi really are just acting like piranhas over that article. And there really shouldn't be any risk associated with the MI6 business, but it will make me feel better. The last thing I want is someone thinking they can get to me through you, and it's not your job to be on the lookout for that."

I fought Dylan the first time he'd hired security personnel for me. It seemed ridiculous at that time. It didn't seem ridiculous to me now. I got it. In fact, I was relieved. One less thing to worry about.

"Okay. Sounds smart."

Dylan lowered his gaze and scrunched his eyebrows in curiosity. "What? No protests? No assertions about how you can vote and walk and run for office without my help?"

I interlaced my fingers, put my elbows on the table, and rested my chin there, batting my eyelashes at him with exaggerated sweetness. "Nope. I'm all for it." Dylan looked suspicious. "What can I say? I've missed my babycakes." I'd loved my routine with Frank, pretend flirting to get Dylan's goat.

Dylan growled, I laughed, and I was so relieved to see the waiter returning with fresh glasses of wine.

* * *

That night, I lay in our bed, the sheets pulled around us, Dylan's heavy warm limbs wrapped around me so completely that I could feel his pulse against my skin. We'd forgotten to close the curtains, and light from the moon cast a column of brightness across our bodies. Dylan's breathing was rich and rhythmic. I looked at him, felt him, and allowed my anxiety about the MI6 operation in, just for a moment. If I opened the doors to it completely, it would engulf me, and I couldn't afford to let that happen. I understood why he had to do it—in some fundamental way, he felt it would make up for so many of the things his father had done, and it was the quickest way of distancing himself from the wreck his father had made of Hale Shipping and the estate. And the fact that a *friend*, Jack, was in charge of the whole thing relaxed me—there was no way his friend would put him in danger. But there was still a small part of me that was scared. I loved him, I loved my future with him, and the possibility, no matter how slim, that I might lose him crushed me.

Chapter 25

Dylan

The rest of that week was decidedly insane.

I'd spent the next couple of days at Hale Shipping in conversation with the board and various VPs. They were aching for leadership—the staff were getting antsy, a few had resigned, feeling uncertain about the company's future. It was time to step up and provide direction. I'd ended the day with my head in my hands, a clear vision of where the company needed to go and absolutely no desire to get it there myself. Fucking hell.

And it was nearly three on Friday by the time the meeting with the International Olympic Committee was over. After a series of scandals involving the banking of tracks in velodromes, we'd have to expand the floor of the west stadium. Fucking nightmare. Couldn't remember how or why I'd agreed to do this, except that they'd given me free rein, initially anyway. The truly shite part was that I was going to have to be in Auckland for three weeks that summer for final tweaks. No way around it. It wasn't for another month or so, and I'd do my damnedest to make sure Lydia was with me, but I was ready to get back to normal. I wanted days to begin with my mouth on my naked wife, include a healthy day at the drafting table, perhaps a run around Regent's Park, dinner somewhere deserving, and to end the day the way it'd started.

Instead I was sitting in my office up to my eyeballs in corporate international Olympic bullshit.

"Sir." Thomas ducked his head in my door. He'd gotten a bit cocky recently, lost all his fear towards me. Gotta say I kind of missed the days when he hid behind his desk—this version was all too brazen for my taste.

"What is it, Thomas?"

"Her Majesty's secretary is on the line for you, and your wife called…" He paused to smile. I was pretty sure my having a wife was allowing him to live out some kind of *Mad Men*–related fantasy of being an assistant, about which I did *not* want to know the details. "And she said she'd invited…" He paused to look down at the paper. "Your sister, over for dinner. I think she wanted you to call her back."

"Thank you. Also, Thomas?"

He gulped, his Adam's apple shifting nervously. *Bingo.* "Please remember to knock."

"Of course, sir." He closed the door and scampered away in the most satisfying manner.

I straightened my tie and sat up in my chair as though the queen would somehow know, via her secretary and over the telephone lines, that I had been slouching during this conversation.

"Hello, Mr. Randolph," I said, ready, eager, accommodating, as I'd been trained to be my whole life.

"My lord." Anyone from the palace, from the butlers all the way up, said titles the same way, as though we needed to be reminded we were lords before the conversation continued, lest we forget the obligations it entailed. "Her Majesty wishes to convey her gratitude for your contributions at His Royal Highness's charity gala."

Was that all? "Of course. I'm glad she is pleased." I relaxed a little, picking up a pen and doodling a vision I was having for an extension to the hideaway house.

"Indeed, sir. In fact she is hoping you may be willing to provide some assistance of a different nature. She is requesting that you accompany Prince Richard on his travels this summer. He is obliged to visit Vancouver, Cameroon, Johannesburg, and Sydney, and whilst Her Majesty is aware that this is a rather…" Mr. Randolph paused, searching for the right word. "Unusual request of someone outside the royal family, she believes you'd set a rather good example for the prince." In other words, the palace didn't trust Richard not to paw his fiancée in public or otherwise fuck up his first royal tour. "Her Majesty trusts you, my lord, and is hopeful that you won't mind." Bloody hell. It was a fucking world tour. "She is aware that you'll be in Auckland in preparation for the Olympics, so surely it won't be an inconvenience."

"I'd be honored, of course." I delivered the acceptance as I should, with grace, etc. But fucking Christ. I'd be gone most of the summer. What a disaster. "When are these trips meant to occur?"

"I've forwarded the schedule to your assistant, Lord Abingdon. Also, I'd like to add that the queen sends her warmest congratulations on your nuptials." Ahh, of course. If I was a good boy, she wouldn't put up a fuss at us having eloped and the accompanying scandals. Hell, this woman was a genius with her diplomacy. No wonder she was trusted with an entire commonwealth.

"That's too kind."

I retrieved the schedule from Thomas, displeased to discover I'd be departing the day after the operation with MI6—in a bloody week—and assuming I didn't have the chance to come home between any of the stops, I would be gone until the week before our wedding.

I ran my fingers through my hair, drawing my nails against my scalp, pressing my thumbs into my temples. The only silver lining was that once it was done, it'd be done.

I'd just have to convince Lydia to come with me. I rang her mobile immediately.

"Damsel." She'd answered the phone on the first ring.

"Hey. How's your day going?" I could tell she had the phone pressed between her ear and her shoulder, could hear the rustling and muffled sound of her shirt rubbing against the mobile.

"Can you be available for two months starting a week from Saturday?" I had a pencil in my hand, continuing to build on the sketch I'd started earlier, an addition to the house Lydia called my hideaway. I could just imagine how the addition might be connected to the main building, how if we had kids, as they grew, there'd be room for them right—

Lydia's sarcastic laughter interrupted my multitasking.

"What?" I asked.

"Two months? Dylan, don't be ridiculous. I was just gone for a month. If we take a honeymoon, I'll be gone from work again in August—we should talk about that at some point. Emily's been hounding me about it. Hannah and the investors just upped the budget for the Manhattan store, and have asked me to take a couple of short trips to supervise. Fiona's jewelry line launches in two weeks. There's no way I can abandon her. Not to mention, we're getting married, which apparently takes a lot work, which I'm finding rather shocking given that we're already married." She was breathy and stressed; her American accent came on so strong during these rants. I had to admit I loved it—it always reminded me how delightfully *not* British she was. Obviously what I had thought was going to be an immediate *Yes, Dylan. Of course, baby, I'll go anywhere with you* was not so simple.

"Wait, why are you asking?" She had stopped moving on the other end.

"The queen's secretary called, and I'm afraid, damsel, that I'm going to be doing some travelling this summer with Richard and Jemma—Johannesburg, Cameroon, Vancouver, and Sydney."

"When? For how long?" I could hear the resignation in her voice, and it fucking killed me. I wanted her with me. Eventually I'd want her to be able to come on these trips, and I was suddenly extraordinarily happy that she'd begun considering a career wherein she was self-employed.

"Starts just week after next, on either side of the Auckland trip, I'm afraid. I'd be back just before the wedding." She sighed, an exhale that meant she wasn't going to tell me how what I'd said had just made her shoulders fall.

"Well, bring me back something nice, okay? A stuffed kangaroo or a picture of you with a koala or on a whale watch or whatever."

"Is that what you think happens on these trips?" I laughed.

"No, but I'd prefer not to imagine you away for that long with whatever vile Olympic volleyball players are going to be like swooning over you." She sighed again. "Okay, well when you get back can we hide from the queen's secretary for a while?" She imitated my accent when she said *secretary* in a way that made me love her just a little more.

"Absolutely, damsel. I think this will be the last of it for a while. I'm afraid I'm a bit indebted after beating Tristan Bailey to a pulp in her Butler's lounge and then eloping without informing the palace."

"Fair enough." I heard more rustling—she'd resumed whatever she was doing. "Also, Emily asked me what we were doing for a rehearsal venue and whether we wanted to book out rooms here in London or near Humboldt for guests?"

"What did you tell her?"

"That I haven't the faintest idea. The point is, she is on top of this. Dylan, really, you should see her. She's incredible at running this show. She's *hired staff*."

"What? How?"

"I don't even know. I'm not sure I even care. All I know is that she's a force. I've handed the planning entirely over to her. You know, Dylan, you might ask her for some help—I have a feeling she is capable of far more than planning weddings."

"Yes, well, I'm sure. But there are more important matters."

"Like what?" I heard something louder being moved around on her end, probably a box of some sort—she had to get better at delegating this nonsense.

"Like is your office door closed?" The rustling stopped again.

"It is now." Her voice had shifted to the pliant soft tone that made my dick hard.

"Good girl. Now I want you to go to your chair, damsel." I slid back in my own seat and pressed the button on my desk to fog the glass of my windows. "Hike that dress up, baby—I want it out of the way."

"Okay." The word was broken, like she was nervous all of a sudden—I liked it.

"Now, damsel. You're going to do everything I tell you to.

And when I'm done, you're going to know that I can take care of you, even from afar."

* * *

"That's the date, yes…Well that's just one of life's real cruelties, isn't it? That you'll have to manage four cakes instead of two?…Well now, there we go—we've figured it out, haven't we?…That sounds reasonable…No, no lilies. What do you think this is? It's a *wedding*, not a bleeding funeral…Absolutely…I'll confirm with the duke and duchess, but sounds classic…Certainly…Send over the sketches by noon tomorrow, and I'll be happy to consider your bid…Cheers."

I'd walked into my own kitchen to find Emily at my table, Molly bringing her dinner, her laptop set before her, not one but two mobiles next to her, and a set of folders in neat orderly piles surround her.

"Shall I get you an office?" I asked sarcastically, rather shocked to see my sister so expertly dispatching my resources in the name of this wedding.

"That *would* make my life easier," she said cheekily as she reached for one of the mobiles, getting ready to dial.

"Haven't you got schoolwork to do?" I looked over her shoulder and saw a pair of bids from bakers side by side.

"Of course, but I've got that handled." She spoke to me while reading an incoming email, as though she barely had time for my interruption. "Did I tell you I've switched courses?"

"No. What are you doing?" For as long as I'd remembered, Emily had said she was going to go into art history—some nonsense about wanting to once and for all be able to confirm that the eyes in the paintings at Humboldt did in fact follow her.

"As I'm sure you're aware, I wasn't exactly devoted to art history. So I've switched to the business course. Unfortunately I missed the entry for some of the key classes, so I've talked with the faculty and decided to take the semester, do some catch-up reading, and resume at Michaelmas."

"Bloody hell, Em." I hadn't been expecting that. Not from the Emily I knew, whom I was quite sure spent her weekends gallivanting around Sloane Square with her schoolmates.

"What?" When she looked at me, her back straight, her focus evident, her efficiency written all over her, I had this sudden realization that perhaps we were far more similar than I'd realized. I'd always thought my drive had stemmed directly from the stifling pressure my father had put on me as the future Duke of Abingdon, but here was Emily, not a child, not a mind-numbing socialite, with what looked like every bit as much drive as I had.

"Dylan, do stop staring at me and say what you need to say or allow me to get back to work. I adore you, for some mysterious reason, but if you want your wedding to happen in less than three months, you're going to have to let me get back to work."

I found myself chuckling. "Fine, madam. But first, have you considered we could simply hire a wedding a planner—"

"I did, twice, and fired both. Completely inadequate."

"Right, then proceed. But check everything with Lydia—"

"Obviously."

"Christ, you're a pill."

She smiled broadly at me, loving that she'd obviously outsmarted me. Loving the respect I was bestowing on her. It felt good to do it, and novel for both of us. Emily was clearly not just my kid sister anymore. "And, if you can fit it into your schedule, you should come down to Hale Shipping with me on Monday."

"Really?" She looked surprised and curious. And honestly I felt both of those things as well. I wasn't even sure where that had come from. An idea was brewing, and she and I would just have to figure out if we could make it work.

"Really. Now where's Lydia?

Chapter 26

Lydia

I was sitting at the vanity in our room when I heard Dylan come in behind me.

Over the six months we'd lived together, the luxurious master suite had somehow morphed into a couple's space. One day I'd come home to find that a small bookshelf containing obscure architecture volumes had been replaced by an elegant vanity and bench, complete with an oval mirror that tilted. Another day, I'd decided to frame and hang a photograph of us that we'd taken at Humboldt, out in the wooded area on a winter day—scarves thick around our necks. I'd added some throw pillows to the couch in the sitting area, which, if Dylan noticed, and I was pretty sure he had, he didn't say anything. My side of the bed had become populated with magazines and books I was halfway through—a habit Dylan was barely tolerating. His side of the bed never had more than a glass of water, his phone, and a single book.

But that vanity was my favorite. On the nights we went out it made me feel like I had a place to move from morning into day, to recover from whatever shenanigans Dylan had roped my body into and get ready for the day. A place to ease from day into night, to leave behind whatever had happened at work, whatever monstrous thing had been said about me on Twitter or in the *Daily Mail* or *Evening Standard*, put on a pretty dress, and let it fall away. At that moment, I had changed into a caramel-colored pleated leather skirt and a thin denim button-down, sleeves rolled up, and was applying mascara when Dylan's suited frame filled the mirror behind me.

"What are you thinking about?" Dylan's lyrical deep accented voice filled the air behind me, and I was pretty sure I sat a little straighter, trying to accommodate the tiny zings and zaps of arousal that darted around my body whenever he was present. His hands rested on my shoulders, adding warmth to the mix and reminding me of his strength.

"Wouldn't you like to know," I said, looking up at him in the reflection.

He leaned over and slid his palms down the front of my shirt and into my bra.

"If it's about our phone call this afternoon, then me too." My nipples pebbled at his touch, but I rolled my eyes for good measure, even if I was involuntarily leaning into his touch. "I like this ensemble. Who knew leather and denim could be so sexy?"

"Um, Bruce Springsteen and every music video from the eighties?" I said, looking up at him. He laughed, withdrew his hands, and sat next to me on the small bench, facing the room while I faced the mirror. He reached over and brushed my hair behind my ear and swept my bangs aside. They weren't really long enough to be covering my eyes, but he still did that occasionally, like he'd be able to see me more clearly.

"I gave Hannah my notice," I said, looking right at him.

His eyes got bigger, filling with awe and concern at the same time.

"Lydia," he started, shaking his head. I knew that his biggest fear was that I would give things up, making too many sacrifices to accommodate my life with him. I could see that fear written all over him.

I put my hand on his thigh. "Dylan, it's what I want. After we got off the phone today I realized how sad I was that I can't go with you on this trip this summer. I want to be with you. I don't resent you going—I resent not being able to go with you. It's not fair to Hannah to prolong it, and it's not realistic to keep working a nine-to-five job, when we both know there will be times I need to leave work early, extended trips we'll need to take. But even more than that, I think I've learned what I can learn from Hannah. I'm ready to move on to what's next for me. I told her I'd stay on until the week before our wedding. I'll get my replacement up to speed. I'll make sure everything is ready to move forward with the Manhattan shop. Two months is plenty of time to do that. Then I'll move on."

"What will you do next?" he asked, a little of the concern falling away.

"Well, I don't know yet, but I'm going to figure it out. I'm going to explore my options. I found this woman who does technology consulting for the fashion industry, and I'm going to take her out for dinner in a couple of weeks, learn about her job. And I'm going to schedule other informational interviews. Fiona even sounds interested in coming aboard."

"Really?" Dylan asked, his eyebrows raised.

"Really. And if I worked for myself, there would be nothing standing in the way of me being with you, travelling with you, doing what we want and need in our life."

"And it's what you want?" He took my face in in his hands, trying to suss out any hesitation in my eyes. I nodded, and he kissed me on the lips, smooth, firm, and slow. "Thank you, baby."

"No 'thanks,' right? We're a team."

Dylan pulled me against him, running his hands up and down my back, and then we both heard the muffled animated sounds of Emily speaking sternly into the phone a floor beneath us. "My sister's a beast," he said, smiling.

I laughed into his shoulder. "Isn't she something? I don't think this wedding will require too much from us, other than to show up on the day. She's a marvel."

"She is," he said, pulling back, and he got a look on his face like he was getting an idea. "She's also probably waiting for us."

* * *

The next morning I was still reeling from all of the wedding plans that Emily had laid before our feet. Reeling and grateful that I hadn't had to do them myself. I sat on the bedroom floor in front of three rather large boxes we'd dragged back from the New York apartment, things I thought I might want for our London home. Dylan had gone to the office—he was trying to sort something out with Hale Shipping so he could free up time to work on a new architecture project he wanted to take on.

I removed the Bubble Wrap from framed photos and put them to the side, thinking that maybe I could get some of Dylan's family photos too and hang them together somewhere. I unpacked a small guitar my father had bought me when I was a child and strummed it just enough to realize how little I remembered about playing and how out of tune it was. Then I dug into a pile of loose photos and papers. I'd been sorting things into "keep" and "discard" piles when I came across a yellowed oversaturated photograph that stopped me in my tracks. I stood from the floor and went to sit at the vanity where the light was better.

My father was leaning against a small blue car on a cloudy day. It was London—I could tell from the British license plates visible next to his legs. He had a mustache, which made me laugh, and he looked so young and healthy. And there, perched on his hip, was me. I was an infant—I couldn't have been much more than six months old, and I was wearing a onesie with little leather buckled shoes and nothing else, and we were both smiling broadly, laughing. The light in his eyes was magnetic, warm. Our eyes were fixed on each other, and you could see how much he loved me—it radiated from the old photograph. I turned it over, and in handwriting I didn't recognize, there was a note.

Rick, I can tell already that she's just like you. Generous with her love and a joy to love in return. I know you'll both be better off without me. Take good care of our girl.

Holy shit. It was from my mother. I had no idea if this was the last note he'd gotten from her or if there'd ever been any other communication. I don't know what happened to her after she gave this to him. I'd never known. I stared at that photo for what could have been hours, and as I sat there, I realized I didn't need to know. Not anymore. She was right. My mother was right: I *was* like my dad. Full of love. And I *wasn't* like her. I *wouldn't* leave.

I had been so *lucky* to have my dad, to be raised by him, loved by him. The man in that photo didn't choose to love me—it was a force, part of who he was. Part of who I was. I knew that now, because I felt it with Dylan, felt what feeling love for another person made possible. What it made impossible. Taking one look at that photo made me realized I had nothing to fear.

Not today, but one day, I'd convince Dylan that he had that in him too, because he did. There was nothing to be afraid of when it came to making a family with him, because we already were a family.

I wiped the tears that had fallen down my cheeks and into my lap. I tucked the photo into the frame of the vanity mirror and silently thanked my mother—something I never thought I'd do—for that note. She never could have known that her message was exactly the one I needed to hear.

Chapter 27

Dylan

For the most part, things had become more relaxed over the previous week. Lydia was calmer since giving her notice to Hannah—she was lighter, and I caught her reading business magazines and filling up her home office with piles that seemed to have purpose. And having Frank around made *me* calmer. Until the wedding was over, and the MI6 operation was far enough in our past, I wanted to know she was safe. In fact, the MI6 operation was the only lurking source of anxiety. That and the weeks-long separation that would follow it.

"I don't want you to do this." Lydia looked up at me with her big brown eyes, searching, as though she could convince me, with just that look, not to go through with the operation. And fuck all, if there were nothing else to consider, I'd have let those brown eyes tell me exactly what to do. Those eyes fucking owned me.

It was finally here—this event that had been looming for the past several months, and we were getting ready to head out the door.

"Baby. Damsel. I will be fine. This needs to be done." I ran my hand down her bare arm. Her skin was still warm and damp from the shower, and she was withdrawn, distracted. She was scared, and I don't think anyone had ever been scared for me in my life. It was so raw, feeling loved like that. I imagined suddenly that's what parents were supposed to feel for their children. Or what children were supposed to feel from their parents. It was family.

I pulled her from the closet to the bed and sat on the edge, situating her so she sat atop me, so those lean endless legs of hers bent next to my thighs, and I pulled the towel from her back. I wanted to be what kept her warm, I wanted her to feel how I wanted to be the one protecting her, that she had no reason to be scared, and I wanted my skin on hers to do that.

She ran her nose against my neck, nesting in the crook of my shoulder. When she did that she was so beautifully vulnerable. I couldn't get enough. Her hair covered my hands, and I kissed her head.

"You'll wait with Jack's staff. Emily will be with you. You'll get every update. And the whole thing won't take more than a couple of hours." I explained the plan as I rubbed her back. I explained how the car would be driven by a trained agent pretending to be my driver. How I'd be meeting King in the back room of a restaurant he owned. How my jacket would be wired, undetectable. How I knew exactly what I needed to get him to say and exactly how I was going to do it. How we'd been laying this plan for over a year, and it was going to work. How the officers would be waiting less than a block away, ready to intervene. How code words were in place. How I'd be in and out, and only a fifteen-minute drive away in Southwark the whole time. It was solid, and I had backup.

"And when I'm done, I'll come right to you, damsel. I'll whisk you off."

"You can't. You're going *away* tomorrow." She said, defeated.

"Yes, well, as soon as I'm back from *that*, we'll get in the car, head to the airport, straight for Ikaria, and stay there for weeks. Just you and me. All right?"

"We can't. After *that* we have the wedding."

"Yes, well, fine, you annoying little thing, *then* I will whisk you away."

What she didn't know was that as soon as this bloody mess was over with and we were safely tucked away in Greece, I had every intention of telling her I wanted a family, not in ten years, but now. I wanted a child. With her. I'd stop being such a pathetic wanker and pray to god it was what she wanted too, that I wouldn't be bloody breaking her in half by asking her to be a mother when she'd said more than once that she wanted more time, that the very idea scared her.

Her head of caramel-colored hair rose, and her damp eyes met mine. "Okay. Just promise me nothing will happen. Say it again."

I took her face in my palms and ran the pad of my thumb across her perfect cheeks. "Nothing will happen."

"Okay. Then let's do this. Go be a hero, Dylan Hale." She rose from my lap and I realized she had her knickers in her hand. "Because obviously being a duke, world-class architect, and devastatingly handsome isn't enough. You just *have* to go off and save Britain *and* Russia, *and* stop human trafficking as well." She began to mock me, doing that thing she did when she was trying to create distance and protect herself, use humor to tell herself and everyone else she was fine. She'd done it the first night I'd made love to her.

I smiled at her daft sarcasm, knowing she needed me there with her, and snatched the knickers from her hands. "I don't know *what* you think you're doing with these, damsel. If you think for one second that after this operation I'm going to want to contend with any extra barriers between me and sinking into you, you've gone completely mad. No knickers, darling." I stuffed the purple silk in my pocket, knowing it was probably demented that I was about to take my wife's undergarments as a good luck token on an MI6 operation.

"Now," I continued as I went to the closet. I fetched her favorite jeans and some kind of loose-fitting shirt and bra and dropped them on the bed beside her. "Get dressed, damsel. Let's get this shit show over with, shall we?"

* * *

I'd been sitting in this fucking empty restaurant for an hour and a half waiting, and King still hadn't shown up. I tried not to look at my watch, tried not to down the whisky in front of me. Tried not to do anything that would draw the attention of the henchmen who'd clearly been assigned to wait with me. And it was bloody hot in there. I had avoided taking off my jacket as long as I could—it was the only thing on me that was wired—but I'd started sweating, and had draped it over the back of my chair. All I could do to distract myself was think of Lydia back at MI6 headquarters waiting for me. When I'd left she'd been sitting on a couch with Emily, whom she'd asked to bring along. "You know," she'd said, in her bloody adorable American accent, "in case I get bored." But I knew it was because she wanted a hand to hold. I adored that she wanted to be strong, and it killed me that I put her in the position at all. But this had to be done. If successful, it cleared the path of being free of the Bresnovs, of finally restoring order with Hale Shipping, for putting Humboldt back in my name. Once this was done I'd have atoned, to some small degree, for the sins of my goddamn father.

At that moment, the door opened and five men walked in—it was immediately clear who King was. The short stocky fucker was flanked evenly by four bodyguards in matching suits.

"Let's go for a ride, Hale. Shall we?" The fucker said it like he knew something was up. Goddammit. I was supposed to talk to him about going over the Bresnovs' head, about offering Hale Shipping services for a better deal. I'd worked the details out with MI6, the script, and they were meant to intervene the moment the ass had incriminated himself by accepting the deal. The plan was for the conversation to take place *there*—why did the fucker want to move?

"I think here should do well, don't you?" I said. "I've got to be somewhere in an hour—why waste, time, right, gentlemen?"

The henchman, the one with the goddamn pistol hanging out his pants, came up behind my chair and tipped it forward. "Mr. King said he'd like to take a ride."

This wasn't supposed to happen, but it would be fine. The tracking device was in my jacket. The officers would be watching my whereabouts and would follow. I reached for my jacket, but the henchman's hand landed on top of mine. I was strong, but Christ, this man was a monster.

King spoke up. "You won't need it." My hand dropped the jacket, and the henchman put his hand at my back and pushed me towards the door.

Fuck.

Chapter 28

Lydia

Something was wrong. I knew it. I felt it.

"Want a cappuccino?" Emily asked, looking at her phone. "Jack called Will, and he's on his way over. He said he'd bring coffee." She said it with a shrug. She didn't know what I knew instinctively—that something was definitely, definitely wrong.

I shook my head and pulled at the hem of my sweater, rolling it between my fingers nervously. "Where is he?" I asked her, as though she could tell me.

"Who? Will? He's just round the corner at the Costa." Emily looked at me as though I had three heads.

"No. Dylan. He should be back by now." I marched to the door of the room and flung it open. The officer who'd been checking in with us was no longer there, and I didn't give a shit that he'd told us to stay there. I needed to know what was going on. My heart was racing. He should have been there—now I knew something was wrong.

I heard voices from a room at the end of the hall, men talking over one another, and a woman's voice speaking over all of them.

"Get Bickford on the phone now. We have to find out where they're taking him. And follow that car, Robert, do you hear me? Do *not* lose them."

I was at the door now, and I could actually feel the color drain from my face; it felt as though the life was draining from my body. Lose? As in, they couldn't find him?

She turned around and saw me, and I was completely frozen in place.

"Your Grace, ma'am. Everything is fine—"

"Don't lie to me. Find my husband." The words were cold and directive. Everything, every detail of the room, every voice, every face became a muted grey, disappeared into the background. All I could sense was my own heart beating furiously in my chest.

One of the other agents approached me. "You should go back to the—"

"I'm not going anywhere."

Right then Emily and Will came up behind me—I could hear them and feel them, and Will's voice came over my shoulder. "What's going on?"

"Something's wrong," I said. "They don't know where Dylan is."

The woman stepped forward. "And you are?"

"Family," I said sternly. "He's family. And we're staying here." I wasn't going to find out a moment later than I had to—whether it was good news or bad news, I was going to be the first to know.

In the meantime, I let Will pull me against him, into his other side. One of his arms was wrapped firmly around Emily, and his other around me.

"It's going to be all right, Lydia. Dylan may be a pompous arse sometimes, but he'll do what he has to do to get back to you."

We stood there for a few moments while the room returned to its frantic state, and then perhaps worst of all, it settled into a thick horrible silence.

Someone brought chairs at some point—they must have, because eventually I was sitting in one.

Someone called Charlotte. They must have, because somehow she ended up in a chair against the wall, holding Emily's hand.

Someone brought food—they must have, because I realized there was an untouched salad on the floor by my feet.

I waited. I paced. I closed my eyes, and willed time to go by faster, willed Dylan to appear in the doorway. He had to.

At some point Charlotte began pacing back and forth, agitated, and one of the agents said to her that we really shouldn't be here. He approached Charlotte and asked her to leave the room.

"No." I stood up and said the first words I'd uttered in over two hours. "She is his mother. Dylan is doing this because of you. He's doing *your* dirty work. He's doing this of his own accord, because he's honorable, because it's the right thing to do, because he believes lives will be saved by doing this. But he didn't have to. And *she*," I said, pointing to Charlotte, "raised the unbelievable man who'd do that. He is *her* son. And if you fuck this up, she has the right to see it happen. She's had enough loss this year, and right now this is the closest she can get to her son, who is missing and possibly harmed. So, I suggest that you stop worrying about who is in this room and get back to work on bringing him back to us."

Charlotte was frozen in place, but sank back against the wall. And I sank back into my chair. Emily's hand was linked in Will's, and her head was on his shoulder. Her eyes were closed, but I knew she wasn't sleeping. I saw him lean down and whisper in her ear occasionally.

The computers at the front of the room continued to buzz and blink. Phones vibrated, and calls were answered, texts sent and received, maps consulted. But for what felt like days, there was nothing.

But it wasn't days. It was minutes. Forty minutes to be exact, before the central line rang loudly into the room, and it was placed on speaker.

"He got him. Hale got the fucker. Recorded him on his mobile, got the fucker completely." The voice was raspy and out of breath, and I could hear commotion in the background.

I flung from my seat again and ran into the center of the room. Some kind of fire spread through my limbs, like they were coming back to life.

"Where's Hale? Where is he?" the officer in the room with us shouted into the line.

"He's on his way back. He got him, James. We finally got King. Hale was brilliant."

I zoned out the rest of the conversation, because I'd heard everything I needed to hear. Dylan was okay. Dylan was okay. He was coming back to me.

I ran from the room and down the hall, and I was in the elevator before I realized I wasn't wearing any shoes. I must have taken them off at some point during the evening.

When the bell in the elevator dinged, and the doors opened, I *ran* through the lobby and out the door. As I exited the glass doors, a town car pulled up in front, and the passenger door flung open. Dylan, his shirt untucked from his pants, his jacket missing, his shirt ripped at the collar, burst from the vehicle with some kind of adrenaline-filled strength. Within a second I was in his arms.

His musky salty smell filled my senses. I could taste his skin as my lips met his chest, then his neck, and his face and then his mouth. My hands were in his hair, on his arms, wrapped around his neck, and I was holding myself to him as though the very turning of the earth depended on my grip.

I'd always loved the strength of his arms, the way he held me and carried me with ease, but this was different. The way he held me against him, the total lack of give in his grip, communicated everything I needed to know. He was never going to let me go.

"Damsel," he said quietly. "You're not wearing shoes."

I laughed a little, just enough to bring me out of my desperate hold and loosen my grip.

"I'm back, baby. It took a little more work than I'd planned, and I'm going to fucking throttle Jack, but did you honestly think I'd ever not come back to you?"

I wasn't crying, but I couldn't speak either. I just needed a few more minutes to revel in the certainty of his presence.

"Shhh," he cooed as he put me down. My chest still pressed against him, but he wedged his hands between us and up my body, taking my face and forcing my gaze up his. "Baby, I'm here."

I nodded and lifted my lips to kiss him.

"Dylan." I started to speak, but I didn't know what to say. That I was so scared he was somehow lost to me forever? That this had been too dangerous? That I somehow lost the one person who'd managed to tether me back to this earth after losing my father.

"I know, baby. But I'm here."

He took my hand in his, and we walked back into the building. By the time we got to the lobby, Charlotte, Will, and Emily along with the rest of the officers were all standing there. The officers were talking rapidly and trying to shake Dylan's hand, but he went to his sister and hugged her.

"Sorry I worried you, Em."

She hugged him fiercely back, but then pulled away, as though she just remembered that hugging wasn't exactly in the Hale Family Playbook. "Oh, please. Who said I was worried? Don't flatter yourself." But I swore she wiped something away from her eyes. He chuckled and gripped her hand one more time.

I stood back and watched as he gave Will a nod.

Then his mother approached us. She stood before us, her misty eyes fixed on Dylan. I'd never seen her look so disheveled. So unmasked. So much like a mother. Her hair was unstyled with a headband keeping the wispy strands off her face. She wore pants and a wrinkled sweater. It was the first time I'd really looked at her all night, and she looked terrible. She looked like a mother who'd been afraid of losing her son.

There was an awkward moment, during which I wondered if I was going to have to tell Charlotte where to shove it, but then she surprised me, perhaps more than anyone else ever had.

"I'm proud of you, Dylan." She reached out to grip his hand, and I saw her squeeze it. Maybe this was as close as they'd get to a mother-son embrace, but it spoke volumes. She stood on her tiptoes to kiss his cheek, and he leaned down to kiss hers. I saw him nod, almost imperceptibly.

"And, Dylan," she continued. "I'm sorry. I've been monstrous. I know that. Tonight made me realize how lodged in my grief I've been, but it's no excuse." Then suddenly she was looking at me. "And I owe you an apology as well, Lydia. And gratitude. Thank you for what you said up there." I could feel Dylan look at me, the way his head had tilted down towards mine. "My son is fortunate to have you as his wife. I can't tell you how grateful I am that he is so loved. Forgive me for taking far too long to appreciate it. I hope you'll pardon my behavior."

"I—" I started to say it was okay, but when I looked at her and saw in her eyes a contrition that could have been mistaken for fear, I simply said, "Thank you."

Then Charlotte gave Dylan an actual hug. I let go of Dylan's hand so he could reciprocate properly, but it was back in my own hand within seconds, squeezing. By threading his fingers through mine, he said all he needed to.

* * *

It was two more hours before we were able to go home. Charlotte, Emily, and Will had left shortly after Dylan's return—once we knew he was okay and the adrenaline rush had dissipated, everyone seemed to need to retreat and recoup. But there was no way I was leaving his side.

I'd never felt this way before, physically unwilling to let my hand go from Dylan's. I knew it was irrational, but it was as though I felt that by holding on to him, I could somehow undo the panic I'd already felt. Or like that panic was still there, its shadow lurking, and the only way to keep it at bay was to literally not let Dylan out of my grasp. Thankfully, he seemed to feel the same way, or at the very least he knew better than to try to make me let go.

At one point, when we'd been sitting in Jack's office for forty minutes, and Dylan was signing a statement, I finally let it sink in. How worried I'd been. How relieved I was that he was back. And what that meant. How was it possible that over the course of a year, another person could become so intimately ingrained in your world? I had always had a little disdain for the "we" couples, those people who when you asked them a question about themselves always seemed to answer in the plural, as though they no longer had an individual identity. It had seemed weird, desperate, showy.

But now I saw it differently. I had become so used to thinking about the world as a place I was moving through *with Dylan* that to think about only myself seemed like a lie somehow, like it didn't reflect reality anymore. And not because I was any less my own person than I had been before, but because the person I was, the Lydia of that moment, was someone who held someone else's dreams, fears, and loves as close to her heart just as he did. And I knew without a doubt that my own dreams, fears, and loves had become his. We had become irrevocably tangled up in each other.

So in those few horrible hours when I thought there was a chance he was gone, I was panicked, not just because I would have found myself grieving the single most important man in my life for the second time within twelve months, but because I would have no idea how to reassemble myself in his absence.

It was after midnight when we were riding back to the house in the car, and I was falling asleep on Dylan's lap, my head resting on his shoulder, his long arms wrapped around me. Feeling like home.

When the car door opened, Dylan somehow exited with me in his arms, and I found myself being carried to the door. "Women can walk you know," I said, yawning, eyes closed, my arms tightening around his neck.

He laughed and hitched me a little higher. "As though I'd let you go."

Dylan carried me up the stairs, and I was in and out of wakefulness until he placed me in the overstuffed armchair in the corner of our room. My eyes fluttered open, and I curled up in the chair, watching him move about the room.

He took off his shoes, and placed them in the closet. His eyes kept fluttering back to mine as he removed his socks, his belt, and I couldn't take my eyes off of him. My body was slowly waking up, heating up, the warmth coming from the looks between us. I was lost in him, and suddenly he was standing before me, in just his pants and his dress shirt hanging open. I looked up to him and saw everything I wanted. The moonlight was casting through the tall windows, lighting up his familiar beautiful form, almost making me question if he was real.

I worked my way up to kneeling in the chair, grabbed him by the belt loops, and pulled him towards me. "I love you," I said, burying my head in his abdomen, inhaling him, letting the smell of him calm me, bring me back to center. His hands were in my hair, his lips on the top of my head.

"I love you too, damsel." He whispered the words, slowly, taking his time. It was like it was our first time again. The very same chair. The same moonlight. But a whole new version of us.

My lips found their way to his bare skin and pressed against the hair on his chest, taking in the heat of him.

Dylan stepped back and took my hand in his own, giving me the space to stand on the floor. When I did, I instinctively raised my arms and let him lift the drapey black shirt over my head. In return, I smoothed my hands inside his open shirt and pushed the crisp material over his shoulders. He quickly unfastened the cuffs, and the shirt fell to the floor. My bra followed suit in a matter of seconds, and then Dylan was on his knees before me.

I went to unbutton my jeans, but Dylan's hands grabbed my own. "Don't. I've been thinking about this ever since I saw you in that bloody bikini."

That's what he'd said the first time we were in this room, and I laughed out loud as he dragged my jeans down my body. I shivered when he ran his fingers and mouth over my bare pussy. "Only this time, no knickers, and…Christ, you undo me, Lydia." He kissed below my belly button, just a featherlight peck.

We moved to the bed, Dylan leaving his pants behind him, and we proceeded to consume each other, find each other, kiss every corner, run our hands along each other's bodies, roll to each get a better advantage. But we always returned to our mouths, to those kisses that made me feel like we were trying to show each other what forever looked like, even though we'd said it.

This was different. It was new. It was old. It was perfect.

Covers had bunched at the foot of the bed, and every sensation or concern outside of us was forgotten. When, mid-kiss, I landed on top of him, straddling him, he interlaced his fingers with my own and brought them to his lips to kiss.

He paused our continuous movement just to look at me, my hair falling over us, creating a tent. He moved one of his hands to tuck it behind my ear, allowing the moonlight to brighten the space between us, and he looked at me as though he was seeing me for the first time.

"What?" I asked, the first word to pass between us in what felt like hours.

"I…I want…" He paused and I saw his throat move with a gulp. "When I get back…" I'd almost forgotten he was leaving the next day. I felt like I'd just gotten him back, which was ridiculous.

"What?" I asked again. But I saw this expression change, leaving whatever "want" he was about to express behind.

"Come here, baby," he said as he rolled us over, him landing on top, caging me in. I wrapped my legs around him, and took in the reverent expression in his eyes. It was as though he was laying me bare with only his gaze. It was almost too much, and I looked away towards the light. "No, damsel, I want to see you. Look at me. Look at us." I snapped my eyes back to his just as he lifted my hips and entered me. I gasped, shocked at the fullness, as though we didn't do this daily, as though he'd never been deep inside me before, but it was as though he was focused on nothing other than binding me to him. His rhythm was steady, intense, and dedicated to getting me off. I could feel him tilting me, angling me, looking for that sweet spot that would have me careening towards an orgasm.

"Dylan," I said, letting his name become part of my exhale, and tightening my legs around him.

"Baby," he said in return, and he kissed me on the nose. Our bodies were warm, sweat making us slick against each other. And there were hands in hair, nails in skin. But none of that amounted to the usual dirty desperation. This wasn't wild frantic fucking, and it wasn't overly sweet lovemaking. It was equal parts intense focus and intimate tenderness. And there was something about it that had my skin humming, an orgasm originating from so deep within me, I hadn't known I could feel there.

"I love you." I wasn't sure if those words were mine or his. They seemed to be shared between us, uttered on each other's breath as we came together.

Chapter 29

Dylan

We'd decided on a big brunch the next day. I was going to be gone nearly two months, and we wanted the family celebration we had yet to have for our wedding, the one that would be quiet and intimate before the fireworks-style affair Emily had been planning.

By eleven, Lydia, Fiona, and Josh were in the lounge riffling through possible website upgrade options for Fiona's business. My mother was oddly quiet and compliant as she sat drinking tea at the kitchen table. I could tell by looking at her expression that she felt contrite. Just that morning, she'd looked at the ring on Lydia's finger and she was "glad it was on someone so deserving." Hell had, apparently, frozen over, pigs could fly, and the fat lady was singing.

Even Frank was there, drinking his coffee at the other end of the kitchen island; while I wasn't concerned about retaliation for the MI6 operation—I knew Jack had it handled—Lydia was still a media target, and I wanted to know she was protected. Especially while I was away.

At that moment we were only waiting on Emily and Will, and I had a handful of hours before I'd have to head to the palace to meet up with Richard and then to the airport. It had been odd that Will was there at all the previous night—kind and all, but odd all the same. I suppose it took something like an intelligence mission gone awry to suss out who your family really included, realize just how big it actually was.

I was finishing up a couple of work-related emails before joining everyone, but I couldn't get my mind off how things had changed, how last night I'd wanted to tell her that everything I'd ever said about not wanting children was shite. That I wanted a family with her. For the first time I'd wished I'd been born a bloody Yank like she had, willing to talk it out at a drop of a hat. Instead I was daftly hoping I could somehow convey the message by shoving my dick in her. *Christ*, I was a moron.

When I got back from this trip I was going to man up and actually talk about this with her and just hope to god that she wanted this as much as I did. Hope I could convince her that she'd be a perfect mother. The truth was, I wanted this brunch to be over, to get on that goddamn plane and get my arse back here as soon as fucking possible so we could get through the wedding of the century and get our life started.

King and the Bresnovs were in custody and would be put away for life by month's end. Humboldt was working properly, I was in the process of putting it back in my name, and one by one the crooked lines left by my father had been smoothed out. I had a plan for Hale Shipping. Hale Architecture and Design was having a banner year. The path was clear, and the only one I wanted on it with me was Lydia.

My own pathetic sigh was interrupted by Emily plopping her enormous handbag on the kitchen island by me.

"Well *that* was a nightmare. I hate to admit it, but I'd generally prefer you not go playing the saint anymore, risking your life, fancying yourself some kind of kung fu–style hero. Can we agree that that was bollocks and you're done playing double-O seven?" She was giving me one of her *I-can't-believe-I-put-up-with-you* kind of stares.

"Have you ever even *seen* a Bond film?" I asked, smiling.

"Ugh, you know I hate the cinema," she said, scoffing. "I mean what *is* the point of sitting in the dark to watch overpaid actors scream at you?"

I laughed and pulled her against me. "Aww, Em. It's nice to know you care."

She made a sound of disgust and shoved me away just as the doorbell rang. She suddenly perked up. "I'll get it," she sang and marched away from me.

A few minutes later, I entered the dining room to see my beautiful wife sitting, coffee in hand, next to her friends, my mother, and my sister.

My sister.

Holding hands.

With *Will*.

I realized I wasn't the only one staring, slightly open-mouthed. I looked around the table and everyone looked slightly confused. Everyone except for Lydia, who was *smiling*. What was going on?

"Will?" I asked, looking at his hand linked with my sister's.

"Hiya, mate," he said, smiling nervously and leaning forward a bit. He should goddamn well be nervous. What the ever-loving fuck? "So, um, about this." He looked at Emily and raised their linked hands to his mouth and kissed her fingers.

"Will and I are dating. Ta-da! That's all there is to say. So, where is the coffee?" Emily reeled off every word at lightning speed, and started to drag Will towards the kitchen.

"Oh no," I said, smiling and moving to block the exit to the room. "Please, take a seat. And by all means, Will, *what* were you going to say? Or perhaps my darling wife would care to elaborate?"

"Oh, no, no, no," Lydia said. "I had no idea. I mean, I may have *suspected*, but have you *met* your sister? I wasn't exactly going to confront her about it."

"You suspected?" I could feel my eyes bugging out of my face.

"Dylan." Lydia came up, linked her arm in mine, and stood on her tiptoes to whisper in my ear. "Leave them alone. Let's have a nice brunch, and then you can take Will out back and give him the old one-two punch mano-a-mano hashing-out thing, or whatever is you intend to do, *after* we've eaten." She gave me a look that said it all. It said *don't be an arse* and *get over it* and *you don't have two legs to stand on* and a thousand other things. As I'd known for some time, that woman had me by the fucking balls, and I fucking loved her for it.

And fucking hell she was right. After five awkward minutes, I did let it go. I mean of course I'd still rip him a new one at some point, give him some fatherly lecture, and he'd probably laugh his arse off as I did it. And the truth was, I knew better than anyone that love came when and with whom you'd least expect it. So, fuck it. He just better goddamn well not break my sister's heart.

Over the course of the meal I realized just how much the flavor of things had changed. Maybe it wasn't just that I apparently wanted to impregnate my wife like some kind of Neanderthal. Maybe there had been some kind of tectonic shift that impacted everyone. I looked at my mother, a woman who was emerging from a grief I was only now beginning to understand. My father was a classic wanker, through and through, but she'd had history with him. She had two children with him. Her life had become inextricably linked to his. I didn't doubt that what I had with Lydia was more intense and intimate by a factor of ten, but if my mother felt even a fraction of what I would feel if I lost my girl, then I guess I bloody well had to accept that she had the right to be out of sorts. If that were me, I wouldn't be held accountable for the damage I'd cause. She hadn't been a perfect mother—hell, she hadn't even been a good one, but I knew her better now than I did before. I knew she loved me.

I felt Lydia's hand squeeze my own, and I looked at her. She looked so calm and replete, even though I knew part of her was buzzing with the anticipation of our separation. I returned the squeeze and slipped my hand around her thigh as she turned to talk to Fiona. She was building a life here. I'd caught her on arrival, been lucky enough to swoop in ahead of any other halfwits who might have tried to claim her as their own, and fuck if I wasn't thankful for it every day. I thought about who she'd been in New York, how it felt as though all of Brooklyn held her up as their sun. She was making it happen here, and it was goddamn beautiful.

A year ago I was a lonely bastard who'd fooled himself into thinking he'd be content with the emotional scraps he'd been handed. From where I sat at that table, looking back on that version of me, I saw a sad bloke, someone who had no idea of the utter bliss headed his way.

Thank fucking god.

Then I looked around and I saw my baby sister, someone who less than a year ago I saw pretty much as a mousy, irritating, albeit lovable child, and saw this competent woman who was my peer, whom I went to for *advice*. When the fuck had *that* happened? In fact…

I tapped my knife against my glass and everyone silenced as I stood up. "Despite this being somewhat of a wedding brunch, I'm *not* making a toast about my incredible bride," I said, looking down at Lydia. "But fear not. I promise you all plenty of that in a couple of months." There were just enough giggles to confirm that they had indeed been expecting a soliloquy about my damsel. "No, I actually have an announcement to make about our family business, Hale Shipping. Our grandfather started the business because he wanted to help build things, make things, do something concrete for people. And he succeeded because he was a damn fine businessman. On the books, I am meant to follow in his footsteps, to run the company that has now been in our family for three generations. However, as you all know, my heart is in a different kind of building, and Grandfather supported my love of architecture, so I know that he'd approve of me handing the company off to another capable business mind. Someone with the savvy and instincts to do the job well and the backbone to do it right." I saw my mother lock her eyes on mine, wondering, but I turned my gaze to Emily. "And if he were here now, I'd expect him to chide me for taking this long to figure out whose hands Hale Shipping should be in." Everyone was quiet for another moment, waiting. "Emily, if you'll have it, the job is yours."

Her eyes went wide for a moment, and then they went soft. I saw Will take her hand, and in that moment I was both utterly confident that I was making the right choice and utterly grateful that she seemed to have someone in her life who might support her the way Lydia supported me.

"Dylan," she started, and for the first time since our father had died, I saw tears in her eyes. "Are you sure?"

"There are few things I've ever been this certain about," I said, and gripped Lydia's hand beside me.

The stunned look on Emily's face lasted only a nanosecond longer, and in typical Emily fashion, she was up and flying out of her seat like some kind of crazed bird with a huge smile on her face. "Dylan," she said, and wrapped her arms around me in a kind of hug I was pretty sure might never happen in our sibling life ever again.

I looked down at her, saw just how right this was, and wondered why it had taken me so long to figure it out. "Emily, you were meant for this."

"I know. I kind of was, wasn't I?"

I rolled my eyes and gave her another squeeze. "It's going to be a lot of work. You'll have put in time there while you finish school, and we'll slowly transfer authority, as you're ready. Are you sure you're game?"

"Completely." Emily's expression revealed the perfect amount of respect for what was ahead of her, and genuine enthusiasm.

My announcement unlocked something, tightened a loose thread, tied a bow that needing tying. I could feel things settling into place.

* * *

It was four in the afternoon. Our guests had been gone since two, and at that moment I lay naked in our bed and watched my gorgeous girl walk back to me from the bathroom completely starkers. Her creamy skin so warm and gorgeous in the sunlight.

After they'd left I'd forced the poor girl to wrap those perfect legs around me and hauled her to bed. I needed to taste her once more before I left, needed to feel her tighten around my tongue, needed to feel her lips around my cock. I needed every sensation to take with me for a bloody two months. I'd been fucking demanding. After I'd coaxed the fourth orgasm from her lithe little body, she'd collapsed against me, and we'd napped. Or she'd napped. Her head on my chest, my hand in her hair. I'd held her against me and loved every second. Not wanting to sleep through any part of it.

Now I needed to leave, and we both knew it.

"Stay," she said, crawling across the bed and nestling back into me.

"Baby, you know I wish I could." She sighed in defeat. "You could come with me?" We'd been through this before, but I figured it was worth one more shot.

"You know I can't." She said it in a way that made her frustration clear.

"Can't blame a bloke for trying." I squeezed her and rolled her so she was atop me, her legs settled outside my thighs, and her perky tits sat there fucking tempting me. Shite. I was going to get another hard-on, and our playtime was over.

"Plus," she continued, smiling. "Even if Emily seems content to run the wedding show, I think she might throttle me if I left completely. The party is set for only a week after you return."

"Right." I sighed. I kept forgetting about that. I was already married, so the idea that we still had to contend with wedding nonsense seemed mental. "Are you going to get lonely without me? Will you take a lodger for company?"

She let a giggle go, and I fucking loved that little laugh of hers, the one she tried to keep in because she knew it would please me too much to give in to my daft humor.

"Not a bad idea. I'll just call up Michael, and see—" As if I would let her get away with that. Her old neighbor who'd professed his interest in her months ago wasn't setting foot in this house while I was gone. She shrieked as I pounced over her, caging her in.

"You saucy little thing. I'm going to have to give you a proper reminder of who's boss around here, aren't I?" She laughed out loud as she rolled onto her belly and tried to hide under the covers. "Someone's got to make sure you're all sorted before I leave, don't they?" I pulled her up by the hips so her perfect round arse was perched in the air, and I landed a smack on that pink flesh that made my dick twitch.

"Dylan!" She screeched, giggled, and flipped to her back. Instead of skittering away from me, the feisty thing wrapped her entire body around me and pulled me to the mattress. We stilled and I held her against me for a moment. "You have to go." She sighed as she said it. She was right. I did.

Chapter 30

Dylan

I hadn't seen her in seven wretched weeks.

The longest seven weeks of my life.

Four sodding weeks of state visits in Cameroon, Johannesburg, Sydney, and Vancouver, with three weeks in Auckland in the middle for prepping the Olympic Stadium. Seven sodding weeks shaking hands, smiling politely, attempting not to explode at the outrageous requests of the Olympic committee. Seven sodding weeks of miserable hotels and empty beds. Thank fucking god they were over—after one week I vowed never to travel without Lydia again. Seven had been a bizarre form of torture.

We easily could have just met the next morning back in London—that had been the plan. It would have been the sane thing to do, wouldn't it? Wait one more day and reunite at home, where we could hide away for hours, days, with no interruptions? But this godforsaken soiree had come up in Paris. It couldn't be avoided, and I couldn't stand the idea of delaying seeing her one more day. And neither could she. So instead of marching through our front door and taking her right to bed, I was going to see her for the first time in a room full of people. She'd flown down that morning, and I hoped she'd gotten her fill of the town, because I wasn't going to let her leave our hotel room once I got her there.

She'd seemed radiant over FaceTime the previous evening, and I needed that radiance in front of me, under me, as soon as fucking possible. I had landed only forty minutes earlier, and I was already in a car headed to the party. Roger had finally proposed to that French woman he shared the Hampstead flat with, and it was an engagement party. I might have skipped the whole thing altogether had he not generously donated over two hundred thousand quid to the suicide prevention charity I'd started in Grace's name. He was a good bloke, and she was inoffensive, a model or something. Her name was Manon, I believed. I hoped. I quickly sent Thomas a text to confirm. Then texted him again to make sure he'd remembered to upgrade our suite at Le Bristol and have Lydia's bags moved.

Then I texted Lydia once more.

SATURDAY, 7:24 pm
On my way. 10 minutes out. You have no idea what I'm going to do to your sweet cunt, baby. Drink up. You may need the liquid courage.

SATURDAY, 7:25 pm
:-)

Huh. That was awfully tame of her. Unusually tame. Maybe she was in the middle of a conversation with someone. I contemplated pushing her further but settled for straightening my bow tie. I'd hurriedly changed into my tux on the plane, but was only now making sure the buttons were lined up properly.

We'd managed to speak on the phone every day at first, but with the shifting time differences, my constant hotel hopping, and her busy schedule with the store and the successful launching of Fiona's business, it had become impractical, so within a week we'd had to settle for daily texting and a video call a couple of times a week. But even then we couldn't manage to line up our schedules. She seemed to be going to bed earlier in my absence—I'd be coming home from an event and would end up waking the poor girl up. I missed her like I was a heroin addict going through withdrawal, and it was even worse now that she was so close. I was minutes away from having those lethal little lips against mine, and fuck, this hard-on was going to be a problem. Who knew having a wife was such a social hazard?

The car pulled into the drive of the stylish bohemian loft space in the Marais, and I bolted from the car. The poor doorman didn't stand a chance—I flung the door open myself before the poor chap had his hand on the handle. I'd have to tip him later for his embarrassment.

On entering the posh space, all high ceilings, lit with small lights and candles, I scanned feverishly for her. Where were those brown eyes?

There.

A floor-length dark green wrap dress with billowing sleeves and a deep V in the front that made her breasts look fucking fabulous. Christ, they were perfect. More perfect than my memory and video chat had allowed them to be. Her hair was in some kind of low side thing, her bangs trimmed—she looked soft, sweet, elegant, and I couldn't wait to ravage her, make her dirty. Make her mine again.

She was chatting politely with an older gentleman—Roger's father, perhaps? I wasn't willing to take my eyes off of her long enough to figure it out. She looked like she had a goddamn halo around her, backlit with those bloody candles. *This* was why we met here, so I could hold on to this vision for the rest of my fucking life and feed off it. Conjure it when I was having a wank, drown in it when I missed her.

She was wearing the earrings I'd bought her on Portobello—that day seared into my mind the way this one would be. I couldn't believe that moment—she'd brought me to my knees then, and now I was hers completely. The woman had destroyed me.

I was closer. She still hadn't seen me, and she looked so uncharacteristically calm, so womanly.

She saw me as I approached but didn't run to me, didn't meet me halfway. Her smile was knowing, welcoming, steady, exactly what I needed. I enveloped her completely in my arms, and sealed my lips against her neck, inhaling her.

"Baby. Lydia," I whispered into her ear, pulling her even tighter against my chest. I wasn't letting this girl out of my sight for at least a decade. Fuck state visits. I was never again doing one without her. Ever.

"Dylan," she replied, tucking her head under my chin, nuzzling into me. She looked up to me, grabbed my face, and pulled my lips down to meet hers. "I wish we were alone," she added.

"Why did we decide to meet here again?" I asked her, stroking her face with my hands, wanting to touch all of her.

"So we wouldn't have to wait another minute."

Just then a waiter approached, offering us Champagne, and I couldn't ignore the fact that both Roger and his father were still standing right there. Roger had the nerve to clear his throat—I wanted to punch the bastard. If I wanted to maul my wife whom I hadn't seen in nearly two months, I didn't care if I was in a church, I'd maul.

"Excuse me," I said to the gentlemen, "I haven't seen my lovely wife in weeks." I took two glasses of Champagne from the tray and offered one to Lydia. She took the glass, but didn't raise it to her lips. "Come on, baby. Toast with me. We're back."

"Might I have a water with gas please?" she asked the waiter. I smiled at the way she was starting to adopt the English terms for things.

"On some kind of health kick, damsel?" I whispered to her as Roger and his father took their drinks. "Am I going to have start all over with you? Reintroduce you to hedonism?" I looked at her, searching for the giggle I knew would come. "I wouldn't mind, you know. We'd start with the pretense that this was all going to be just sex." I smirked and wrapped my arm around her waist, pulling her even closer. She kissed me and smiled again. That goddamn smile.

"Where have you been, Hale?" Roger asked, slapping me on the back. "Travelling the world without this lovely creature? Don't you think that's rather cruel?" His loud voice pissed me off. Nosy bugger.

"You have no idea—cruel for me," I said. "Where's the blushing bride, Rog?" I asked on autopilot. I wanted to be with Lydia, alone. I wasn't even sure what he said but I know I replied, and I must have said something to exit us from the conversation, because the two interlopers were now walking away. I only hoped I hadn't been rude. All of my attention was on the woman in my arms.

"Baby?" I pulled her even tighter to me and looked down between us. Was it just me, or… "Fuck me, Lydia, are you wearing a push-up bra or something?" I asked, surreptitiously stroking the edge of her breast with my thumb, my palm wrapped clear around her back to the other side. Her being so tiny had its advantages.

She shook her head, and when I looked in her eyes I saw apprehension. Wondering. Pleading.

Wait.

I looked at her Champagne glass—she still hadn't touched it. Her breasts were definitely bigger. I felt the blood drain from my face. Was she fucking with me?

"Lydia?" I whispered, looking right into those gorgeous brown eyes, willing them to tell me what I was now eighty-five percent sure she was telling me. I moved my hands to her hips and stepped back to get a better look at my girl.

"I'm—"

"Pregnant. You're pregnant." I could hear my own words, and they sounded as though I was meeting Elvis or the president of the United States, mystified, questioning, not believing that this unbelievable thing before my eyes could be reality.

"Pregnant," she said, and now it was her turn to look at me imploringly. Oh god, she was nervous. This beautiful woman—my wife—was *pregnant* with our child and uncertain about me, how I felt. I rushed in and pulled her into me. I wrapped myself completely around her. I felt the world fall away—this was happening. It was happening with *her*, and I'd never have been able to anticipate the joy that was pulsing through my limbs. The utter satisfaction.

"Nothing. Nothing in the world has ever been more beautiful to me than this," I said directly into her ear. One hand holding her head against my shoulder, the other wrapped around her perfect waist. I could feel her chest rise and fall in quicker succession. She was crying.

I took a swig of my Champagne and then deposited our glasses (mine empty, hers full) on the tray of a passing waiter. Then I quickly moved Lydia to the edge of the room, pulled her face into my hands, and laid a kiss on her lips that I hoped would convey everything that needed to be said. I stroked her cheeks, her neck, her shoulders with my palms as I sank my lips into hers.

"Really?" she asked, those big brown eyes looking at me with relief and hope. "I wasn't sure. We never got a chance to talk about it again before you left, and then I found out, and I didn't know—"

"Shhh, baby. Really." And urged her back against me. And then I realized I still didn't know how *she* felt. "Baby, do *you*…I thought you weren't ready…" I couldn't finish the sentence, but I didn't need to. Lydia was nodding, a tear slipping down her cheek.

"I am. I knew I was before you left, and I figured we'd talk about kids when you got back." She laughed a little, looked down at her belly and shrugged her shoulders. "But it's a little late for that." She smiled the most calm, beautiful smile I'd ever seen on her.

"Baby," I said again, holding her against me. I smiled back at her, suddenly realizing that that term of endearment was also a statement of fact. "How long have you known?" I pulled away again so I could see her face.

"I found out the day after you left. I think I missed some pills when I was in New York—I was so distracted, and the timing makes sense."

I wasn't surprised often, but somehow I was almost more surprised by this than the fact that she was pregnant. "The whole time? You knew the whole time I was gone? Why didn't you tell me?"

"I wanted to tell you in person. It was never a good moment on the phone, and I just wanted to be in the same room as you when we finally talked about it, and I—"

"Shhh," I said into her ear as I rocked her subtly against me, "let me take you out of here."

"But—"

"Fuck the lot of them, the sorry bunch of wankers." I gestured towards the room, and she laughed through her tears. "I haven't seen you in seven weeks, and you just told me I'm going to be a father. You've made me the happiest man alive, Lydia. And you've had to think about this all alone, and now I'm here I want it all. I want to inspect every millimeter of your body. I want to catch up on every ounce of you. I want you tell me everything about when you found out. Everything."

"Thank god," she said, laughing and wiping away her tears. "I'm so happy too. And I might have had to consider having a major blowout fight with you had you suggested we stay at this party. And since I haven't seen you in almost *two months*, and I'm so goddamn horny…" She slipped her hands underneath my jacket and held me tighter. I laughed—she tells me she's pregnant, and all she can think about is sex. I knew I'd married her for a reason.

"No rows. Only us, damsel." I could feel her smile against my lapels, and I placed my hand against her stomach. "Only us."

Epilogue

Lydia

The Canadian air *was* different. I hadn't been imagining it. Or maybe it was because I was now standing in the very spot where Dylan had first kissed me.

It's not that we hadn't been back there in the five years we'd been married—we had, but it wasn't often enough, and we'd always been busy. This time I'd snuck out of the house to find this spot. The place, the slight curve in the narrow dirt path that connected the estate, La Belle Reve, to the main road, was burned in my memory. I stood under the canopy of trees, as I had before, only this time the sun was peeking through instead of the moon. And I was alone.

It was late afternoon, a quiet time of our day, and I'd gone for a walk. I wanted to stand there and see if I could feel it, could smell it, if there really was something special about this place.

There was.

The smell of chamomile drifted from the lawn. The smell of roses and hydrangeas and lavender were carried from the gardens. I stood there, my eyes closed, head back, listening to the trees rustle, feeling the warm breeze meander over my skin.

Then I felt hands on my hips. Dylan's hands.

"What in heaven's name are you doing out here?" he asked as I felt his warm tall body press against my back, allowing me to lean against him. My head fell back into his chest, and my whole body relaxed there, eyes still closed.

"I wanted to remember," I said.

"Our first kiss?" he asked.

"Mmm," I said, sinking into the moment. Dylan wrapped his arms around my torso, and his hands landed on the light linen sundress covering my swollen belly.

"That kiss has led to a lot. In fact, it changed everything," he said, stroking my stomach and allowing one hand to cup the bottom of my pregnant bump, the other the top. "Without that kiss, we wouldn't have Eleanor," he said, moving his lips to the side of my neck. I tilted my head to accommodate him, to invite him. Our almost four-year-old daughter, named for Dylan's grandmother, our firstborn, was hopefully still napping safely back at the house, *her* grandmother nearby if she woke up.

"Without that kiss, we wouldn't have Aiden," he said as his hand moved from my belly to my breast. He slid his broad palm into my dress and cupped my sensitive flesh. Our two-year-old son was hopefully napping happily with his sister.

I groaned a little, catching my breath as he enveloped me. We'd discovered that pregnancy made me insatiable. And something about it made me crave him, want to curl up in him.

"Without that kiss, we wouldn't have our girl here, our Anna," he said, running his hand over my stomach.

"Chloe," I said. We still hadn't agreed on a name for our soon-to-be-arriving daughter. We had three more weeks to decide, plenty of time.

Then I forgot all about baby names. Our children conveniently left my mind completely.

His hand hitched up my dress, and his kisses to my neck, my cheek, my lips as I turned to face him, were paired with his hand slipping into my panties.

"Thank god for that kiss, damsel. Without it, I wouldn't have you." I turned to face him completely and stood up on my toes to kiss him. "Fuck, I love you like this," he breathed quietly. "I love your body, round with our child, so responsive."

"Well you'd better enjoy it—we only have another few weeks." I hummed.

"You think I can't convince you to have a fourth?" he asked, smiling.

I laughed. We'd been over this, and he knew better. I was already stretched thin between the fashion consulting firm I ran with Fiona, being a duchess, and our family. Plus, I knew our family was about to be complete. He murmured agreement and backed me towards the tree behind me, possibly the very same tree I'd leaned against six years earlier, when our lips had touched the first time. As I had then, I stepped onto the roots, bringing our eyes to the same height. Only this time, my belly hung between us.

Dylan leaned over it and kissed me as he had then. His tongue sliding along the seam of my lips, prying them open. One hand against my rib cage, his thumb strumming against the edge of my breast. The other hand cupping my cheek, allowing Dylan full control of this kiss. Until I kissed him back. It was patient—we had nowhere to be. But it was also potent, full of fever, of purpose.

"I love you," he whispered into my mouth. "I love you so fucking much."

"I love you too," I said.

"Let me take you back to the house. Let me show you," he said.

"Show me here," I said, and he looked at me, eyebrow raised. "It wouldn't be the first time you've made love to me outside," I said.

He nodded his head, smiling. "I'll love you anywhere," he said, but he didn't resume his attack. Instead, he paused. He placed his hand at my back, and pulled me towards him.

"Anywhere, always."

About the Author

PARKER SWIFT grew up in Providence, Rhode Island, and then grew up again in New York, London, and Minneapolis and currently lives in Connecticut. She has spent most of her adult life examining romantic relationships in an academic lab as a professor of social psychology. Now, she's exploring the romantic lives of her fictional characters in the pages of her books. When she's not writing, she spends her time with her bearded nautical husband and being told not to sing along to pop music in the car by her two sons.

Twitter: @the_parkerswift
Instagram: @parker.swift
Facebook.com/ParkerSwiftAuthor

You Might Also Like…

Looking for more great digital reads?
We've got you covered!

Now Available from Forever Yours

FATE HAS A WICKED SENSE OF HUMOR.

Alexis's new life was made up of two things: baking and hiding the details of her old life in Chicago. The first allowed her to finally find some happiness. And the second is about to be destroyed by a man who knows all her secrets.

Marshall Rawlins was prepared to do anything when he moved cross-country to launch an upscale cocktail bar—anything except work with Alexis, his best friend and business partner's ex-wife. Adding Alexis's boozy baked goods to his menu would be a major feat for his bar. But striking a deal means getting in bed with the enemy.

Battling between distrust and desire, Alexis and Marshall give in to a passionate, forbidden affair. They know if they're discovered the consequences would be bad—it's just hard to remember that when being together feels so, so good.

SOMETIMES, GETTING IN TOO DEEP IS THE ONLY WAY TO SURVIVE...

As darkly charismatic as he is unpredictable, Ethan Ash knows me better than I know myself. He's spent years unraveling the family scandal I've tried desperately to escape. I once thought that made us adversaries. Now he's the closest ally I have left.

Ethan's both the chaos around me and the deep, calm center where I feel safe. People warn me about him, tell me he's dangerous. Don't fall for him. But it's too late. Because I can't tell where my addiction ends...and his obsession begins.

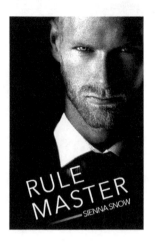

HIS RULES. *HER PLEASURE.* HIS WAY.

Italian heiress and international financier Milla Castra knows she can't avoid him forever. Irredeemably confident and controlled Lex Duncan once shared her craving for things deliciously forbidden. He was her lover. Her Master. And the husband she's kept secret from everyone.

But Lex will never relinquish what's his—and Milla is definitely his. And he knows she can't resist the exquisite pleasure that awaits in his arms. When the violence of her past threatens them both, Lex will risk everything to keep Milla safe...before she submits to the cruelest master imaginable, *Fear*.

RULES ARE MADE TO BE BROKEN…

If England had yearbooks, I'd probably be "Arden St. Ives: Man Least Likely to Set the World on Fire." So far, I haven't. I've no idea what I'm doing at Oxford, no idea what I'm going to do next and, until a week ago, I had no idea who Caspian Hart was. Turns out, he's brilliant, beautiful…oh yeah, and a billionaire.

It's impossible not to be captivated by someone like that. But Caspian Hart makes his own rules. And he has a lot of them. About when I can be with him. What I can do with him. And when he'll be through with me.

I'm good at doing what I'm told in the bedroom. The rest of the time, not so much. And now that Caspian's shown me glimpses of the man behind the billionaire, I know it's him I want. Not his wealth, not his status. Him. Except that might be the one thing he doesn't have the power to give me.